Dance On His Grave

Sylvia Dickey Smith

L & L Dreamspell

Spring, Texas

Cover and Interior Design by L & L Dreamspell

Author's Note:
This book is a work of fiction. The characters are pure figments of my imagination. Any similarity to real people, alive or dead, is strictly coincidental and speaks only to the commonality of us all. Orange, Texas, however, does exist, lying alongside the meandering Sabine River just across from Louisiana's southwestern border. The area claims a rich history. First occupied by the mound building Atakapa Indians and pirate and slave-trader Jean Lafitte, today, cowboys, Cajuns, and chemical plant workers keep the place hopping. For the most part, I have accurately described the area, however I did take the occasional liberty and beg the resident's forgiveness.

ISBN: 978-1-60318-006-1

Library of Congress Control Number: 2007923009

Published by L & L Dreamspell
Printed in the United States of America

Visit us on the web at www.lldreamspell.com

Acknowledgements:

I couldn't have finished this work without the aid of so many people it is difficult to remember them all. So I will start with the one who has offered the most, my husband, William (Bill) Smith, Colonel (Ret.) U. S, Army. Never has he failed to encourage, support, and celebrate each accomplishment along the way, offering total, unconditional love at every turn. Next, my friend, Beverly Tackett, had grown weary of listening to me talk about writing, ordered me to sit in my chair and write, and I did. Persist & Publish, my online critique group from Writers Village University, has given me fabulous support and help. Among the members, Nancy Connor, of Ithaca, New York, copyedited an early version of the manuscript and helped make sense out of a disjointed work. Rebecca Hanley walked me through early writing lessons, teaching me how to write a story. Carolann Malley not only did the same, but also gave a final read of the manuscript. Austin Mystery Writers, led by Karen MacInerney, provided endless critique and guidance. Friend and fellow writer Tammy Petty Conrad gave the manuscript a final read, as did my beautiful sister, Glenda Merrell, who stood by me all the way with advice, detail, and encouragement, as did my brother Pete Dickey. That man knows more about the Orange area than anyone I know. I have missed others, I'm sure, who contributed so much to this work, I pray you forgive my oversight, and know how much your help has meant. Last, but most definitely not least, I want to especially thank my four children, sons, Jim, Jon Mark and Russell Hogg, and my daughter Anissa Hogg Russell, for they are the lights of my life.

I can't say enough about the fabulous duo, Lisa René Smith and Linda Houle at L & L Dreamspell, the best publishers in all the world.

Dedication:

**Dedicated to the brave women who inspired this story.
You know who you are.**

On the continuum of light and shadow
Black and white
Right and wrong
There is truth.
Not only at the ends
But at each point in between.

PROLOGUE
Thirty years ago

The Stud, as he called himself, slammed down the phone, sure Mama'd get the message. "Bitch," he swore. Damn woman put hair appointments before even God. You'd think those underdrawers she wore on her head at night would keep that hair in place a little longer, but he guessed they didn't, not to her satisfaction anyway. It seemed like she went to that damned beauty parlor every other day. Didn't do her no good, still uglier than dirt.

Goosebumps popped out all over him. He yanked on a pair of blue jeans from the pile of dirty clothes in the corner and pulled a T-shirt over his head.

The girls would just have to go with him, that's all there was to it.

He marched to the roll-away bed and shook Emma and Jewell, both curled under the blanket in tight balls. "Get up, kids. Grandma ain't coming." He jerked the covers off the bed.

"Do we have to?" Emma whined, red hair poking straight up. Emma always whined, drove him nuts.

The Stud slung the covers to the floor and grabbed Emma by the arm. "Yeah, you have to," he whined, mocking her. "Come on. Get up, get out of here." He shoved her toward the door.

"Go?" Jewell sprang straight up in the bed. "Where we going? Can I take Teddy?"

"No, just get the hell out of bed. Hurry up! We're gonna go for a ride."

Jewell crawled across the bed, her eyes stretched wide. "To feed the horses?"

"No, dammit, not to feed the horses, that's all you girls think about!" This kid was his for sure, always ready to go anywhere and do anything. All Emma ever did was whine. Crazy Nancy still tried to convince him Emma was his.

He shoved the girls out the door, anticipation running a foot race in his chest.

The other men were such pussies. Not him. He liked the doing. He wondered if God got turned on when *He* killed people. The Stud sure had.

He boosted the girls into the pickup, and then shoved on the faded green carpet he and his buddies had rolled up and stashed in the truck bed the night before. Satisfied, he secured the can of gasoline and slid behind the wheel.

The beat-up Ford truck rumbled down the dusty road jarring his insides like a damn cement mixer. Just watch, one of these days he was gonna be county commissioner and get these shit-ass roads fixed.

When The Stud reached the Levine Cut-off he made a hasty right turn, cringing as the oyster-shell driveway crunched under the weight of the vehicle.

So much for being quiet. Hell, he might as well blow the damn horn and let all the neighbors know he was coming.

Gravel shot out from underneath the tires when he threw on the brakes and swung the truck into a quick u-turn, tossing Emma and Jewell to the floor like a sack of unwanted puppies.

He jerked the truck door open and turned sideways, swinging his legs out. Smoke curled into his eyes as he took one last, quick, puff from his Camel and pitched it to the ground.

Shit! His hands still shook.

Reaching behind the seat, he pulled out a burlap bag and threw it at the girls. "Here," he yelled. "Get down under this and stay down!" Then, bounding out, he pulled and tugged on the carpet until, finally, he got it on his shoulder.

Staggering under the weight, now carried by one instead of three, he grabbed the side of the truck and held on until he got his balance.

Slow, careful, he freed one hand, collected the gas can, and stumbled up to the house.

Wheezing by the time he reached the front door, he kicked it open and flopped the carpet, and its contents, to the floor.

Soak it good. Leave no evidence, he'd been warned, as if he didn't have the sense God gave a goat.

The fumes stung his eyes, burned the back of his throat while he dowsed the carpet. By the time he'd soaked the floor and splashed the walls with fuel he couldn't breathe, couldn't half see.

Hurry.

He snatched matches from his pocket, struck one and tossed it behind him as he ran, but before he even reached the front door, hell raged in the room. The roar deafened him. Flames lapped at his feet.

He pounded out the door and down the gravel path, head tucked low, rocketing away from what he'd heard the preacher call perdition.

He just called it hell.

The hot smoky air made his lungs feel like an incinerator. He smelled singed hair and touched his head, scared his own burned.

When he reached the truck, he hurled the gas can into the bed of the pickup; it banged against the back wall.

Only then did he see two tiny feet attached to two blue-mottled legs.

Emma stood beside the empty gas can, eyes locked on him, red hair sticking out.

"Dammit to hell," he bellowed, "where's the other one?" There she was, head poked out the passenger window, staring at him, pig-tails waving in the breeze.

"Damn kids. I told you to stay down. If you don't stay down I'm gonna burn you up, just like I did her!"

One
The present

"What on earth are you doing?" Sidra Smart yelled over the sounds of an electric drill boring a hole in the bottom of the eye sign.

The wizened man on the ladder glanced down at her standing there with her fists crammed into her hips, then switched off the drill. "Mornin' ma'am." His voice sounded like a rasp pulled across a two by four. "I'm hangin' this here sign."

She chuckled at the old man, but her irritation didn't budge. "I can see that. But who authorized you to do that work?" She slammed her car door and stepped up to the sidewalk, squinting in the bright morning sun.

"Why, Mr. Chadwick did right after hurricane Rita messed up the old one. I just had a lotta work piled up. Told him I'd get to it when I could. Today, I could."

"But didn't you hear that my brother—Mr. Chadwick—died in a car accident?"

Died. The word felt glib on her tongue, didn't anywhere near match the pain squeezing every drop of blood out of her heart.

"Yes'm, but ain't somebody else gonna run the business for poor Mr. Chadwick? Figured I'd jus' get it ready for 'em."

"No, somebody isn't. The business is for sale, or will be as soon as I can list it. I wish you'd checked with me before—before hanging a new sign."

"Yes'm, but..." The old man reached a finger into the hole he'd made and swiped out sawdust. "I reckon if he bought and paid for it, least I could do is finish the job, God rest his soul." He freed one hand, crossed himself then switched on the drill and made another hole, and in short order had the grotesque sign swinging in the breeze.

Beneath a giant blue eye, the sign read, *The Third Eye*, then in smaller letters, *Intuitive Investigations*.

"What the world is intuitive investigations?"

"Beats me," he shrugged. "They order it, I paint it." He climbed down, tossed the ladder and toolbox into a jalopy-of-a pickup then wiped his neck with a red kerchief and stuffed it into his pocket.

With a bow, he touched his fingertips to his forehead and smiled. "Demoiselle, with your permission I take my leave."

While Sid stood with her mouth open, he climbed into the truck and with a blast of exhaust, backed out and rattled off. She watched the truck until it turned the corner, taillights disappearing behind a building.

She sucked in a deep breath, turned and stared at the office door, her stomach a stampede of cattle charging over a cliff.

What had Warren been drinking—to leave her this business? She'd made it clear to him years ago—no way, Jose!

She reached in her pocket and pulled out the keychain his lawyer, slash, executor, had given her the day he'd read her the will. After several false attempts, she found the right key and unlocked the door.

It creaked open.

Stale, moldy air accosted her before she crossed the threshold. She ran her hand across the wall, flipped the light switch, and spied a can of air freshener on a desk. Grabbing it, she sprayed, shook the can a couple of times then dropped it in the trash basket.

A clay pot with a few brown sprigs of mint sat in the front window. She rummaged in her bag, pulled out a partial bottle of Evian and dumped the water into the flower pot. A sudden whiff of mint rose from the almost indestructible herb. At least something of Warren's still lived. Feeling more an intruder than the new owner, she explored the office like an alarm might go off if she touched the wrong thing.

Or land her in *Oz*.

One thing for sure, she certainly wasn't going back to *Kansas*. Some Baptist preacher's wives might spend their whole lives totally happy following along in the tight, narrow shadow of their husbands, but she wasn't one of them. She'd spent thirty years in the deep, deadening rut of being the perfect, submissive, unambiguous preacher's wife. Thirty years being pulled, stretched, molded like Play-Dough.

Just thinking about it made her ill, literally nauseous. She slumped onto the hearth of a small fireplace and waited for the queasiness to pass, forcing herself to think of something different.

The Third Eye—she remembered the day Warren had called, excited about the name he'd chosen for his new business, how it matched his philosophy of working with the whole person. She guessed that was why he'd added the wording to the sign.

Intuition—if she'd ever had any, it was long gone.

Her first job, the lawyer had advised, was to pay Warren's overdue bills. She forced herself into action. Rummaging in the desk, she found the checkbook and pulled it out. After sorting bills from junk mail, she stacked the bills, latest on bottom, oldest on top, and spent the next half hour writing, licking and sealing. By the time she finished, she was pleased the balance wasn't red, not black either, more a medium gray. But not nearly enough to keep her head above water until the business sold.

Next, she went through the huge pile of junk mail, tossing some, stacking others. At the bottom, she found a postcard addressed to Warren, but with no return address. She flipped it over. Scratchy tight letters, strung together, made one short sentence. *An eye for an eye.* Weird. She tucked it in her pocket.

But the storage closet gave her the creeps. Crime scene kits, cameras, recorders, binoculars, polygraph equipment, and listening devices—all these reminded her that it was an ugly business. Yet, she didn't have to run it, she told herself. She had no idea how to use any of the equipment and didn't care to learn. Damn Warren. She slammed the closet door.

Despite the lingering odor of air freshener, she still smelled Warren in the room. That bothered her more than anything. He seemed so near she thought she felt his hand on her arm, urging her forward.

But, dear sweet brother, I don't want to go there, she thought. She'd wither and die in a town like Orange, Texas. Besides, private detective wasn't a job for an ex-preacher's wife, at least not one her age.

Okay, what should she do? Sell the business? Burn the building to the ground?

Or busy your butt learning the detective business!

She had no idea where those words came from, but she quickly shoved them out of her brain, for that was not an option.

She'd noticed another PI office on Sixteenth Street. Perhaps the owner would buy Warren's caseload—if you could sell such a thing.

The front door opened, but preoccupied with her misery, the squeak didn't register in her brain until after the woman spoke.

"Excuse me Ma'am. Can you help me?"

Sid whirled around, startled. "What?"

A young woman, seven shades of white, stood so close to Sid she felt the woman's fear prickle the hair on her own arms.

"Are you okay?"

"He killed her! I know he did!" The blonde woman came at Sid like she was the sole flotation device between breathing and drowning. Instinctively, Sid stepped back, half-expecting an attack.

"Do you work here? I'm looking for Mr. Chadwick." The woman patted her heart while she talked. "Is he in today?"

Sid grabbed the woman's elbow, deposited her in a chair, and asked again. "Are you sure you're okay?"

The woman nodded. "It's just that coming back to this town scares the hell out of me."

"I'll get you some water." Sid yanked a paper cup off the water dispenser, filled it and offered it to the other. She waited until the woman drained the cup before answering her earlier question. "No, I don't work here."

The woman's expression tumbled further than Sid thought possible.

"My name is Sidra Smart, yours?"

"Jewell Stone." She offered a limp hand.

When Sid hesitated, a sickly smile played across Jewell's face. "Yeah, I know, but it's not an alias, honest. I married into the last name. At the time, I took it as a sign." She shrugged and a short, sad laugh slipped out of her throat. "I guess it was."

Sid looked away. Of late, her own roller-coaster-life left no energy for another person's problems. "It's Sunday, you didn't have an appointment with Mr. Chadwick today did you?" She hoped her question sounded aloof. She wanted to keep her distance.

Jewell's words erupted like rapid-fire ammunition. "Not an appointment, but I was hoping to catch him. He told me he often worked weekends. I'm a new client of his. I used to live here when I was a kid." She glanced out both windows before turning her gaze back to Sid. "I live in Goose Creek now." She pointed south with a bright red fingernail that had a thin white stripe painted diagonally across it.

Jewell stood and paced the room. "But, if you don't work here," she turned back to Sid, "where the hell is Mr. Chadwick?"

"He's dead—" Sid paused, half-expecting the young woman to feign sympathy, but none came forth.

"Dead? Oh. I hadn't heard." Jewell's face crumpled, tears welled in her eyes. "What happened?"

Sid got the distinct impression Jewell's tears were for herself, more than for Warren. "My brother was in a car accident." She cringed over the words, hating them more every time she said them. "Let me see if I can find a file on you." She strode over to a metal file cabinet and tugged on the top drawer. Thumbing through several records she located a folder with Jewell's name. "Here it is." She pulled out the file and with a push of her hip, the drawer banged shut.

Flipping through several pages, she looked up at Jewell. "It looks like he'd barely gotten started, just your contract, intake form, that sort of stuff." She closed the file and dropped it on the desk. "I'll reimburse you the retainer. There's another detective agency on 16th Street. You might try them." The desk drawer screeched open as Sid retrieved the checkbook, opened it, and grabbed a pen.

"I don't want my money back, I want answers. Why can't you help me?"

Speechless, Sid stared at her.

The woman stared back while tears ran down her cheeks and dripped off her jaw. After a moment of visual standoff, Sid marched to the door.

"I truly am sorry, Ms. Stone, but I don't know anything about this business. You'll have to find someone else to help you." She held the door open. "Now, if you'll excuse me..."

Jewell didn't budge. Instead, she tapped her forehead with her fingertips. "This photoflash keeps going off in my head, but I can't see the picture. It's like—when you have a dream, and the next day you can't quite get your mind around the details, but the sense of it keeps going off in your brain. But it isn't a dream. It's a memory—I know it is! Something I know, but I don't know how I know it, or even what the hell it is!" She leaned forward, elbows on her knees, and buried her face in her hands. Sid eased the door shut, took a couple of steps back into the room.

"My family has always had this big fucking secret no one will talk about. I've got to find out what it is because it's driving me crazy." Jewell raised her head and shoved her thick, curly hair out of her face. "I see this naked woman flashing in my mind. I think my dad killed her because—"

As Sid stood in the middle of the room staring at Jewell,

wondering what the hell she should do next, a soft blue flame appeared above Jewell's head. Sid's breath caught in her throat. She blinked, convinced her eyes played tricks, and sure enough, the flame disappeared. Or had it been there at all?

"Something happened, though, when..." Jewell stopped mid sentence and looked at Sid. "Is everything all right? You had a funny look on your face."

Sid shook her head. "No, no, I'm okay, go on."

"Something happened when we lived here in Orange. That's what I want to know. What?"

Sid resumed her seat and waited, uneasiness crawling up her backbone.

"Whatever happened, it made my mother sick, and then the next thing I remember we're living with my grandparents. They always protected my mom. Any time I asked about my dad, Grandma shushed me up and shooed me out of the room. 'You'll make your mother sick' she'd say. Sometimes my mom sat on the floor in the living room pulling her hair and screaming, 'don't kill them, Roy,' over and over."

"Is Roy your father?"

Jewell nodded. "Roy Manly."

"You're afraid of your father?" Sid's last word squeaked out.

Jewell nodded. "A house burned down—I believe a woman died in it."

Sid stiffened. "Your house?"

"No—I don't know whose house it was."

"How do you know that?" Now Sid was the one leaning forward.

"I have no idea. No one ever told me, but I know my father had something to do with it." She flung her hands out in front of her, palms up. "I can't explain, I just know it."

Sid opened her mouth, decided against interrupting, shut it.

"The old house had a lot of junk in the yard," Jewell continued, "and I see this doll's head stuck on top of a fence post."

"You sure this isn't a nightmare? It sure sounds like one."

Jewell shuddered and sat up straighter. "It might sound like one, but I know I didn't dream this. That's why I hired Mr. Chadwick. I have a little savings, plus I got a settlement in my divorce last year."

"I see." Sid stalled, wondering how in the world she could get out of this.

Jewell smiled for the first time during their meeting. "So you'll take my case?"

"Oh no! I can't, Jewell. I'd be cheating you. I don't know diddly about this business. I'm not an investigator. You need someone experienced. I wouldn't even know how to start."

Not to mention the story scared her witless.

Jewell stuck out a trembling lip. Without another word, she grabbed her bag and stomped out the door, head down, shoulders slumped.

As Sid watched her go, guilt and fear seeped into her heart.

Dammit Warren, she thought, what'd you expect me to do?

She put her head on the desk and fought back tears. Chiming bells off in the distance reminded her it was Sunday. She knew the tune—*Count Your Blessings*. She lifted her head, listened a moment, and then snorted at the idea. For years she'd stood in church, sung every song, word for word, without needing a hymnal. Lately though, she'd made an agreement with God. She wouldn't go to church, and God wouldn't bug her about it.

What she needed, more than counting any blessing, was a margarita on the rocks, the rim loaded with salt. She glanced at her watch. Twelve noon on Sunday seemed a perfect time for her first-ever alcoholic beverage. She grabbed her bag and keys and climbed into the rental she'd leased shortly after the divorce. It still galled her that Sam had gotten the Avalon. As professional clergy, the lawyer argued, Sam needed the nicer-looking car. Bullshit!

She'd passed a quaint place earlier, now she backtracked her

way down Green Avenue, past the carillon still chiming atop a
pink granite church. With stubborn determination she forced her
eyes on the road, but old habits die hard. Her eyes wandered up
to an opalescent glass dome and stained glass windows. Some-
what of an expert on church buildings, she recognized the modi-
fied Greek Revival architecture. She pushed her foot harder on
the accelerator.

Capistrano's restaurant looked like it had been around as
long as the old San Juan mission she'd seen in pictures. The beige
plastered building hunkered alongside a railroad track.

"Welcome to The Cap," the burly man said as he ushered
her across the dining room, weaving his way between well-worn
tables and chairs. The place rang of a camaraderie that natives
love about familiar haunts. A few couples reminded Sid of the
dinner-after-church crowd, distinguishable from the alcoholics
by suits and ties, high heels, panty hose, and attitude. Sid hoped
she looked like neither one as she slipped into a small booth in
the corner and ordered her drink.

When the margarita came she sipped it slowly, waiting until
the tequila dulled her misery.

A blob of dried ketchup stuck to the wall. She flicked it with
her fingernail and wiped her hands on the moist cocktail napkin
under her glass. A jukebox blared out some song about a perfect
world gone awry and lost love. At least it wasn't a hymn.

Her perfect world had certainly fallen away. Like a baby bird
inside an eggshell, growing until the exact, perfect moment when
the shell no longer fit. When one tiny peck led to another, and
then another, until its world cracked and shattered in a heap.

She'd been so compliant, accepting without question Sam's
belief that he was superior. Until a vague discontent dislodged
the anesthetizing sleep-dust he'd sprinkled in her eyes, and one
peck led to another. At least she'd just divorced, instead of shooting him, like the pastor's wife in the news had done.

She touched her tongue to the salty rim.

Nothing tastes like salt, but salt.

A Bible verse popped in her head unbidden. *But if the salt has become tasteless, how will it be made salty again?*

She felt tasteless.

Okay, enough alcohol. She sat the glass down and ordered a cup of coffee and a Creole chicken sandwich.

Tomorrow she'd take her own advice and visit the owner of the detective office on 16th. Hopefully he could tell her how to go about selling The Third Eye.

When the food came, she nibbled it then ordered dessert and a second coffee before heading back to Houston and home.

Sam had moved out of the parsonage temporarily, but the deacons hadn't been happy about that. They pushed him to set a time limit on Sid moving out. Her fast-approaching deadline, like water torture, had dripped on the middle of her forehead for weeks.

An hour and half later, she turned onto her street and there sat Sam's car parked at the curb in front of the parsonage. Every time she saw him, she felt like a marionette jerked around by its strings.

She turned into her drive, punched the garage door opener and drove in, refusing to glance his way, irritated at the unbelievable control her ex-husband still held over her gut. More accurate—it pissed the hell out of her.

Her stepping to the other side of the Baptist line had been more than Sam could live with. It called into question his authority over her—over everyone. But he had been hurt, and the sight of him still ripped her heart out.

By the time she exited, he stood just outside the garage door, waiting. "Christine called and told me Warren left you his private detective business," he called out, pain evident in the ruts across his forehead, around his eyes, the stiff line of his mouth.

"That's right." If she'd had hackles, his words would have raised them. She hadn't asked Christine or Chad not to tell their dad about her recent inheritance, now she wished she had. Sam was all about mind-control. He'd been jealous of Warren, of anyone that might dilute the power he held over his wife. It still pissed her off, the way he'd looked down on Warren, tried to keep them apart—as if Warren cavorted with Satan.

"You don't want to get mixed up in that world, Sid." Sam's words pulled her back to the present. "It's all crime, killings—working with heathens, infidels!"

Still handsome, despite the grief of the last few months, he pushed his fingers through gray-sprinkled brown hair. "As a Christian, you're supposed to separate yourself out from the world—that is if you still call yourself one! Besides, how's it going to look, my wife—okay, ex-wife—running with the dregs of society?" He slung his hands out in front of him. "Please don't do this, teach school or something—anything respectable."

Always about Sam. Everything.

"I don't plan…" She swallowed what she intended to say, that she planned to sell the business. Full realization hit her, The Third Eye was her baby now, her decision, not Sam's. A smile stretched across her face.

His face crumpled, along with his shoulders. He turned on his heel and headed to the Avalon. She watched as he climbed in and drove off, shoulders slumped. She felt like shit, but it boiled down to him or her, and she'd sacrificed her all her life. She had nothing left to give him.

She punched the garage door closed, walked into the kitchen and stood on the doorjamb, speechless. The room looked like a gang of thugs had been inside. The cabinet doors hung open, empty; the contents lay on the floor broken to smithereens. Flour, sugar, coffee, macaroni, potato chips, and crackers, everything she'd had in her pantry was broken open and spread around the room. Tomatoes were squashed on the wallpaper, eggs thrown everywhere.

Trancelike, she stepped through the mess and closed her refrigerator, where, on its white door, someone had written two words with a black magic marker.

Sam's Delilah!

Two

It didn't take a private detective to narrow down who'd do such a thing. She could name any one of five hundred people—possibly more. She almost called the police, but didn't, weary of feeding local gossip. Whoever it was had already condemned her to hell, what worse could they do?

Sam hadn't done it, of that she was sure. His methodology was guilt and shame, not vandalism. She'd almost called and demanded he come back and look, find out who did it—put a stop to it. But pride stopped her, for he believed she'd betrayed him too. She could still hear him say, "Can't you just go back and be like you used to be? I don't like you this way."

An overpowering sense told her, had she done so, she'd cease to exist.

She shoved the mess into the garbage, along with the loss of what she wished her marriage had been, more determined than ever to get her life going.

After she'd tied the last trash bag and delivered it to the curb, she went to the bathroom to clean up, but as the warm soapy water rinsed the grime off her hands she glanced in the mirror. A boring image of a woman with conservative, platinum-colored hair stared back at her. How pathetic. Early fifties, and she hadn't decided what she wanted to be when she grew up.

She shook the water off her hands, wiped them on her pants and stepped across the room to the linen closet. Determination running hot through her veins, she yanked open a drawer beneath the towels and scrambled until she came up with a pair of black-handled pinking shears.

One quick step back to the mirror and, without so much as taking a breath, she lifted a sprig of hair and started chopping.

👁   👁   👁

The next morning, ominous storm clouds hung overhead, droplets already spitting in the dust, as Sid raced to the front door of Léger Private Investigations and Bail Bonds. The bright yellow prefab building in the middle of half a dozen palm trees looked as if it sprouted out of the ground.

The owner, George Léger, was in.

If ever anyone looked like an archetype of a private eye, George did. He stood, maybe six four, broad-shouldered and big bellied, blue jeans slung underneath the belly. Thinning hair lay plastered over a shiny pate. Jowls hung loose, but his smile was broad and friendly.

"Come on in, sha. What can I do you for?" A Cajun accent thickened his speech. He tucked his hand into the small of her back as he escorted her into his office.

Sid cringed. She hated it when men did that. It felt so patriarchal.

"My name is Sidra Smart, just Sid, please." She offered her hand. "I'm Warren Chadwick's sister. Maybe you knew Warren? He passed away recently."

"Warren? Hell yea, I knew him. Fine man he were, too. He and I done been drinkin' buddies from way back. He'd give me a holler mos' Friday nights. We'd done get us out some of dat good ole Cajun food, then we'd go out to Sparkle's Paradise and do us a little dancing, don't you know. We pass us a good time drinkin' beer mostly, but eyed de pretty girls a lot, too. Ah-eey."

His eyes crinkled at the corners. "Sure sorry about his death. A car accident, they say, huh?" He moved out of the Cajun accent as easily as he'd moved into it.

She nodded. "Seems so."

He shook his head and wiped his nose then stuck the hand-kerchief in his back pocket. "Let me catch you a cup of Seaport. Okay?" George excused himself to a back room and returned with a cup of the blackest, thickest coffee Sid had ever seen. "I hope you like chicory," he said, offering her several lumps of sugar and a small pitcher of thick cream. She plopped in every lump offered and poured in as much cream as the cup allowed.

He pulled a decanter out of a cabinet and raised it toward her, "I like a little nip in mine. Care for some?"

"No thanks, not this time." She couldn't help but smile, for she was getting a clear picture of Warren's friend—he liked his booze.

He unscrewed the cap off a bottle of bourbon, poured a chug into his cup and screwed the lid back on. "Well, what brings you to The Gateway of Texas?"

"Excuse me?"

"Orange! Bayou country! Where a gator can bite a man's leg off before he can paddle his pirogue out of Adams Bayou. That is, if the mosquitoes don't eat him first." He chortled, running his hand through his gray hair. "I tell my bride, when God wants to give the earth an enema, this is where he inserts the enema tube." His belly shook as he laughed at his own joke. "Now don't get me wrong. I like Orange. You just have to catch the flavor of the place, and then it grows on you. That and mildew." He laughed again. "You're not from these parts are you?"

"I live in Houston." She raised her voice to get above the noise of the rain now coming down in sheets. It hammered on the tin roof and whipped the palm trees against the windows.

Coffee cup in one hand, the other in his pocket, George ambled over to the window and stared out. "Look at that rain, will you?" He half-turned and beckoned her to the window. "Looks like a cow peeing on a flat rock."

Sid walked over and looked out at the rain, her hand over her mouth to hide a smile, glad he'd turned back toward the window.

"I came by to see if you'd be interested in buying Warren's caseload."

George looked over his shoulder at her, turned from the window, and headed to his desk. "Aw, sha, I'm sorry, but I'm in no position to buy any caseload. I'm up to my hairy ears already!"

"I see." Sid's hope dropped to the pit of her stomach.

"I know you need the money, sha. Why don't you just run the business? Warren told me about your divorce and all. Hope him telling me don't bother you none. Your brother was just worried."

"I know he was." Sid fidgeted with her handbag.

"Look at it this way." George stood and headed around his desk. "You've done the hardest job in the world. Why, running a private detective business should be as easy as eating a piece of crawfish pie." He snorted with laughter. "Tell you what. I can teach you everything you need to know."

"But don't you need a license or something to run a private detective office?"

"Well, sha, it boils down to this."

George held a manager's PI license. Should she decide to work as a PI, his license allowed him to manage the business until she qualified for an individual license as an investigator. In other words, she'd be his employee, but work out of her office. Her degree in sociology added to her credentials. She'd be okay, George said.

"As a matter of fact, that's how your brother got started," he smiled, as if remembering old times. "Warren worked under me the first three years until he got his own license. Besides, you can get all the training in the world, you know, but one day, you just have to play your own game. You'll do good, though. That white hair and air of innocence will work for you, make people more likely to trust you."

What a flip flop. She'd hoped to talk George into buying Warren's caseload and instead, he'd talked her into giving the business a try.

As she left she thought of Jewell and almost told George she'd referred the case to him, but stopped short. If she told, he might turn down the case. She may give the business a try, but that case would not be her first. Jewell had George's name, she'd leave it at that—mail back the retainer. If he didn't take the case the woman would just have to find someone else.

Three

The rainstorm had passed by the time Sid headed to her vehicle. She climbed inside and sat with her hands on a steering wheel as cold as her feet. What had she just committed herself to do? This was crazy! She snickered at her audacity until the thought of Warren's car sobered her. Until now, she had resisted seeing the wrecked vehicle. Dealing with his death had been enough to handle, the vehicle could wait. But now seemed the perfect time to get it over with. She drove out MLK, crossed over I-10 and after a couple turns, spotted the car graveyard crouching under a grove of pine trees looking as if it belonged there as much as the trees did.

A cyclone fence surrounded the lot. She drove through the open gate to a guard shack just inside the fence. Piles of wrecked vehicles, snuggled up along the edge of a weed-lined gravel path, reminded her of tadpoles nudging along a river's edge. She stopped the car when an addled-looking attendant tottered toward her. Sid rolled down her window, and following a gut instinct she hadn't anticipated, smiled broadly and pulled out everything she'd learned about winning people over to her side. "Good morning. I'm lost—made a wrong turn back there somewhere, just need to turn around if I may."

The man's smile revealed toothless gums as pink as a baby's butt; attraction burned in his eyes. Sid knew he liked what he saw, a diversion from what must be a boring job. He leaned over and stuck his head at Sid's level. The man oozed Cajun from his dark leathery skin, too long in the sun, to his thick accent. Harmless old coot, but maybe good for information.

"Afternoon, ma'am, where is it you trying to get to? I be glad to help."

"Now aren't you kind," Sid cooed. "Your name is?"

"Well now, folks always call me Couillon, but I ain't nuts like de nickname sez. Crazy neither."

"Crazy? Why you look quite sane to me." Sid hoped her words made him so. She opened her car door and smiled innocently, stepped out and headed to the shack. "Do you have any water? My mouth is so dry." She licked her lips for effect, fanned her face with her hand.

"I know what you mean. Dis here Texas weather takes it outta ya. One day hot, next day, freezin' cold. Come on in, I got *eau fraîche*, I fetch a clean glass for ya." He walked over to a rickety cabinet and pulled out a water-spotted glass, filled it with water from a dispenser and passed it to her with a slight bow and a "Ma'am."

Sid had heard Spanglish before, where a bilingual English/Spanish-speaking person intermingles the two languages as they talk, but this was the first time she'd heard anyone speak Frenchlish. Cajunlish?

"May I sit a moment?" Not waiting for an answer, Sid stepped over to a rough-hewn wooden box and sat. Couillion sat across from her, keeping one eye on the gate.

"He don' like me lettin' jus' anybody in here."

"I'm not just anybody." Sid flashed an innocent smile. "And who doesn't like it?"

"The boss. I likes to keep 'im happy."

"Tell me, how long do you keep these cars before you crush them?"

"Oh, we's cain't crush 'em, till folks sign what dey call a release."

"I'll bet this is the lot where they brought my brother's car." Sid stretched to look out a small, dingy window. "Warren Chadwick's car? Think I could see it?"

The man's face turned red. "No'm, cain't do dat les boss say-so."

"Can you ask him?"

He hesitated, tickling his chin with his fingers. "Reckon I can, if'n you wait a minute."

Sid nodded. "Sure."

Couillon picked up a wireless phone, punched in numbers and turned his back. He mumbled something into the phone then grew silent. She watched his shoulders go up toward his ears. Evidently someone on the other end was not pleased he'd called.

His body nodded a couple of times in reply.

Finally, he turned back to Sid. "Yes sir. Got it. I tell her dat." He laid the phone in the cradle and sighed. "Ma'am, he say not today. Come back tomorrow an' he have it ready."

A dull pain throbbed behind her eyes.

"Thank you. I will, and thanks for the water."

"Aw, dat's nothin'. You a nice looking woman—if'n you don't min' me sayin' so. You come back an' visit any time."

They stepped outside. He opened her car door and held it for her. After she slipped in and started the engine, he closed the door. Resting his hands on the window ledge, he bent down and smiled.

"I'm just going to drive back there and turn around." Sid pointed to the rear of the lot and waved as she eased down the accelerator. Couillon straightened, tipped his hand to his forehead.

She coasted to the back of the lot, craning her head for a glimpse of Warren's car. Noise from a huge machine drowned out all other sound.

She stopped to look. A car dangled from a crane, ready for its descent into oblivion. Warmth flushed her face as recognition set in. Throwing the gear in park, she jumped out at the same instant the jaws of the crane released its burden, and Warren's car met its fate in the belly of the crusher.

Four

Blinded by the throb in her head, Sid reversed and eased out of the fenced yard, certain she, nor Warren's lawyer, had signed anything authorizing the destruction of the vehicle. She glanced over at the passenger seat. The scrawled words on the postcard jumped out at her. An eye for an eye.

An involuntary shudder shook her as she realized someone had been out to get Warren. Perhaps they had gotten him.

Shaken, Sid headed back to The Third Eye determined to comb through Warren's files.

Instead, when she drove up, a familiar, older-model maroon-colored Oldsmobile sat diagonally parked in front of the office. A red head bobbed above the rear of the driver's seat.

"What does she want?" Irritation burned hot on Sid's cheeks. She parked next to the car and stared straight ahead, building up courage, hoping the woman would vanish.

The woman didn't.

Instead, she opened her car door in sync with Sid's.

Aunt Annie crawled out sporting a raspberry beret, of all things, and a bright green pantsuit. Combined with gaudy costume jewelry, wide hips and red hair, she reminded Sid of a Christmas tree. Guilt from her uncharitable thought washed over Sid.

"Hell-o, Siddie, surprise, surprise! Fancy seeing your *Aint* Annie here, huh?"

Most people called her Sid. Only Annie had her own pet name for her niece. More than once, the woman had barged into Sid's life and left her self-esteem in tatters. Annie's greeting usually started off by telling Sid how fat she looked or how unbecoming her white hair was—color it, curl it, grow it longer, cut it shorter.

But family was family. That magical, sometimes dreaded, word obliged politeness and tolerance, or else Sid's dad would haunt her from his grave. He'd been big on family—and his family had been big. Now that the woman was here, Sid's upbringing demanded she invite her aunt inside.

"Aunt Annie, what a sight for sore eyes." Sid stretched her lips wide, hoping they turned up at the corners. "What on earth brought you to Orange, Texas?"

"Good news, honey," she patted Sid's shoulder. "I just moved here a few weeks ago. I bought one of them old antebellum homes downtown. It's just a couple miles from here." Annie grabbed a large metallic-gold purse off the front car seat and slung it over one shoulder. She opened the back door, scooped up Chesterfield, a huge tabby cat, and slung him over the other.

"Why didn't you let me know? Why did you buy a house in Orange? The farm's a couple hours away. You don't want to leave the farm, do you?" Questions tumbled out of Sid as fast as her heart pounded.

"Yep." Annie patted Sid's arm. She and Chesterfield smiled up at Sid. "I just signed the paper yesterday; it's a done deal. We're in the middle of getting contractors to fix up the place, aren't we sweetie?" The orange cat grinned up at Annie as if he had planned the clandestine activities.

"I didn't tell you because I wanted it to be a surprise. I knew you'd be excited. I thought you might even want to move in with me."

Sid's body went rigid. No way in hell would she move in with this woman. First she'd sleep in a homeless shelter—or starve to death lying on a bed of fire ants.

"It's a big house," Annie begged, "and I have plenty of room."

"That's kind of you, but…"

"We've been looking to buy the place for quite a while, as an investment you know. The deal was just too good to pass up. So I told Husband…"

Annie always called Uncle Frank *Husband*.

" …'Siddie shouldn't be there all by herself. She needs family around.' Besides, I come to help."

"Help?" Sid felt like she floundered in floodwater without a life jacket.

"Yeah, you know, with the office work and all."

"But what about Uncle Frank?" Frantic words stumbled through Sid's brain and tripped out her mouth.

"Well, I says to him, 'Husband, you can come if you want, but I'm gonna help Sid.' He just grunted." Annie flapped her hand at Sid. "He's got his chickens and pigs—sometimes I think he likes them more'n he does me, anyway."

"Okay, what's going on? You're not telling me something. Are you and Uncle Frank having problems?"

"Never you mind," Annie huffed, shutting the door on the topic. "You just tell me what to do. By the way, what in the world is intuitive investigations?" She said the two words like she had vinegar on her tongue.

Sid shrugged. "I have no clue."

She didn't have the nerve to outright reject Aunt Annie's offer of help, or to dig deeper into possible relationship problems between her aunt and uncle. Besides, Annie looked like a kid on Christmas morning. "Well, great, let's get off this sidewalk and go inside. I'll put coffee on."

"Come on Chesterfield," Annie purred, "let's us go see what we can do to help Siddie." The orange ball of fur purred back at Annie as she sucked in her breath, squeezed wide hips between the two automobiles and slammed shut the car door. Using the fender for support, Annie pushed herself up to the curb, and put her free arm around Sid's waist.

Sid reciprocated, choking on Annie's Tabu cologne as they

walked across the sidewalk and through the office door.

"Ain't this excitin'," Annie plopped her purse and Chesterfield on top of the desk, "us working in a private eye office?" She grinned, shoulders hiked up to her ears like a tickled little girl.

Sid stopped dead.

"Work? I thought you said help."

"Of course, work! I know you'd never let me help for free. You don't have to pay me much. I'll answer the phone, pay your bills, and clean up—that sort of thing. Won't it be great, the two of us working side by side, day after day?" Annie caught her breath, clasped her hands in front of her. "Warren would be so proud—God rest his soul."

"But—you've never worked outside the home. You—you can't…"

"Now don't you tell me I'm too old to do this job, Missy. I happen to know you ain't no spring chicken yourself."

"Wait a minute," Sid plopped her own bag on the desk and pushed her palms out at Annie. "There's a big difference between fifty-one and seventy-one." Damn, the woman got under her skin. She hadn't felt this controlled since she'd been married to Sam. Being a preacher's wife did that to a woman—or being married to Sam did that to her. Sometimes she wasn't sure which it was, or if it was both.

Ever since her dad died, she'd felt responsible for the only surviving member of his family—Aunt Annie, his youngest, and favorite sister. She meant well, she was just a busybody—and an expert at crawling under Sid's skin.

Besides, how the hell could she pay the woman, much less keep up with her bills? Texas wasn't an alimony state, and Sid had spent a lifetime caring for family and fulfilling a multitude of responsibilities as the Pastor's Wife, which didn't pay a cent.

But who was she kidding? She knew her elderly blood-kin held the upper hand. "If you do work here—I'm not saying you can, you understand—but if you do, you've got to do what I say. You can't just go off on your own and do things like you want.

You must remember this is my office. I set the rules."

"Of course, of course. You won't even know I'm around."

"You can live with that?"

Annie's head bobbed. "Sure I can."

"Okay then, I'm willing to give it a try—but if it doesn't—"

"Now, honey, don't you think we ought to change that sign out front?" Annie pointed outside, shivered for effect. "That big blue eye follows me everywhere I go. Gives me the creeps."

"See, there you go already trying to change things." Sid stood tall, locked her knees. "You said you wouldn't do that."

"No, no, it's okay, never mind." Annie perused the office, scowling at the scarred furniture, the rusted-metal file cabinets, the oversized sofa shoved underneath a side window, and then she snatched up the cat and marched to the back office.

Sid cringed. Oh hell, why hadn't she checked the bathroom? Annie already thought she was a slob.

But Annie bypassed the bathroom and marched right into Sid's small office in the rear. After a cursory glance, she sniffed and marched back into the reception area, her nose tilted upwards.

"What do you think, Chessy? Think we can get this place shaped up for Siddie?" She plopped the cat on the floor, pulled out the desk chair and parked her wide green derriere. "The place could definitely use some sprucing up. Look at that old chair over there," she pointed, "looks like something a dog drug up. This is my desk, huh? You do need help getting this place organized all right." Annie opened the drawers and pulled out pens, stapler, tape dispenser and other odds and ends. The reorganization had begun. "But Siddie, that eye on the sign irritates the hell out of me."

"Oh, I don't know. It sort of grows on you after awhile." A sugar-sweet smile stretched her lips until they cracked. Annie's dislike of the sign generated Sid's interest in keeping it. "And, if you're going to help out here, don't you think you should call me Sid, instead of Honey or Siddie? Those names aren't very professional."

"Sure, honey, sure."

Yeah, right. Well, guess we'll just have to work on that one. The image of Annie growing roots through the chair and down into the floor flashed in Sid's head. Tidal wave or hell wouldn't uproot the woman now.

When the phone rang, both women reached to answer, but Annie snatched it up before Sid got halfway there.

"The Third Eye," Annie announced impressively, her chest swelling higher than her abdomen for the first time in Sid's memory. "Yes, Ms. Smart is here, may I tell her who's calling, please?"

Sid stood, hands on her hips, mouth open. The fact hit her in the face. She'd never again have a chance to answer her own damn phone. Chesterfield purred, rubbing up against her leg, attempting to win her over to his and Annie's side.

Sid didn't budge.

"Hold on," Annie said, and held the phone to her chest. Pointing to the device, she whispered at Sid. "Sounds like someone disguising their voice, won't give their name. I doubt it's anything important. Want I should take a message?"

"No, no, I'll take it." Sid raced to the phone before Annie ran off a potential paying customer.

"Good morning, this is Sidra Smart. How may I help you?" Sid felt herself automatically engage the voice and style she'd learned from Sam, and she hated it. A wave of nausea washed over her, and she clutched the corner of the desk.

After a long pause, the voice on the other end hissed into the phone. "You better think twice about what you're doing, you filthy bitch! You've brought a great man down," the obviously-disguised voice continued, "and God's going to make you sorry."

Sid handed the receiver back to Annie, who dropped it on the base without taking her eyes off Sid. "You look like you've seen a ghost, honey. Who was that? What'd they say?"

"Someone blaming God for what they plan to do." Sid's voice quivered. Who wanted her gone—some fundamentalist zealot? Or maybe someone responsible for Warren's death? If it was the latter, they certainly knew her background.

Just as Sid turned to go into Warren's—her—private office, the phone rang again.

"I'm just gonna let it ring this time," Annie said, her face turning as red as her hair. "Probably same caller. No sense in you listening to that garbage again."

"No, that's okay. Go ahead. Answer it. If it's them, just hang up."

Annie did as Sid instructed while Sid watched her aunt's face.

"Says he's George Léger," Annie said, the phone on her chest again. "Checking to see if you're in. He'll be here in a minute. Oops, he hung up." She returned the phone to its cradle, her eyes still on Sid. "I don't know who he is, but he sure don't sound too happy."

👁   👁   👁

Fifteen minutes later, the door squeaked open and a hulk of a figure framed the doorway. Sid saw him from her office and headed to the reception area. "Hi, George. Come in. Meet my aunt, Annie LeVeaux. She'll be helping me out for a little while."

Smiling broadly, Annie stuck her hand out to George. "I'm her new office assistant."

"Nice to meet you, ma'am." George stepped over and clasped Annie's white hand between his large, dark-skinned ones, then turned to Sid. "Can we talk?"

Sid swore she saw steam coming out of his ears. "Sure, come on back. What's up? You look upset."

After they settled into chairs, the tight smile slipped off of George's face. "What's going on?" he demanded. "Jewell Stone just came by, said you'd sent her. I told you I was up to my ears, besides, I thought you decided to learn PI work—you've hired an assistant and everything. Looks to me like you're open for business."

"Hired is an overstatement." Sid gave a small shrug. "Wheedled her way in is more accurate."

She took her time with the next question. She too had whee-dling to do. "Yes, I decided to give the PI job a try, but I've got a lot to learn before I take on a difficult case. I thought I'd start out with easy ones—those that don't involve murder or violence. And another thing I won't do is sit outside a cheap motel that charges by the hour and snap photos of a cheating spouse." She shuddered from that image now plastered in her brain.

George sucked through his teeth, jerked his coat off the chair. "What a pantywaist. Now I've heard everything. You gonna hire a PI to watch your back while you're watching someone else's?"

He stomped to the window and stared into the back alley. "Dammit, you'll never make it that way, Sid. If you're scared of your frickin' shadow you might as well close up shop and go find a nice job teaching school or something, 'cause this job ain't for sissies. I never pictured you for one, but guess I was wrong. You been carried around on a dang feather pillow so long, you don't want to get off and get your lily-white butt dirty—live in the real world." He harrumphed.

She sat speechless, George's anger seeping into her pores. Chad, at ten, had upset her virgin ears the day he came home from school and said a teacher pissed him off, but now pissed-off fit her mood to a tee. She stiffened her back, lifted her chin. "So what do you suggest, Mr. Léger, that I go fall off a cliff to prove I've got guts? You know my background."

"Hells bells, Sid, cliff-jumping ain't required. Just take Jewell's case, dammit. She don't want me, she wants you. I'll be there if you need me. Right now, you don't know if a murder even hap-pened. It might all just be voices in a crazy woman's head. Find out. Walk it through. If it gets too tough, call me. Until then, run this business like you was Warren's blood-kin—like he be-lieved you would."

"Here." He reached in his pocket, pulled out an object and stretched his arm toward her.

"What is it?" She opened her fist to the offering. A rust-col-ored potshard lay in her palm.

"Pottery from the area's shell middens left behind by the Atakapa Indians. Gree-gree, mojo, whatever you wanna call it, think of it as your own personal PI." He snorted a laugh and walked out of the room.

"I am not taking that case George, I don't care what you give me, or what you say." She slung the words at his retreating back.

"I'm not gonna help her, she's your client." He waved over his shoulder at her as he left the building.

Damn Jewell. The whole case scared the hell out of her—until Sam's opinion of Warren came to mind. "Christians don't mix in that. Remember, we stay above the world, not in it." He'd said those words so many times just the memory of them gagged her.

Annie walked in just as Sid gulped down a glass of tepid water. "Couldn't help overhearing." Her eyes glistened with curiosity. "He was a coming down on you pretty hard, huh? I don't think you're a sissy, hon. I think you're the bravest woman I ever did see. Takes a passel of courage doing what you done. He don't know the half."

Sid gave a sickly smile. "I just wish I didn't feel so scared—confused."

She remembered the last time she'd felt that way—confused. A church member had called, excited to share the latest gossip. Sam was dating Nora, a widowed church member, and they planned to marry as soon as his divorce from Sid was final.

After she'd hung up, Sid had called Sam. Did he indeed plan to remarry as soon as they signed divorce papers?

"Texas law requires us to wait sixty days. But yes, I do. Why?" he challenged.

"It's just—I'm confused." Divorce, after thirty years, felt like ripping out her heart, or slicing herself in two.

"You've been confused a long time, Sid."

Not only did his reply stun her senseless, it clarified the problem. All these years she'd thought Sam loved her, needed her. That wasn't the case.

Sam needed someone—anyone—who let him speak for God. And with God speaking through Sam, and Sid unwilling to listen—the results would be the same.

The decision to take Jewell's case made a sound so clear Sid thought someone had called her name.

Five

Jewell rushed into Sid's office in a pant, fanning her face with her hand. "Excuse me. Traffic got me flustered this afternoon," she said, shrugging out of her jacket, "but at least I'm on time." She dusted a spotless chair and sat, taking the proffered cup of coffee. "Thanks. Your call took me by surprise." She lifted the cup toward Sid, sat it on the table between them while she scooped her hair into a ball and clipped it behind her head.

A spider crawled across the floor and up the table leg. Sid watched, too nervous to go after it, but relieved no flame flickered over Jewell's head this time.

"Mr. Léger and I've talked. I've decided if you really want me to stay on your case, I will. First, you must know—"

"Great, I was hoping you would." A big smile crossed Jewell's face.

"Wait, hear me out. You know I'm a newbie at this detective business. I don't have a license. I don't have any experience. I know nothing. But I do want to know if your memories are true."

Jewell's face grew brighter as Sid talked.

"The bottom line is I made arrangements to work under Mr. Léger. If you want me to take the case under these circumstances, I will."

Jewell's head bobbed like a cork in water. Without hesitation she asked, "Do I sign anything?"

"Yes, you do." Sid passed her a folder. "Read this agreement and see if you're ready to proceed. It covers my fee, which is by the hour, plus expenses. It's the same rate as my brother's. I'll be as frugal as possible, but you'll have to trust my judgment on that. You've paid your retainer, so that's all covered.

God, she sounded like she knew what she was doing.

Jewell read it hurriedly, signed, and handed it back to Sid. "As long as you're the one doing the investigation. I don't want contact with anybody else. I'd rather you not give anyone my name either." Jewell wiped the palms of her hands down the front of her blue jeans.

"Okay, I'll promise you this. For now, I won't give anyone your name. First, we need to find out if a murder and a fire occurred. There may not be records on file from that long ago, but I think it's time we found out. Confirmed or not, it'll tell you what direction to take so you can get on with your life. Right now, you're stuck. Let's see what we find." Her own palms felt sweaty.

"I'm scared enough, just coming here to see you. I keep my sunshades on when I drive through town, my car doors locked. At traffic stops, I look straight ahead." Jewell appeared indecisive, then pushed her shoulders back, stood and paced the room. "I don't know how I know what I know," she repeated, slinging her hands out in front of her, "but I'm not making this up."

"The memory of my father and the dead woman is clearer, though." Jewell's words caught in her throat. "God, I don't want this to be true."

"I can understand that," Sid admitted, handing Jewell a tissue. "I don't either. Maybe it isn't. Let's just keep working and see where it leads us. Now, start at the beginning—what you remember, we'll go from there."

"I must've been about three," she said, sitting again. "I guess Emma would've been five. I remember looking for presents. Maybe I thought leftovers from Christmas or something—I don't know—but I had the bright idea that mother had hidden presents in the storeroom." Jewell slipped her hands under her thighs. To keep from wringing them, Sid guessed.

"We had this storeroom off the back porch, a junk room,

actually. You went out the kitchen and turned right," she motioned with her hands. "Emma and I were in the living room. I said something like I knew where presents were hidden. We ran through the kitchen and out the backdoor, into the storeroom. But as soon as we got inside the room, Emma stopped dead in her tracks. I yanked her hand, but she wouldn't budge, so I looked over at her to see why. She had this strange, far-off look on her face. My eyes followed hers.

A woman with no clothes on hung by her wrists there in the middle of the storeroom. She was so white, stark white, and her feet were tied. I can still see her looking at me with these golden brown eyes. They seemed to say, run, but then again," Jewell frowned, "they also seemed to say help." Jewell choked on the last word. "She might have had something over her mouth, I'm not sure… I-I can't get past the eyes.

Daddy always told us the neighbors ate little kids, so I was too scared to run there. Emma and I just had on our little panties." Jewell stared past Sid, as if the woman hung there in the room with them.

Sid resisted the urge to look over her shoulder.

"Her hair's soft-looking and pulled up," Jewell demonstrated with her hands. "Sort of in a topknot, or had been. Strings of reddish brown hair kind of hung loosely around her face."

She shifted in her seat.

"My father's there, squatting down, like he's looking for something. Two other men are there, one of them is dark, wearing overalls. The other one I can't see, he's behind the woman, but I hear him. I get the idea they're making preparations to do something. Does my father see me? I don't know. Maybe I just knew we needed to run. I grabbed Emma's hand—she just stood there like a zombie—and pulled her with me.

No question about where to run, through the kitchen, to the living room, and into the closet. We always hid in the closet when we needed to get away from him. I wanted my big sister to hold me but she wouldn't, she just curled her knees up to her chest, put her arms around them and rocked, blank-eyed."

The thick air wrapped them both in a cocoon of stillness. Sid heard the furnace come on, finish its job, and cut off again. She held her blouse out from her chest and fanned. Remembering the potshard, Sid rammed her hand down into her pocket.

"I remember thinking we'd be safe in the closet until Mother came home."

"Where was your mother?"

"I don't know, I guess at work. I think she worked at a bag factory, although I don't know how I know that, no one ever told me. As I told you, my family never talks about the years we lived in Orange." Jewell stared off in the distance.

"I don't know how long we stayed in the closet. Emma kept rocking back and forth. She wouldn't talk to me. I know I left the closet at least once, maybe twice. I remember seeing blood all over the kitchen floor and table. Then Mother came home and screamed what had he done now. He yelled at her to clean it up and threw a shirt at her."

Silence.

"Everything goes blank there."

Sid sucked in a long breath and heard Jewell do the same. The coherent barrage of memories struck Sid as believable, too believable.

Jewell sat up straighter, her eyes open wide. "I see myself standing in the backyard staring at a piece of junk metal. You know—the kind they used to put on roofs?"

"Galvanized tin?"

Jewell nodded. "A woman's head is sticking out one end. Her skin is white, stark white, like before. Her hair is brown, soft looking. Her eyes are closed."

Jewell spoke first in past tense, then present, then back to past again. Sid just let her talk.

"One arm stuck out from under the metal, like this," she demonstrated, "and her head lay turned to the side. I remember thinking—she's dead—but I didn't even know what dead was. I

was three for Christ's sake. The woman looked peaceful. I wished
I could feel that way."

"Have you seen this woman before, Jewell?"

"Yeah, it's the same woman I saw hanging in the storeroom."

An uneasy feeling slid into Sid's belly. She wrapped her arms
around her abdomen.

Jewell looked spent, but energized, like she'd just finished a
long-dreaded task. "Remember I told you about a house burning down? I see myself sitting in the front seat of a pickup truck.
That doll's head is over there on a fence post. My father tells me
to stay under some type of old bag he throws at me. He gets out
of the truck and takes a piece of green carpet into this old house
and pours something out of a can onto it, I guess gasoline. Then
there's smoke and flames. I remember horses running around as
if terrified of the smoke.

"We drove off in a truck and he hit an old bag lady. Emma
and I called her Minnie Trombone. She always walked the road
wearing an old brown coat and pushing a cart. Maybe she slept
in the old house, I don't know, but I can still see her face coming up against the windshield. Emma and I are standing in the
seat as he strikes her. We fall forward and our faces are next to
hers. Then she falls off into a ditch or something. She'd been
walking by the side of the road and looked back as my father approached. It seems like he had threatened to hit her before. This
time, the expression on her face looked like a dare. He took it,
and kept driving."

A puzzled frown wrinkled Jewell's forehead. "I don't know
for sure if this is related to the fire. It seems jumbled all together
in my mind. The sun is shining; we're out on a paved road. The
grass is green. No, maybe this is another time," she tried to clarify,
"because the grass seemed brown at the fire. He'd play this game
with Minnie Trombone. 'Let's try and run over the bag lady,' he'd
say, and just laugh. Except this time he really hit her."

Jewell grew quiet. Sid wondered where she had gone, but

didn't have long to wonder. "When I stood in the backyard look-ing at the woman, my father stuck his head out the back door and yelled at me to get away. These two men helped him roll the woman up in an old green carpet and load it into the back of my father's old truck."

"What did the men look like?"

"One, white, the other was dark."

"Had you seen them before?"

Jewell sat quietly for a moment, head down. When she lifted her head and looked Sid in the eye, Sid knew what she'd say.

"Yeah, one of them is the man I saw in the storeroom where the woman hung from the rafters."

Oh my God. Knowing what to expect didn't half prepare Sid for the shock on her senses when it got there.

"Three police cars came to our house one day," Jewell con-tinued. "I don't know if it's related to the other incident but I re-member standing by my mother at the front door when these three policemen asked to see my father. They wanted to arrest him. Mother told them Daddy wasn't home, like he'd told her to when he saw the cars drive up, while he hid under the bed.

"One policeman must not have believed my mom because he stuck his foot in the door and pushed in. About that time I looked back and saw my father running out the back door. I ran after him, scared of what the cops might do to my daddy. They caught him in the alley, handcuffed him and carried him away in the patrol car. I don't have any idea how long they kept him or what it concerned, but—I cried when the car drove away. There must be a record somewhere of that arrest. My father threatened to kill my sister Emma a few years ago. I want answers for my-self, for my own peace of mind, but I want absolutely no contact with the man."

Sid's stomach felt like a pretzel.

"I wrote to the County Clerk's office here in Orange, to see if they had record of the arrest, or if he had ever been convict-ed of anything," Jewell blurted out. "I also sent for a copy of my parents' divorce. If my family won't give me any answers, I'll get my own!"

Sid's admiration for the young woman grew.

"There's some way I can find out why he didn't get any custody rights. My mother always said that she hated Christmas because one year he'd raped a girl on Christmas Day. Maybe that's why the policemen came. But wouldn't there be a record?"

Sid shrugged, puzzled, too. "I don't know, but at least now we know the questions. Let's see if we can find the answers."

If only she knew where to start. She stuck her hand in her pocket and found the potshard.

Six

"But why now, Jewell," Sid asked, curious as to what set her client off on such a search now, after all those years. "What happened to make you come in now?"

Tears made Jewell's eyes sparkle. "The other night my boyfriend was on the sofa, and I had my head in his lap, telling him about my memories of the fire and all. Then this new scene plops in my mind—it's in the kitchen in the green house. A nude woman has been spread across our kitchen table; blood is everywhere. Then my boyfriend asked me to stop talking, that I scared him, and the scene vanished."

Jewell closed her eyes, held her hands out, palms up. "I don't know what these memories are but I want them gone, they're awful."

The tears now pushed over the rim of her eyelids and down her cheeks. Her lips stretched into a tight line. "I don't think I'm making them up, but if I am, I'm as crazy as my mother!"

Clueless how to proceed, Sid said the first thing that came in her head, "Jewell, I've got to talk to Emma. You remember these things, but does Emma? If a woman was murdered surely she can confirm it. I don't want to spend a lot of your money," and mine she thought, "if she can't do that."

"Yeah, I figured as much. Oh, and by the way, I drew this floor plan of the green house." She handed Sid a piece of paper.

Sid stared at the floor plan—hastily drawn on a piece of paper torn from a green legal pad. An uneasy feeling crept into her bones. The detail startled her, doors, windows, and the tree in the middle of the sidewalk at the front door. How old was Jewell when she moved from there?

Until now, she'd treated this whole story as a figment of Jewell's imagination. What if an unsolved murder did occur? The unfathomable pain of such an event hammered her gut as she imagined a parent's grief of not knowing whether a missing daughter lived, squirreled away somewhere by a maniac, or lay dead in a shallow grave, unidentified, the guilty still out there, perhaps still killing.

"I'm confused. How old did you say you were when you were last in this house?" Sid asked, rattling the paper in her hand.

"Three. Max four, somewhere in there. I told Emma to draw what she remembered and to send it to you. She said she would. Here's her phone number." A slip of paper passed from one to the other. Static electricity sparked between them as their fingertips touched; they both jumped in surprise. The mood in the room shifted, almost as if the electrical charge acted as a conductor. Sid saw Jewell's body tense, like a porcupine ready to defend itself. Energy, almost tangible, dared Sid to come close.

"I just remembered more," Jewell said, twisting her hands.

My God, how long was this horror going to continue? "Tell me." Sid softened her voice, straightened her back, and cleared her throat. She wished she knew how to act like a private detective.

Jewell uncrossed her legs and sat up straighter. The tissue in her hand shredded as she twisted it. Tiny pieces fell in her lap unnoticed. "One day I played in the back near a shed. I heard whimpering. I just knew I'd found puppies and took off running. When I got closer I realized it wasn't puppies. It was my father and Emma in the shed. Creepiness crawled inside me and I stopped."

She paused.

Her voice grew softer. "I ran back to the house." Shame oozed between every word. "He sexually abused her then. I know that now, and I did nothing to help her."

Maybe he'd have stopped if I'd gone in."

"I doubt it Jewell."

"He always made us lie down and take a nap. I'd get excited thinking he'd take a nap with us. But then he'd put pillows over our faces. He abused her then, too."

"How do you know that?" No assumptions.

"I heard her cry. He did something to her, I just didn't know what. I go mad thinking about it."

With hardly a breath Jewell jumped to another subject. If she'd been hesitant before, now her words tumbled over each other. "My father told me to throw baby chicks into a barrel of fire to see how pretty they looked when they exploded."

Sid cringed, but forbade emotion in her face.

"We lived next door to this chicken hatchery. He got the chicks from there. At first I felt horrified, but…then I decided it must be okay so I threw them in too. They did look pretty, the sparks flying and all." A defensive laugh erupted. "I didn't know better." Jewell looked like a dog whipped into submission, head hunkered down, tail between its legs.

What kind of man did such things to a precious child, a defenseless chick? But Sid knew what kind. She waited, fearing what might come next.

"I've never trusted anybody since." Jewell's eyes looked like those of a dead person, staring, vacant.

Sid said nothing. Not because she had no words but because she had too many. Good God, how much did one man get away with? She shuddered and hoped Jewell hadn't noticed.

She had.

"So you think that's wrong, too?"

"Hell yes I think it is wrong. I can't imagine someone doing that to a child."

"That's a relief." Jewell wiped the palms of her hands on her blue jeans. "It helps me know I've been right all along—seeing it confirmed in your face like that. Over the years I've begun to doubt my own sense of knowing."

Sid shifted in her chair and yanked up her jacket. Jewell's words hit too close for comfort. Many times she'd doubted her own sense of knowing. She'd accepted others' opinion or judgment, usually Sam's, over her own.

"We never told anyone about these things my father did. We had no one to tell. No one would listen, and if they did, they'd have thought we made it up. I never knew right from wrong." She turned her palms upward, appealing. "Even if it felt wrong, when I saw him do it I figured it must be okay. Surely these memories aren't true. Deep down though, I know I'm not making them up."

She paused.

Silence moved in like dense fog.

"They're not like regular memories. I can't sit here and say I remember so and so happening." Her eyes glazed over. "It's more like I just see pictures in my head—there's no feeling associated with them.

"I called Emma the other day. I thought maybe she could help me. I wanted her to tell me that she didn't remember the stories about the chicks. I didn't think she'd talk with me about it but she did. She remembers them almost exactly like I do."

Jewell paused. When she took a deep breath the sound filled the room. Sid realized she'd held hers, too.

"I'm worried about my sister. She won't talk about it but I know that's why she married a Trinidadian and moved with him to the Caribbean. She's deathly afraid of our father. Her phone number is unlisted because of him."

Indecision battled off the walls inside Sid's head. Should she, or shouldn't she go see Emma? If she didn't, she might never know the truth. Stalling for time, she headed over to the coffee pot and refilled her cup. By the time she got back to her chair she'd made her decision. "I'm going to see Emma after Christmas. I want to talk to her face to face."

"But she might agree to meet with you, and then just not show up. I'd hate for that to happen, all that way for nothing."

"She'll meet with me—even if I have to camp out on her doorstep."

☞   ☞   ☞

When Sid awoke the next morning, her body lay curled in a fetal position, recovering from dreams leached from Jewell's story. She showered and just towel dried and moussed her delightfully easy new do.

What day was it? She'd lost all track of time. She guessed going to church on Sundays did help one keep track of weekends. Flipping pages of a day calendar it hit her that Christmas was just a couple days away. She'd made no preparations other than mailing off packages to Christine and Chad.

She missed the days when her kids were small, their eager faces creating her best and brightest decorations. Maybe if she spent a couple days at home, where they'd grown up, the holiday spirit might show up. She'd call Annie and tell her to close the office until after the holiday.

Annie answered on the first ring.

Damn. She kept hoping it was all a bad dream, but her aunt had indeed taken up stake and moved in.

"Good morning Annie, just checking in."

"Morning, Siddie. Where are you?

I got here bright and early." Annie's voice blasted through the earpiece.

"I'm staying in Houston for the holidays, why don't you go to the farm and spend some time with Uncle Frank. You have my cell number if anything comes up."

"You just go about your business, honey. I have everything here under control."

Annie's declaration sounded good, but Sid knew she still hadn't paid the devil. The day was coming when she'd regret letting Annie barge into her life.

Sid's move-out deadline loomed right after the new year. She'd spend the day packing. She chuckled at herself. She always waited until the last minute—for everything!

When she opened her closet, a wardrobe full of familiar, church-lady-clothes chided her. She yanked them off hangers and shoved them into trash bags, promising the Salvation Army they'd have them before the sun set tomorrow. She pitied the next woman who put the damn things on.

Panty hose were next, she pulled out every pair she owned and crammed them into the trash basket. She'd always hated the damn things, made her sympathetic with men's complaints about condoms on their dicks.

By the time she finished the chore, all she had left in her closet were blue jeans, sweaters, shirts, blouses, a couple pair slacks, and a jacket or two.

That evening, exhausted, but somehow cleansed, she carted out her bedraggled artificial tree and ornaments and spread them around the room. That way, she'd have to finish the job or walk around the mess for days. A warm fire and a cup of cocoa made her feel normal again. She stuck a Neil Diamond Christmas CD in the player then unwrapped the tissue paper from around her favorite snow globe. Turning it upside down she wound the crank then watched the flakes fall as Jingle Bells played on the music box inside.

As she slipped the tissue from the figures of the crèche she'd had since childhood, the baby Jesus slipped through her fingers and fell to the floor. The head broke off and rolled under the sofa, a metaphor of her. Broken.

She'd always looked to Sam for validation, for his approval. Her own sense of identity had depended upon his role in the church and community. How stupid could a woman be? She walked over to the trashcan and dropped in the broken figurine.

Always the dutiful wife, she'd ignored her own wishes. All I want is your happiness. I'll go wherever you want, as long as you're happy. You believe dancing, drinking, cursing and mixed bathing are all sins? Okay, I'll believe that too. Women are inferior and subordinate? Okay, I'll be that for you. Eggs and toast for breakfast on Monday, Wednesday, and Friday. Three meals a day, seven days a week. You'll give me my opinion? Sounds fine to me.

"Gag me with a spoon," she said as she opened the front door and rushed out in the cold night air.

"Good evening, Sid."

"Oh, hello, Mr. Taylor. Walking your dog, I see." In no mood for conversation, she turned to go back inside.

"Wait a minute. I wanted to ask you something." He came up the sidewalk, dog in tow.

"I'm in a hurry. It's cold out here." She shivered for effect.

"Just wanted to see how you were doing, with Sam gone and all. Sure hated to hear about the divorce." He stuck out his chest and tugged his pants up over his belly. A whiff of alcohol floated on his breath.

"I wanted to tell you if you ever need anything you just call me." He made a point of looking her right in the eye. "I mean anything, if you get my drift." He took a step closer and reached out to touch her arm, but she'd anticipated his move, entered the house and shut the door with his hand still in motion. He yelped as the door pinched his fingertips.

She'd gone to happy hour the other day with a good friend who'd warned her about this sort of thing. "You're going to have a lot of men after you," he said. "Because you're a minister's ex-wife lots of men will think you're hungry for a good time."

Bile filled her throat. She bolted to the bathroom and vomited. Easing herself down on the bathroom rug, she allowed herself its comfort, her head a jumble of fuzz. What was her problem? How'd she get in this situation in the first place? More than that, how in the world did she ever find her way back to her soul? Something inside her felt severed. It wasn't Sam, more like an inner repository of herself. It left her long before she'd left him.

⬿   ⬿   ⬿

Christmas came and went. Sid had begged off going to her

children's homes, preferring to hibernate and regroup. Now, she had only one day left before she flew to see Emma on the island of Trinidad. One day left to find a newspaper clipping of a murder or arson or anything tangible about a fire in the early '70s. She might not be a detective, but she wasn't stupid either. If someone had died in a house fire the newspaper would have recorded it.

The next morning she jumped up at sun's first peep—showered, dressed, and shot out I-10 again—heading for Orange. Preoccupied with a fast-approaching deadline to move out of the parsonage, she contemplated Orange as a new address and shuddered. She had to be practical about this, she told herself. If it looked like this case was going anywhere, it only made sense to live in Orange, at least temporarily. A friend had suggested she move into Warren's old place, which still sat with a for sale sign in the front yard. Maybe she'd drive by later.

☙   ☙   ☙

The brand-new red brick library on Fifth Street surprised her. She'd expected a ramshackle old house piled with dusty books. The empty parking lot left plenty of space available as she wheeled the car into a spot next to the front sidewalk. The lease is up on this little puppy soon, she thought, as she sighed, pushed the gear into park and stepped on the handbrake. Another decision to make.

Inside, she requested newspaper records from the late '60s forward. The microfiche machine rolled until her eyes were bloodshot and her fingers numb. Nothing. She'd worked straight through lunch, but hunger pangs won out somewhere around supper time. She took a break to search for dinner.

Options were limited. She settled on Crazy Jose's on Mac Arthur Drive and ordered chicken enchiladas with mole sauce, rice, and beans.

The server sat the hot plate down in front of her, smiled and walked off. Just as she lifted her fork she heard a familiar voice.

"Sid?"

"Mr. Léger?"

"Aw, just call me George, Sha." He pulled up a chair without waiting for an invitation. "Everything going okay on the case?"

Sid suppressed the fact she was still pissed at George. "Well, I don't know if it's a case yet, but yes, I think so. I'm flying to Trinidad, West Indies tomorrow to see the sister. Maybe I'll know if there's anything to the story by the time I get back." She dug the fork into the hot, gooey food. "Right now, I'm trying to find a newspaper story or something about the fire, but I'm not having much luck. I've spent the day going through microfilm."

"Yeah, I thought you had that glassy-eyed look of someone who's had her head stuck in a machine all day." He laughed, patted her hand. "If there's anything I can do for you, call me, you hear? Oh, and stop by my office when you get back, okay?"

"I will, oh, and I also want to talk to you about Warren's car when I get back."

"Great." George said, and headed out the door.

She finished dinner and returned to the library. With a full belly, fired by renewed determination, she dug back into the files.

The picture jumped out at her first.

Three men stared at the charred remains of a fire at Millersfield farm near Hartburg, the date, thirty years ago. A woman, identified as Ethel Elaine Perry, died in a mysterious house fire. Questions remained about why she was in the area and in the house, and what started the fire.

It was being investigated as a crime due to the suspicious nature of the scene.

Bingo.

Seven

Sid held a copy of the old newspaper clipping as if the ashes in the photo smoldered still, thirty years later. She leaned her head against the cold airplane window and gazed out at nothing but aquamarine water far below. A trickle of fear dribbled down between her shoulder blades. She reached over her shoulder and pulled the plastered rayon shirt loose from her back. She didn't have to do this. She'd just go to Trinidad and have a nice vacation. Maybe she should have just called Emma, like she'd first started to do, but after Jewell had told how skittish her sister was, Sid wanted to meet her face-to-face.

The plane engines drummed in her head.

None of it made any sense. In her previous life, separated from the real world, people shut their eyes and hoped bad things didn't happen. They used pat, meaningless clichés. Quote scripture and pretend you live in a perfect world. Like Sam.

A metallic taste coated her tongue.

The warm tropical air and a light breeze welcomed her as she disembarked, located her baggage, and eased through customs with her suitcase still intact.

In the hot, humid air her clothes clung to her damp skin as she walked through the airport terminal to a rental car company.

After the deposit that almost maxed out her credit card, the white-teethed clerk handed her keys to a small two-door British-made car and driving instructions to her hotel.

The steering wheel on the right side threw her for a moment. The feeling intensified when she drove out of Piarco International Airport in the left hand lane, cars coming at her on the wrong side of the road.

Following the map, she headed toward the north coast. Air conditioners, optional, jacked up the price of a rental, so she'd chosen a car without, and drove with the windows down, wind in her face. The magical spell of the island added an extra beat to her heart's rhythm.

The rain forest, lush with bananas, coconut, cocoa and coffee, lined the winding, narrow road. Occasionally she passed rough-hewn tables on the roadside displaying stalks of bananas in varying degrees of ripeness. She wished she'd stop and buy a hand of them, but lacked the courage, unsure where to stop on the narrow snake-like roadway. By the time she arrived at the hotel, windblown and warm, she felt as lightheaded as if she'd consumed a bottle of rum.

Fresh red anthurium greeted her in the lobby of the Laguna Mar Beach Resort, a hotel on the north coast outside the Upper Village of a town called Blanchisseuse. The car rental clerk had described the town's name as French, and the English translation meant 'washer woman'.

She checked in, dumped her bags in her room and flipped on the ceiling fans. Louvered doors ran the length of the cottage. She slid them open, stepped out of her shoes, and strolled onto the private balcony, pulling her shirttail out of her slacks as she walked. Tempted to unbutton her shirt, she glanced around, saw no one, and yielded. A light wind blew the shirt open and tickled her skin. Hypnotized by the island, she unfastened and stepped out of her hot slacks, kicking them aside. She shivered in the breeze, and pulled the shirt around her.

Reluctant, but determined, she turned and walked inside to an old fashioned telephone on the night stand. She plucked a damp piece of paper out of her shirt pocket and dialed.

The phone rang on the other end. Sid turned and faced the balcony. Through the open drapes, the peacock blue ocean waited for her, just like the surfers waited at water's edge.

�   ⚫   ⚫

The day started off warm and balmy but did nothing for Emma's sharp-as-a razor nerves. She wanted to meet with this woman—to help Jewell of course, but if she put her childhood into words, she'd relive it all over again.

The clock on the wall dragged around the numbers. She begged it to hurry, anxious to get the call over with, but every time she looked, the long hand, taunting her, stood still. By mid afternoon, cigarette butts overflowed the ashtray. When the phone finally rang, she jumped like a frog on an electrified lily pad.

"Hello."

"May I speak to Emma Barfield?"

"This is Emma Barfield."

"Hi, Emma, this is Sidra Smart. I think you were expecting my call."

"Oh. Hi. Yeah, I figured you'd call today." *But I hoped you wouldn't, I hoped you'd never call.*

"Can we get together tomorrow?"

"Actually tomorrow won't work for me, the kids and all."

"When can you meet? You know I flew here just so we could talk."

"I've decided I don't want to talk about any of this." She heard the woman suck her teeth in exasperation, but Emma didn't care. They could all just go to hell as far as she was concerned. "You can call me tomorrow if you'd like. Maybe I'll change my mind. Maybe I won't." Emma clipped out her last words and slammed the phone down.

⚫   ⚫   ⚫

"I can do that," Sid said to the dial tone buzzing in her ear. She hung up the phone and walked barefoot across the sisal rug to the balcony and flopped in a lounge chair.

Now what the hell did she do?

A donkey brayed. She peered around the corner of the building following the noise. Piled high with freshly cut sugar cane, a cart sat up to its axle in mud. An old man in a dilapidated straw hat stood in front of the donkey pulling the animal forward. Just as determined, the donkey pulled backward, yellow teeth bared, hooves dug into the ground.

Sid felt like both the old man and the cart. What if she'd come all this way for nothing? She thought of Jewell and the pain the woman strung up in the storeroom must have felt.

"Well, Emma's just going to have to deal with me, that's all there is to it," she broadcasted to the bird perched on the railing in front of her. She jumped out of the chair, startling the bird, and marched back to the phone and dialed Emma again.

Without greeting or preamble when Emma answered, Sid launched in. "Emma, I know you're afraid of your past. But this is important; you need to meet with me." She heard heavy breathing on the other end, but stood resolute, the phone at her ear.

Again, Sid heard the dial tone.

She dialed again.

Emma picked it up on the first ring and yelled. "Why? Why should I?"

"Because Jewell is your sister, and she needs your help."

"No one's ever been there for me my whole damned life. Now you expect me to just drop everything, change all my plans, meet you and spill my guts? I don't think so. What's in it for me?"

"Maybe nothing. Maybe a lot. I don't know Emma, but Jewell needs to put some issues to rest for her own sanity. We think you can help. You don't have to tell me anything you don't want to. You're in control. Just come talk with me for a few minutes. You can leave when you want."

"Okay. So what if I do meet with you, then what?"

"I honestly don't know. It depends. But after we talk, I can give you a better idea." Sid stood straighter and held her breath, conscious of the pulse beat in her ear.

"Tomorrow morning, nine o'clock, in the lobby of the Laguna Mar Hotel?"

"Alright," Emma spat the word out. "I know where the hotel is. Look for someone with screwed-up hair. I chopped it off and dyed it red. I don't know why I do that. He always chopped my hair off—so short it embarrassed me, and yet I keep doing it to myself. Crazy, huh?"

❧   ❧   ❧

Emma awoke hyperventilating, digging her nails into her palms. The bedcovers trapped her legs; her pillow lay on the floor. She flung her hand to the other side of the bed. Empty. What time had Rahim left for work?

What kind of questions would this Sid woman ask? She hoped they only talked about Jewell. "I'm fine," she proclaimed to the breakfast dishes, but defensiveness followed her into the bathroom like a specter, and helped do her face and hair.

Jewell had asked her to draw a floor plan of the green house and give it to Sid. On the bus ride over to the hotel, she dug into the large brown envelope and pulled out a pen and stenographer's notebook. Her mind snuck back to Finnell Street, her eyes focused on nothing.

The green house waited for Emma, as clearly as if she were standing in the front yard. Chills crept up her spine and down her arm as the pen moved across the page, giving life to that house again. She'd spent years trying to forget the green house ever existed. Now, the floor plan wrenched her right back inside it. The pen slipped in her sweaty palm. Emma stopped drawing and stared out the window, her eyes desperate for something to anchor her in the present moment.

The bus climbed up the windy Paria Main Road. Rain fell heavily now and cascaded off the mountain. She hurried to finish the floor plan before the revulsion returned.

She wasn't ready, but the bus stopped anyway.

Time to get off.

With each stride she felt one step nearer the hangman's noose, but even that seemed a better place than her past. Her greatest fear, the past and the present now one, loomed fast and furious.

She checked her watch. A few minutes left. She stopped at a roadside vendor, bought a Buljol and forced herself to eat the coconut bake filled with salted codfish. Maybe the food would settle her stomach. Besides, she still needed more time to think. About what, she wasn't sure.

What did this Sid-woman know about her? What questions would she ask? Humiliation and shame heated her cheeks. She could just not show up. "Dammit, Jewell, stop bothering me!" She swore aloud at her absent sister just as a man walked by with his Roti and juice. He looked at her oddly, and then gave her a wide berth.

No, she at least owed it to Jewell to keep the appointment. If she didn't get up right now, she'd change her mind. She stalked down the road towards the hotel. With every step, she begged the obeah woman to snatch her up and make her disappear.

Jewell had described Sid as a "gentle-looking woman in her fifties." Not much to go on. She hoped the woman was five minutes late. If she was, Emma was leaving—and it'd be Ms Smart's fault Emma didn't show.

👁   👁   👁

Sid walked into the lobby, selected a seat near the glass-topped rattan coffee table and scanned the room. Workers disassembled a gigantic Christmas tree in the corner. Poinsettias bloomed in brightly colored foil pots.

There she is. Sid watched the young woman skulk across the lobby like a fawn ready to bolt. The flip-flop of rubber thongs slapping against her heels resonated on the terrazzo floor. She wore a one-piece, short jumpsuit of dark-flowered material. Sid saw no purse or handbag, simply a large brown envelope clutched in Emma's hand.

She glanced toward Sid, and then quickly looked away.

Give it time. Give her time. The room scan continued. Emma's eyes and ears seemed her weapon of choice, alert for the first movement of an enemy.

Emma snuck into the lobby and balanced on the edge of a wicker chair. Where was the 'gentle-looking woman in her fifties'? A sigh slid past her lips as she watched the tourists. They had a certain look about them, an air of self-importance, superiority. Emma focused on the silver-haired woman across the room who sat with her hands in her lap. Her head of white hair reminded Emma of the old Barbara Stanwyck movies on late night television. Except this woman's was cropped close, chic, like the British movie star, what was her name? She gave the woman a condescending look. *Isn't she Miss La-tee-da?* Emma needed a cigarette, bad. *Screw making a good first impression.* She scrambled through the envelope until she found one, lit it, and inhaled.

Across the lobby, a woman stood and stared at Emma. The stupid, way-too-short purple polyester pants the woman wore combined with tennis shoes and tube socks looked tacky. The white ruffled blouse looked like something out of the seventies. Oh boy, if that's her, I'm going to say I'm not me and leave.

Miss La-tee-da walked toward Emma. *She's coming to complain about my cigarette, I know she is.*

Emma stubbed it in an ashtray. Now let the woman moan about her smoking.

The woman looked at her, questions in her eyes. "Emma?"

Emma jumped. "Yeah?"

"Hi, I'm Sid."

Boy, who would've thought–Miss La-tee-da. At least she's not Miss Purple Polyester Pants.

Emma and Sid walked around the building and found a quiet corner in a hall lobby. Sid sat on one of the wicker chairs with her back to an outside wall of windows.

"Okay, we're here. How do we start?" Emma blurted out as she sat on the sofa.

"Thank you for meeting with me, Emma. I know you came because your sister asked you to. That takes a lot of courage."

Emma nodded. She stubbed out a Virginia Slims Menthol Light and with a shaking hand lit another. "You don't mind if I smoke?"

"No, that's fine."

"Are you sure? I really need my cigarettes." She laughed again, and then pinched off the laugh with a wheeze.

"It's okay. Do whatever it takes to make you comfortable." Sid did mind but suppressed the feeling.

Emma lit the cigarette, took a deep draw, and exhaled. "How was your trip?" Her voice sounded tinny.

"Smooth, just long."

Not a muscle moved on Emma's face, only her eyes revealed secrets hidden inside. They looked weary. Finally she spoke. "I know Jewell hopes I remember a murder, but I don't," she said in an affected nasal twang, "but I do remember a fire."

"Tell me what you remember."

Emma started to speak, then stopped and looked at Sid blank-eyed.

"Look out the window if that helps." Sid leaned back in her chair, giving Emma lots of personal space. "Just think back on that day and tell me what you remember. Don't pay attention to me, forget that I'm here."

Turning sideways, Emma pulled her legs into the chair. She wrapped her arms around her knees and then reached and slid the ashtray across the table within easy reach. She took another deep draw on the cigarette. Ethereal-looking smoke curled around her face. "I'm in the back of a pickup truck. I don't know how I got there. I don't know if anyone is with me. I don't know if anyone is not with me. I'm watching Roy Manly. I just remember being in the back of the truck, watching. I must have crawled around or something, I don't know. I see him coming toward the truck. He has something in his hand." Her voice droned, detached.

"He?" Sid asked. Again, she made no assumptions.

"Roy Manly. I won't call him my father. Fathers don't do to their daughters what he did to me." The mask disguising Emma's emotions weakened.

Sid agreed. "Okay, so he's coming toward the truck. What happens next?"

"Yeah," Emma said.

There went the nasal thing again.

"He's taken a piece of rolled-up carpet into this old house and thrown gasoline on it. There's trash around the yard."

Emma paused.

"What else do you see?" Sid pushed her harder.

"A fence."

"What kind of fence? Anything unusual there?"

"Yeah, like—glass bottles—blue, you know the kind…and," she turned and looked at Sid, a puzzled frown across her fore-head, like she didn't believe her own eyes. "A doll head? That doesn't make sense. Why would someone put a doll head on a fence post?"

Sid's heart felt like it flipped out of rhythm. Her toes curled inside her shoes.

She settled down to listen, comparing Emma's memories to Jewell's. "Keep going. What else do you see?"

"I see him walking away from the burning house." Emma paused, a strange expression on her face. "It's like—the devil's coming out of the flames." Emma looked at her, startled. "He's angry. He's angry!" she cried, her face bright red, her eyes squint-ed into tight lines.

Sid pushed past the panic cramming up into her throat. "How do you know he's angry, Emma?" She made her words soft, encouraging.

Emma grew quiet and stared out the window. Her eyes looked hollow—like they'd been scraped raw and left sightless. "I hear him. He's yelling at me." Emma slapped her legs. "He did it. I know he did it!"

"Tell me what you see." Sid wished she, too, saw into the past. Decisions would be simpler.

"She's right." Emma's eyes widened. "Jewell's right! Oh, my God, I hear him!" She screamed, drew into a tight fetal position, head burrowed down between her knees, shoulders quivering. Her keening wail echoed off the walls.

Pain twisted Sid's heart until it felt squeezed of the last drop of blood.

Two chubby men in swimsuits walked by and glanced nervously, first at Emma, then at her, and then hurried off, beach towels dragging the floor.

Sid scooted over and wrapped her arms around Emma, spooning her body into her own, shielding her from the curious eyes of onlookers.

Emma's sobs settled into snubs and she wiped her eyes with the heels of her hands. She pulled a tissue out of her pocket and swiped it across her nose.

"I know this is difficult, Emma," Sid straightened in her chair, "but you must tell me what you heard him say."

"He yelled, 'I told you to stay down. If you don't stay down I'm going to burn you up just like I did her!' Jewell's right, he did do it!"

"Emma," Sid urged, softly firm, "tell me what you saw."

"I saw him walking back toward the truck. He carried something."

"What was he carrying?"

"I don't know. It's metal, though."

"How can you tell it is metal?"

Emma thought for a moment and then looked at Sid, her eyes wide. "I hear it hit the bed of the truck!"

Sid cleared her throat. "Okay, what happened next?"

"He yells at me to get back in the truck, says if I don't he'll 'burn me up just like her.' We take off and then he throws on the brakes and I go flying to the floor. He's mad because I didn't sit down, the bastard."

Silent for a lifetime, memories rushed forward. Sid sat back in her chair and listened.

Emma talked.

Eight

"The fall I turned four, he took me and my little sister out for a long drive. We ended up at a farm way off the main road. I remember shuffling through dead leaves. I can still smell them. My little sister and I were tickled at all of the sheep in the big pen. I ran over to the fence and called, but they ignored me, so I climbed through the rails and stood in the middle of sheep of all sizes and shades. We were in our own little world. It was so neat. I was in a sea of sheep!

I heard him, off in the distance. He stood over there with his buddies. They all wore cowboy boots and hats and drove pickup trucks. They sat on the truck's tailgates and drank beer, laughing and listening to loud music. I have the sense they were there to kill a sheep and cook it outdoors. I don't think the sheep belonged to them.

I kept an eye on him while Jewell and I named the sheep. One lamb in particular drew me. Her wool was snow white and she had the kindest eyes I'd ever seen. She rubbed her head in my hands and looked up at me. I knew she trusted me. I wanted to take her home and keep her forever. My fingers kneaded deep into soft, warm wool."

Emma's fingers kneaded back and forth, synchronized with her memory.

"I heard him calling from behind me. I pretended I didn't hear him, hoping he'd go away.

'What're y'all doing?' He yelled.

'Nothin'.

He walked over to us. 'What'd you think of that little girl?' he asked me, gesturing toward the lamb. I didn't answer. I didn't want him to know I'd fallen in love with it. Finally I squeaked, 'she's cute.'

'Well, you want to take her home with you?'

'Really? I can take her home?' I let down my guard. For a moment I truly believed him. I wanted that lamb more than anything in the whole wide world. She'd be my friend forever and I'd love her more than anything I'd ever loved in my life.

He got in, wrapped his arms around the lamb's legs, and carried her out. Jewell and I tagged behind. I knew he'd lied to me as soon as he left the pen because he headed away from the car. We raced to keep up with him. I can still feel my heart pounding." Emma laid her hand on her chest. "He walked over to a shed and came back carrying a sickle in his hands. It all happened so fast!"

Emma squeezed her eyes shut. Her chin quivered, and soon tears poured down her cheeks. She reached for another cigarette, lit it, and took a quick drag. The ashes dropped in her lap, but she didn't seem to notice as her staccato words punctuated the air.

"I will never, for as long as I live, forget the smell of the blood of the lamb." She moved to the edge of her chair, stubbed out the cigarette, reached for another and started to speak, but choked on the words. She shook her head, swiped the back of her hand across her nose and sniffed.

Sid started to speak, but Emma waved her off.

"He grabbed me by the back of the neck and pushed me forward. I can smell his sour odor, all mixed up with the blood." Emma's lips curled. "His voice—it sounds so far away—but he is standing right in front of me. 'Emma? Emma? Do you hear me? Hold out your hands, Emma!'

I raised my hands. He took them in his and held them under the dripping blood, brought them back up and rubbed them over my face and neck." Emma rubbed the palms of her hands down her clothes as she talked.

"He said, 'if you ever tell anyone I did this I'll do the same thing to the likes of you!'

To this day, I feel guilty. I'll never forgive myself for doing that to my lamb that fall day. I think if only I'd picked another one it wouldn't have hurt so much." Emma shuddered. "It's her eyes, so trusting. They still haunt me."

Emma reached for another Virginia Slims Menthol, but her hands shook so badly she couldn't light it. She threw the cigarette and lighter on the table, wiped her eyes with her fingertips, and straightened her shoulders. "When we lived there I went to this church down the street where they sang about being washed in the blood of the lamb. That's the stupidest thing I ever heard of, washed in the blood of the lamb," she mocked. "Been there, done that. Believe me, it ain't so fucking great." She shuddered. "It sure turned me off of religion—I'll tell you that!"

She ain't stopping now, Sid thought. What Emma had refused to even think about for a lifetime, now demanded verbalization.

"Last May, Rahim talked me into taking scuba lessons. We flew over to Speyside, on Tobago. I've always been afraid of water and he wanted me to get past the fear. Well, my first dive was my last.

I'd reached thirty feet and the instructor, who was beneath me, thought I was having buoyancy problems and yanked my fin. When he did, my head jerked back. I saw thirty feet of water on top of me. The sunlight played in the water and danced with the shadows below, sending me into this time warp. Suddenly I was back in Orange, in the bathtub of the green house, and he was holding my head under water. I looked up through the water and saw his hateful blue eyes and missing tooth. I'd forgotten about the missing tooth until then. Jewell was beating on him, telling him to stop. Water filled my nose and ears. My chest burned.

I panicked and let go of the regulator. When I did, I shot toward the surface. Rahim grabbed me and forced his safety second in my mouth, and charged through the water like a misfired torpedo.

When we got to the surface I still thought it was him with his hands around my throat. Only when someone from the shore yelled at Rahim to leave me alone did I realize it wasn't him, it was Rahim."

Sid didn't even bother asking who *he* was. She knew. Roy Manly, Emma's dad.

"I ran down the edge of the water like a wild woman. Something chased me; I felt it breathing close, hard. I even smelled its stale, sour breath. As long as I can remember, it's chased me.

I ran until I dropped, exhausted, onto the cold, wet sand. The tide inched higher up my legs. I wished I was dead, but the rise and fall of my chest reminded me of my luck. I watched my fingers grip the sand and dig tiny oceans that submerged again in the rising tide. A seagull flew overhead, dinner in its beak.

I'd thought all that shit was behind me. I'd promised myself I'd be happy. The only way I knew how was to pretend nothing ever happened. But every day proved harder than the one before. I had my secret weapon, though. I knew how to leave my body and mind, how to find a zone somewhere in between time, where nothing existed."

Emma turned her arm over and stared at the inside. "You know Jewell and I mutilate ourselves."

No, Sid didn't know. Jewell hadn't told her that part.

"I burn myself with cigarettes," she stuck her arm toward Sid, pointing to scars, "to see if I'm alive. Jewell cuts herself.

When I was a kid and he raped me, he always put a pillow over my face. To this day, when Rahim and I make love I have to put a pillow over my face. Isn't that stupid?"

"No, Emma, it isn't. Adults, abused as children, frequently follow the same patterns inflicted upon them in the abuse." She learned that working with Sam when he counseled parishioners.

"Jewell and I had to visit him once when I was a teenager. It had something to do with my mom trying to get child support, I think. I didn't want to go. I threw up on the plane the whole way. While we were there, one day he sent Jewell outside, and he raped me, and got me pregnant. A few weeks later I borrowed some money from Jewell—she always had money—and went to another town by myself and got an abortion. My grandparents never knew."

The ashtray overflowed with cigarette butts and ashes.

"I always tried to intervene when he came after Jewell. I had to protect her; after all, I was the oldest."

Emma hopscotched to another subject. "You know what I fear? Turning on the TV one day and my face is on the evening news. I don't want all of this to come out. It hurts too much. I'm afraid of him. I never expected to tell this to anyone until after he died."

A different mood entered Emma. Sid heard no twang now, only intensity, long suppressed. Once again Emma's cigarette-held hand punctuated the air. "When he dies, I literally will drink tequila and dance on his grave."

Sid had no doubt Emma meant every word.

"I'm not kidding," she repeated, "I'll drink tequila and dance on his fucking grave!" She stuck the cigarette in her mouth then lifted her chin and exhaled the smoke.

Sid thought she'd left the planet.

"He won't be able to hurt me or Jewell anymore then."

The cigarette in her fingers smoldered.

"I kid you not—I want nothing to do with that man. I want to help Jewell, but I want nothing to do with him. Nothing!" Her voice rose in pitch and her hand sliced the air, leaving behind a smoke trail of exclamation.

She paused again.

"I have smell triggers."

Sid raised her eyebrows, surprised at the professional term. Jewell had said Emma adamantly refused counseling.

"Odors that cause a strong reaction," Emma explained.

"No, I haven't been to counseling," Emma snorted, "but I do my own research. Besides, I have friends who've gone."

She's proud of herself, Sid thought.

"Anyway, I lost it one day a few months ago in an elevator. It stopped and a woman got on. She had on some kind of perfume or something that sent me into orbit. I panicked and punched every button on that elevator until it stopped. When it did I bounded out. Rahim had no idea what had happened. I didn't know, either.

Oh, before I forget. Jewell asked me to draw the floor plan of the green house we lived in on Finnell Street. I drew this on the way over here earlier today." Emma threw the paper over to Sid. "I haven't been in it since we left. But I'll never forget it." Her breath came and went in quick puffs.

After three hours, Emma was spent and ready to go home. Sid walked her back to the lobby. Emma grunted something that sounded like thanks and took off. She neither slowed down nor looked back.

Sid walked out the lobby and through the hotel garden until she found a bench under a magnificent Immortel tree covered with red flowers. She sat and soaked up the energy from a tree she'd read represented eternal life.

She felt sullied from Emma's childhood. Although the victimization occurred decades ago, for Emma, today was still yesterday, for she hadn't gotten past it. And until she did, her tomorrows would all be yesterdays.

Sid and the world had no choice but to carry Jewell and Emma's pain, to help find healing for the sisters, else they'd all keep on paying for the sins of another.

She'd come seeking confirmation of Jewell's stories and she'd gotten it—in bone chilling detail. Jewell and Emma weren't through, however. They'd have to tell the same story over and over again before justice was done.

A judge's duty was to provide justice, fairness, rightfulness; the very title indicated such. But that wasn't possible this late in the game. There was no fairness, nothing could come close to making these heinous acts fair. The laws of a civilized society prevented full Old Testament retribution—an eye for an eye and a tooth for a tooth—and thank goodness it did. She wouldn't want to live in one that didn't. But how did a society provide justice—fairness—to victims of crimes committed decades ago, victims who spend a lifetime trying to recover?

She had no answer.

The flight home seemed endless. Sid tried to nap, but a teen-aged sports team, heady from a big win, romped up and down the aisles. The three poorly attended children in the seats behind her didn't help either.

It was past midnight by the time she pulled up at the parsonage. She dumped her bag on the floor, stripped, slipped a nightshirt over her head and crawled into bed. She had never before slept without first washing her face and brushing her teeth. Tonight, she didn't care.

After a fitful night, she arose early, showered, dressed and forced down coffee and toast, and then headed to The Third Eye, eager to call George.

But she didn't beat Annie to work. Thanks to her, the office was toasty warm, coffee perked, and the furniture spotless. But Annie created the bright spot of the room, or at least a hot-pink dress that stretched across her wide hips, did. A royal blue silk corsage covered her shoulder and Tabu cologne saturated the room.

"Morning sweetheart," Sid smacked a kiss on the top of Annie's crimson head. "You smell powerful and you're mighty dressed up today. Going to a funeral?"

"If you must know, I'm having dinner with a friend."

"Oh? Anyone I know." Sid asked, pouring a cup of coffee and stirring in sweetener.

"Did you have a good trip?"

Sid let the change of subject go. "Can't say good, but productive. I need to call George. You have his number there, huh?"

"Here, let me dial him for you." Annie flipped open her address book and started dialing.

Sid headed to her office and sat behind her desk, impressed by Annie's newfound office skills.

Early morning sunlight filtered through the mini-blinds and cast light and shadow across her face as she took a deep breath. She held it a long moment and exhaled slowly, forcing every bit of air out of her lungs. Where did she start?

When Annie buzzed, Sid picked up the phone. "Good morning, George. Remember, you told me to call you any time I needed help with this private investigation thing?"

"I sure do, sha. Have to keep you working. What's going on?"

"Well, that's just it, I'm not sure. At first I wasn't sure I had anything, but this hole's getting deeper. I'm yelling uncle. Can you make time for me today?"

"Let me see. Tracking a big dude this week and I've got my whole damn office hot on his tail." Sid heard the sound of flipped pages and Cajun music playing in the background.

"Let me see. Not today, sorry. Looks like I'm booked." Sid opened her mouth to beg but he continued talking. "Wait a minute. Oh—yeah. I have a cancellation later today."

"Great."

"It's late, though. Six o'clock?"

"No problem. Thanks for working me in." Jewell and Emma's memories begged sharing. No, demanded it.

She felt comfortable with tough, gruff-spoken George. She liked the crinkles around his eyes, and the way he eased back and forth between using his Cajun accent and plain English. She even liked his Cajun jokes. "I'll be there. See you at six."

Nine

George put his hand at the small of her back again as they walked into his office and closed the door. Sid shut her mind to her dislike of the gesture.

"Hey, sounds like your aunt's doing you a fine job."

"I guess. I really can't afford the expense, but…" She chuckled, holding both palms up. "When your dad's favorite aunt claims squatters rights, what can you do?"

"She reminds me of Annie Christmas. Heard that story?"

No, she hadn't, nor was she in the mood to hear it now. She wanted to talk about Warren and Jewell.

"Annie Christmas was this Creole woman who stood six feet, eight inches tall, weighed two hundred fifty pounds or more. She wore men's clothes and did a man's job. Had this little bitty trim mustache and the voice of a foghorn. Man, when she snapped those shiny black fingers, men jumped. Story goes she could tow a keelboat from Natchez to New Orleans and not even break a sweat."

Sid had a vague idea what a keelboat was but didn't dare ask for clarification.

"Dressed like a man, worked like a man, fought and drank like many a men wish they could. Then, ever once in a while, she'd get in the mood to act like a lady, and she'd dress frilly-like and seduce any man she wanted. One day, Annie met a man who could whoop her, and she fell in love for the very first time."

"Sounds pretty close to my aunt, she's married, but she leads my uncle around by a ring in his nose." Instead of a period, Sid put a proverbial comma at the end of her sentence and continued. "I've got to talk to you about the case, George. It's a weird one. Maybe I'm missing something."

"Shoot."

George listened quietly as Sid recounted Jewell and Emma's stories. At one point, he reached up and ran his hands through his hair and down the back of his neck. His dark eyes creased around the edges and his mouth pressed itself into a thin line.

"In the dark of night, I wonder if I'm being taken as the biggest fool in town even listening to these incredulous stories." A fly buzzed down and landed on Sid's arm, she waved it off.

"I understand what you mean, done that before too." He smiled, as if a memory of such an event flashed in his head. "What I look for, in cases like this is, one, is the client's story consistent in detail, in timing? Two, does she set the story up as an attention-getter, or does she genuinely search for the truth? When all the details are laid out, letter perfect, then I'd get suspicious."

"I watched for that. I saw Jewell struggle with the details. Much like anyone would, grappling with dim childhood memories. At times she admitted some of them didn't make sense. I just don't see her drawing attention to herself."

"You said she holds down a job and socializes with friends?" George scratched his head and smoothed his hair back in place.

Sid nodded.

"Sounds pretty normal to me." George leaned back in his chair and propped his legs on his desk. Mud clung to the bottom of his clodhoppers.

A little tension eased out of Sid's shoulders. "What about the possibility of a murdered woman, perhaps never reported? What would you do about that?"

"I'd check with the local authorities, report what she remembered. You say you have a newspaper clipping that appears to fit the story?"

"Right here in my bag." She dug it out and passed it to him. "The sister confirmed this story?"

Sid nodded. "And more!"

"All the better." He grew quiet, picked up a pen, flipped it back and forth in his fingers, and laid it back on the desk. He walked over to the pot and poured coffee, added sugar and milk, and handed Sid's cup to her. "You need a big shot of brandy today," he laughed and poured in a shot. "This is a tough case. Think you're up to it?"

Sid shrugged. She didn't have an answer to that question.

"My thoughts, too," she said, "about calling whomever you're supposed to call with something like this. Only thing is," she continued, "she's afraid of her father and suspicious of the authorities in this town. She's not going to want to call the police. If anything, she'll want me to. Would you?"

"Sure. That's part of a detective's job." He turned in his chair and stared out the window. "The Police Chief is Quade Burns. I'd call him. Good man."

Sid followed his gaze and watched out the window as two men walked through a fine mist, newspapers over their heads. She thought of Sam and brushed a wisp of hair out of her eyes. At least she thought of him less than before. She still loved him. She always would. But that wasn't the same thing as living with the man.

George turned away from the window. "It takes a lot of courage to do what you've done, Sid. A few months ago Warren and I were drinking a couple of brew and he told me how proud he felt for you. I mean the divorce from Sam—him being a Baptist preacher and all. I know what church groups can be like. They get their hooks in you and brainwash you until you think like they do. No variation. By the way," he said, changing the subject, "you mentioned you wanted to talk with me about Warren. Did you find out anything?"

"A couple of things. Earlier, I received a threatening phone call. It sounded more like a religious fundamentalist angry that a preacher's wife would divorce her husband, but…"

"Some people can't handle a strong woman." George chuckled to himself. "They take everything they read in the Bible as literal, regardless of whether it fits the world as they know it today or not. No ambiguity, no contradiction, no fallibility." He walked to his desk, leaned on it, crossed his arms over his chest and stuck his legs out in front. "They need things in tight, neat bundles." He uncrossed his arms long enough to point a pencil at her. "And if everybody believed like them, then that'd mean they were right. So they judge everybody else by their standards. Thing is, they pick and choose what they want to believe, and then accuse us of doing the same thing."

As George talked, Emma's words about the blood of the lamb echoed inside Sid's memory. Horrors inherent in the song crawled inside Sid, but she forced down the revulsion and refocused on George's words.

"They lose the power of the metaphor, the symbolism, don't you see? They don't want to think, sha. They want rules handed down on tablets of stone."

Sid laughed with the last comment. "Perhaps you're on to something. You just described me, a few years back."

"No, Sid, you're too genuine a person."

"But I wasn't, for too many years. That's what ate away at me. Perfection—perfect role model for the world— was the goal, instead of just being." She cleared her throat, stood, and adjusted her pants legs. "You wouldn't believe the pressure I put on myself to accomplish that goal."

Straightening shoulders that had slumped as she sat, she grabbed her car keys from the corner of George's desk. "Sorry, I gave away more information about myself than I intended to reveal."

He shook his head and waved her off. "One thing about this job, sha, you got to know the person you work with. Your life depends on it. And to tell you the truth, I only trust *Les femmes* who done been *Sorcière,* you know, up on a broom."

"Guess that gives me permission to fly, huh?"

"Sounds good to me!" George snickered.

"Lost my train of thought," Sid said, also snickering. "Let's see—what was I saying—oh yes, the phone call. Then I wondered if the caller wanted me to think he was a religious zealot just to scare me off running the Third Eye. When you and I met, you weren't sure Warren's death was accidental. That comment nudged me out to the junk yard to see Warren's car. Just after I arrived, they dropped it into the car crusher. Odd coincidence, don't you think?"

"I'd say so, yeah."

"Something else is going on there, too." She pulled out the postcard and showed it to George. "This was in Warren's mail when I first got there."

Warren read it, flipped it over. "Hmm," he said, and handed it back to Sid. "Something smells."

"You know who owns the junkyard?"

"No, but you can sure find out. Check the County Tax Office records. You can even check 'em on line. I'd help you, but right now I'm up to my ass in alligators."

A ringing phone and a knock on the door underlined the pressure on George.

He walked her out of his office and to the front door, side-stepping three people in the lobby.

The rain had stopped, but not for long.

"Stay in touch, you hear?" George held her by the shoulders and looked square in her eyes. "Call me when you need me, and for sure call Chief Burns."

George hadn't said what she'd hoped. Drop the thirty-year-old case. Police have enough work today, with neither the time nor the interest in a case that might have occurred years ago. But he didn't. Shit.

"My name is Sid Smart," she said out loud, practicing her

phone call to Chief Burns. "I've got a client who remembers her dad murdering a woman when she was three." She shook her head. "Hello, I'm Sid Smart. A woman was cut into pieces and burned in a house fire over thirty years ago, and my client, who was three years old at the time, remembers it—hello?' She imagined the man's reaction. 'Lady, you're crazy,' he'd say and slam the phone down in her ear. Perhaps she'd investigate a little bit more before she called Chief Quade Burns.

From what she'd heard from Jewell and Emma she couldn't, for the life of her, understand why their mother, Nancy, married the jerk in the first place. Didn't her parents see him as a loser from the get go? Next visit? Maybe Dallas. Hopefully, Nancy and the grandparents, Martha and Will, would talk with her.

👁   👁   👁

Sid wanted to call Nancy, but Jewell begged her to get the grandmother's approval. The daughters were well-trained to protect their mother.

Martha answered the phone. At first she sounded friendly, but after Sid explained who she was and what she wanted, her voice grew tight, wary.

"Well, let me talk with Will and see what he says. Can you wait a minute?"

Sid heard Martha lay the phone down and walk off. Hope faded, but when she returned, Martha said yes, come the next day before noon while Nancy worked.

It was late by the time she drove into Dallas, located a room and settled in for the night. She crawled in bed, nibbling on a sandwich, but after the first few bites her stomach clenched into a tight fist. She flung the covers aside and marched to the bathroom, dumping the sandwich in the wastebasket on the way. Her reflection stared back at her as she brushed her teeth. Dark circles under her eyes looked swished on with a paintbrush.

👁   👁   👁

The white frame house sat behind a low fence. Flowerbeds had been prepared for Texas winter and rested beneath a thick layer of mulch. A row of freshly pruned trees looked ready for new growth. Sid stepped out of her car and walked up to the front door, forcing confidence into the set of her shoulders. She rang the bell and waited. No one came. Perhaps the bell didn't work. She knocked.

Next door, an older woman watched her from a car in the driveway. "Do Martha and Will live here?" Sid called out. Evidently the woman didn't hear her, for she looked behind her, backed out of the driveway and drove off.

Sid returned to her car and sat staring at the house, as if staring delivered someone to the door.

It did. The door opened and a gray-haired woman stuck her hand out and into the mailbox. When Sid opened her car door, the woman glanced up and watched as she strode up the sidewalk to the front steps.

"Ms. Smart? I'm sorry. Have you waited long?" Martha asked. "I was in the shower. Will walked out back with the trash."

"A while," Sid nodded. "I thought I'd been stood up." She smiled and offered her hand, pleased at the firm grip of the elderly woman. Ushered into the living room, Sid and Martha completed introductions. Will walked in as they spoke, wiping his hands on his coveralls before he offered one to Sid.

"Thanks for seeing me." Sid sat in a chair across from them.

"Can I get you a glass of water, or a beer maybe?" Martha brushed her hands across her skirt.

"Water would be great."

"Sure you don't want a beer?" Martha walked toward the kitchen. "I think I'll have one. I like my beer." She laughed nervously.

"Water's fine. Thanks."

Finally settled, Sid began.

"I'm working for your granddaughter, Jewell."

They nodded.

"She has memories of a crime she thinks she witnessed as a child. I wanted to talk to Nancy and see if she has any knowledge of it. I understand you've cared for her and the girls since the divorce. Anything you can tell me would be helpful."

Martha leaned forward in her chair, rested her forearms on her knees, and twisted the beer can around in her hands, staring at it. "Nancy's not well, you know, hasn't been since before the divorce. She might talk with you, but I don't know anything about a crime, except what that man did to her."

"Are you talking about Roy Manly?"

"The bastard." Will jumped into the conversation for the first time. He reminded Sid of a puffed-up bullfrog.

"I take it you don't think much of the man." Sid sat her glass of water on the table, smiling at Will.

"I guess you can say that." A sneer twitched his lips.

"How'd she meet and marry him in the first place?" Sid stopped—afraid she'd pushed too far. "I hope you don't think I'm rude, but you seem like good people. I've been curious as to how Nancy happened to marry a jerk like Roy."

"I'll tell you how." Will's words sounded bitter and full of regret. "She'd just graduated from high school when she met him at the skating rink and brought him home to meet us. I didn't like him from the get-go. 'He's a blow-hard', I told Martha. It's all just a cover up."

"I remember that night," Martha said. "After they left, Will slammed the bedroom door so hard a mirror fell off the wall and shattered into pieces. I can tell you word-for-word what you said," Martha looked at her husband, eyes full of regret. Will stared at the floor and shook his head. "Mocking Roy you said, 'where I come from, you can walk down the street and shoot somebody and nobody will do nothing to you.' Then you pounded your fist on the table and asked me, 'what kind of person says something like that?' " Martha looked at Sid.

"I can see and hear it as if it happened yesterday."

Lament, almost tangible filled the room. No one spoke. No one had to.

"I don't know what good it's going to do," Martha said, "bringing this up all over again."

Will ignored Martha. Sid suspected this wasn't the first time he'd disregarded Martha's wishes. "By the time Roy brought Nancy home that evening, he'd talked her into moving with him to his parents' home in Orange." Will paced the floor like a wild animal caged for the first time.

Martha reached into her pocket and cringed as she pulled out a hand-written envelope addressed to her. "I threw up the first time I read this. Why I've kept it all these years I'll never know. But you need to see it. Maybe then you'll understand what Nancy got herself into. Nothing we did stopped her. Martha's hand quivered as she handed the wrinkled envelope to Sid.

The postmark was from Orange, Texas.

Sid pulled the letter out, opened it and read.

Orange, Texas   August 25, 1964

Dear Mrs. Hubbard,

I am Roy Manlys Mother. and he wanted me to write and tell you about him.

When he first went to Huntsville there was a girl he had taken out and she was from Livingston & I think he went with her once this year. And then she went with anything that would go with her. And then she come up pregnant and she tried to blame it on Roy. and I would not let him marry her. She is 24 years old and had a child before and gave it away.

So Roy is under bond and will be for a while, then he will have to go to court.

He sure thinks a lot of Nancy & that is the reason he wont'ed you to know. Nancy would not tell you and Roy wouldn't either.

I sure was glad to know Roy was going with some one like Nancy. and she can stay at my house any time. Well guess I had better sign off.

Yours truly, Maybelle Strong

Sid refolded the letter, slipped it back inside the envelope, sick herself.

"He's a pig," Will said, "that's what he is."

"Two days before Christmas Nancy called to tell us she and Manly were getting married after the holiday."

"The man made my skin crawl." Will brushed his hand down his shirt sleeve. "I couldn't— just couldn't go watch my only daughter marry the scum bag."

"I had misgivings, too, Will," Martha said, "but I had to support our daughter."

She seemed to plead for Sid's forgiveness, permission—anything to lift the burden of guilt she'd carried since then.

"I knew they'd never be rich, but at least they both worked." Her eyes begged Sid to understand. "You don't have to be rich to be happy. We're not rich."

"Martha went to the wedding by herself. I damn sure didn't go." Will said, sitting again.

And that made what difference? In some ways Will reminded Sid of Sam. Always right. She debated whether or not to reveal Emma's secret, but decided she had nothing to lose. "Did you know that Roy sexually abused Emma?"

Martha's face turned white. Will's turned red. "Oh God," Martha groaned, and doubled over, clenching her belly. "I didn't…she never told me that."

"Not only raped her, but impregnated her when she visited him as a teenager."

"What?"

"Emma says she borrowed money from Jewell and took a bus to Fort Worth and had an abortion. You thought she spent the night with a friend."

Martha whimpered.

"If I'd a known that I'd a killed the bastard." Will pounded the chair arm with his fist.

Sid and Martha, both, jumped.

"I'm sorry to bear bad news. I know this is difficult for you, but what about Nancy? How much do you think she knows?"

Will stood again. His countenance had changed since she'd arrived. Before, he'd been gruff, but friendly. Now Sid thought he'd kill somebody if he could. She hoped it wasn't her.

"Nancy's sick." Will waved his hands over his head as he walked. "She has been ever since she married that man. Martha's worn herself out, dragging her back and forth to doctors. They've had her on all these drugs for so long I think the drugs have made her sicker."

"Did she ever say anything about her husband murdering anyone?"

"Is that what this is about?" Martha looked drained. Guilt tugged at Sid for dragging them through the muck of their past.

"I remember Nancy used to go into her bedroom and talk about blood all over the floor." Tears welled in Martha's eyes.

"I'd go in there and look around but I didn't see anything. Nancy insisted though, she saw blood. I just told her there wasn't any—she was safe, just put the past behind her."

Yes, ignore all you want, and it'll go away, Sid thought. How many times had she done that? "May I talk to Nancy?"

Martha made all the decisions, it seemed, regarding Nancy. "Let me talk to her when she gets home from work. I'll call you tonight. Are you staying in town?"

She was now.

Ten

A simple, small-town wedding, in a church still decorated with the hope of Christmas. Sid stared at the photo Nancy pulled out of an album and shoved at her. Innocence sparkled in the shy smile of the bride, dressed in a pink dress with a box-pleated skirt. Roy wore a striped jacket and dark trousers, white shirt and tie. He looked decent enough, except for the creepiness behind his eyes.

Short and thick around the middle now, Nancy showed no resemblance to the young woman in the wedding photo. Sadness seemed to saturate the woman, as if she'd made one bad choice and been screwed by life. At times she retreated into her own world and Sid wasn't sure if she spoke to her or talked to herself. Her hoarse voice hinted at years of cigarette use. The habit had also left her with a constant cough. Her brown hair, sprinkled with gray, was permed and cut short. Heavy hair growth on her chin and upper lip confirmed Jewell's report of psychotropic drugs. Now she sat across the kitchen table from Sid, disheveled, hands in her lap. She started to light a cigarette, then threw the pack on the table and instead took a swig of coffee.

Sid didn't worry about contaminating testimony. Nancy would never make a credible witness in a court of law. But hopefully Sid would pick up a clue of some kind.

"Maybelle, Roy's mother, gave us a wedding gift of a honeymoon night in the local hotel." Nancy sipped coffee and chain smoked as she talked.

"I was tired and hungry by the time we checked in, and I begged Roy to go buy me a hamburger. He came back with two bags, opened one and pulled out a piece of cold toast and threw it at me, cackling at his own joke. Then he opened the other bag, peeled the white, greasy paper back, opened his mouth wide and crammed the whole burger into his mouth. After he finished, he smacked his lips and wiped them on his sleeve."

Nancy licked her lips, and then wiped them with a tissue.

Sid leaned over the table and laid her hands on Nancy's. "A beautiful part of you must have died that night."

Nancy sniffed. "I snuck into the bathroom, took off my wedding dress and put on my nightgown, and then crawled in bed. I pulled the bedcovers up to my chin real tight." She sat quietly, caught in the memories of that evening. "Later that night I got pregnant with Emma. I know that's when it happened." She ducked her head, looking embarrassed. "Roy never believed Emma was his." She looked up at Sid. "He said I must a been pregnant when we married. But I swear I never slept with anyone but him."

"This may seem a rude question, but why'd you marry him in the first place?"

Nancy's hands lay in her lap, fidgeting. "I was a good girl, you see. Good girls don't have sex until they're married. He made me have sex, I had to marry him."

The old patriarchal double standard again. Woman as commodity. Should've known.

Sid didn't interrupt Nancy as she stared at her hands and talked of her past. "We moved into a small green house on Finnell Street. I remember we had a plastic black-and-white cat with a white clock in its belly." Nancy smiled. "The cat's tail swung back and forth like a pendulum. After the girls were born, they slept on a rollaway bed we put in the closet during the day. The kitchen sat at the back. I remember large white enamel pans, with red around the rim, sat over here." Agitated, she motioned with her hand, as if she saw it all in her mind.

"One day, I came home from work and Roy had a blow torch

turned on the floor. He burned a hole in the linoleum. I never knew why. I never knew why he did anything."

A smile played across Nancy's lips. "We had this curtain that kept getting caught in the kitchen door every time we closed it. Out the kitchen we had a porch, the left end, screened at the top and boarded up at the bottom. The right end was a storeroom."

Sid sat, patient, waiting for the right moment to nudge Nancy deeper. Dare she? Pushing this woman over the edge seemed a real possibility.

"Maybelle made me take a job at the bag factory. They gave me the first shift, which meant I left the house before dawn. When I first met Roy he sweet-talked me, flattered me, and nudged me into doing what he wanted. After the wedding he turned into a monster. Why'd I stay?" Nancy stole a quick peep at Sid. "Fear, that's why.

'You goddamm bitch!' He yelled at me one day, just as I came home from work, tired, big pregnant with Emma. He stood right next to my face. His beer breath made me sick to my stomach. I headed to the bathroom to throw up, but he shoved me into the bedroom. 'Open the goddamned door,' he yelled, and pushed me toward the closet. I didn't know what to expect, but I knew I didn't want to see it. I can still see his eyes glaring at me. 'Take your time, baby, I've been waiting all day,' he said, 'I can wait a little longer.' I opened the door, but nothing jumped out at me or fell on my head." Nancy scraped her chair against the tile floor, stood and walked over to the bay window and looked out. The ashtray overflowed.

Sid thought of Emma. Now she understood why Emma smoked so much.

"I've never told this story to anyone," Nancy turned and faced Sid, her face crunched like a wad of paper. "My dolls—I'd kept the dolls that my parents had given me as a kid." Tears dripped out of the corners of her eyes and rolled down her cheeks, but she forced herself to continue. "They were all on the floor of the closet—their heads torn off. Their eyes stared up at me."

Nancy shuddered and wrapped her arms around her chest. "He'd taken a kni—a knife and slashed their faces and their bellies. There was stuffing all over the floor. All these tiny pieces of cotton floated in the air."

Nancy sat at the table again and laid her head on her arms; gut-wrenching sobs shook her body. Sid wasn't sure whether to let her cry or comfort her. Or cry, too. Overwhelmed herself, she walked over and laid her hand on Nancy's shoulder and waited. So much for delusions of a sick mind. No doubt about the truth of this story.

Nancy continued, her words muffled. "He laughed at me, a hoarse, sick laugh. I got the message. You wonder why I didn't leave him. That's why. My girls were the most important thing to me. I wanted them safe."

Sid gave Nancy a couple of minutes, and then asked, "How did you finally get away?"

"I got sick."

Desperate times require desperate measures.

"They put me in the hospital. After that, my parents took me and the girls home. They never knew how he treated me. When I tried to tell my mom, she'd say 'don't talk about it, it's over now, you're safe, just forget it'." Nancy lit another cigarette. Her hands shook as she blew out the match and dumped it in the ashtray.

Okay, the bastard powered over Nancy, abused her, but Sid hadn't asked the big question. She stiffened her back. "What about a fire and a murder? Did you ever see him with a woman's body in your kitchen?"

Nancy shook her head.

Instead of driving to Houston that night, Sid headed to Orange and got a room at the Holiday Inn, determined to beat Annie to work. However, her resolve faded when sunlight glowed around the bottom and sides of the hotel drapes. She turned over, willing the sun away until the thought of Annie's incessant chatter added motivation. If she didn't get to the office early, she'd have little opportunity to make notes on her trip before Jewell arrived.

Forcing movement, she slung back the covers and dressed quickly. After a quick, hotel-flavored coffee in a Styrofoam cup and a bowl of boring cereal, Sid headed to the office.

A cold front had blown in overnight and, chilled, she sprinted to the door, key in hand.

Dammit, Annie hadn't locked the door the evening before. This wasn't going to work at all if she couldn't depend upon Annie.

She pushed open the door and made a quick check of the freezing-cold office.

Computers, copier, equipment in the surveillance closet, everything was there. File drawers looked undisturbed. As far as she could tell, nothing looked tampered with or broken into.

The room felt like icicles hung from the ceiling. She shivered, rubbed her hands together and blew in them. She headed to the thermostat and peered at the temperature. Je-sus, no wonder she was freezing. She stuck her index finger under the control box to adjust the little lever, but it was gone, like a fingernail broken off past the quick.

Being cold was beginning to piss her off. She put on her reading glasses and looked up into the thermostat but saw only darkness. She grabbed a paper clip from Annie's desk and jiggled it inside in the empty slot. Still nothing.

Frustrated, she looked around until she spotted the fireplace. Up until now, she'd viewed it as Warren's folly—a fireplace in a PI office.

She crumpled a pile of old newspapers, crammed them under the neat stack of wood. After a couple of clicks from the small lighter she carried for just such emergencies, a small blaze danced across the wood. Sid blew on the fire, and then turned and sat on the hearth, awaiting the warmth, trying to ignore a sudden pounding headache.

She looked over her shoulder toward the fire and noticed wisps of smoke circling into the room.

Dammit, she hadn't checked the damper, but where was it? Where was she? Waving away fast-rising confusion, she stumbled around, reached inside and pulled on the damper, but found it already open.

Not much smoke, but she couldn't breathe—sweating.

Her stomach felt like a bear ripped at her gut. She groaned, grabbed her middle, sunk to the hearth, and slid to the floor, as night swallowed day, smelling garlic. Then she smelled nothing.

Squares, white squares hurtling at her. From all directions, rushing, rotating on invisible axis, head-on, rod-straight, see through boxes, solid boxes, large, small squares charging at her, looming—larger, receding—smaller, and then stampeding at her again, geometry on drugs. Squares, squares, stop, Smart.

"Ms. Smart? Ms. Smart? Can you hear me? Can you open your eyes?"

Oxygen returned before light. People were talking, something covered her nose and mouth, someone nudged her arm, shook her gently, but nothing halted the squares.

"Siddie, honey, it's ya Aint Annie, baby, wake up."

Sid sucked in gulps of air.

"Just breathe normally," she heard someone say. "That's it, slow and easy."

Gradually the onslaught of squares slowed, disappearing into the black void.

Like awakening from a bad dream where some unremembered horror hangs like a cloud inside your head, Sid opened her eyes and struggled to sit up, to flee.

"Its okay, Ms. Smart, you're okay," a young man the size of a linebacker leaned over and spoke to her in a voice that soothed the savage beast banging her skull.

She shoved aside the face mask and struggled to sit. Strange arms and hands encouraged her to lie still. Her vision cleared and she saw Annie standing behind the linebacker, mascara-colored tears running down her white cheeks.

"You're in the hospital, Ms. Smart. You inhaled some kind of poison. I'm Adam, your nurse," said the linebacker dressed in scrubs.

Images flittered around inside her head but couldn't take root, couldn't form themselves into questions.

"I think she'll be okay." The nurse patted her hand.

"There wasn't that much smoke," another voice spoke up. "We got to her pretty quick."

Sid followed the new voice and saw a tall blonde, in uniform, speaking to Adam.

"But what concerns me is her breath. It smells like garlic."

"Ms. Smart?" Adam leaned closer to Sid. "Have you eaten garlic in the last few hours? Yesterday?"

"What? Garlic, um, garlic, no, I don't think so."

Annie pushed her way to Sid's bedside. "What's garlic got to do with this?"

"When arsenic gets hot, ma'am, it turns into Arsenic Trioxide, which has a garlic smell." The young man answered patiently. "We'll do a urine and blood test to see if she inhaled arsenic."

"If she did what will happen to her?" Annie asked.

"Lower levels, which is all I think she got, makes a person confused, sick at their stomach, headache."

"But arsenic can kill you." The explanation had not lessened Annie's concern.

"If you get enough of it, yes. She got just enough to make her sick. If she'd inhaled much more though, she'd have been dead in a matter of minutes. We'll give her something to help clean it out of her system. You might make sure she eats a lot of sulfur the next couple of days."

"Sulfur? Where the hell am I going to get sulfur?"

"Eggs, fiber, onion, beans, lentils, garlic, that sort of diet," he explained.

Hearing she inhaled arsenic cleared out any leftover squares of confusion. Sid swung her legs to the side of the stretcher just as a pot-bellied police officer walked up.

"Ma'am," he said, "we checked your flue. There was a lot of rags stuffed in it. They looked like they might of been there a while—dusty, that sort of thing. You're one lucky lady 'cause whoever put 'em in there left a couple large gaps around the corners. Either that, or over time some of the rags slid down the flue. Most of the smoke escaped into the air, that's probably what saved you. I've collected the burned pieces of wood, and we'll test it for arsenic. Mind telling me where you got it?"

"I didn't. My brother must have put it there before he died."

"Did he have any enemies?" The officer glanced first at her, and then at his notebook where he jotted down a few notes.

"I have no idea."

"Do you?"

"Enemies? No." Sid shook her head. Maybe later she'd have an enemy, but Roy Manly didn't know about her yet. At least she didn't think he did. Or should she count the zealot who made the threatening phone call?

Eleven

The hospital dismissed Sid from the emergency room. She was to eat her eggs and fiber, check in with her family physician, and wait for the police report.

By the time Jewell arrived, Annie had a new thermostat installed, had forced three boiled eggs down Sid, and headed to the beauty shop, reminding Sid to pick her up later.

"I've got a throat infection," Jewell announced as she walked into Sid's office sans makeup, hair unkempt. "I don't care how I look."

She flounced into the chair. "Every time I remember something new I get sick with a sore throat." Running away, she said, seemed her best option, from her job, her family and friends. "This isn't getting easier. It's getting harder. Remember I told you I wrote to the Clerk of Circuit Court of Orange County? This is what I got back." She read the letter out loud.

Dear Ms. Stone:

Enclosed you will find copies that you requested of Orange County Case No. 737-S-6. We searched for cases involving Roy E. Manly between the years 1965-75. We did not locate any cases involving him during those years. We did find a divorce case was filed in 1970 for your parents, but it was dismissed.

I am enclosing a refund check in the amount of $50.50.

Sincerely,

Chester D. Wilson

Orange County Circuit Clerk

"I can't understand this." Jewell shoved the paper at Sid. "I saw him arrested. Why are there no records? I know there's a conspiracy in this town. By the way," she said, "my grandmother called and said you'd met with them and my mother. Did she remember anything?"

"She talked with me, and wanted to help, for her girls, she said, but when I asked her about the murder, all she remembered was walking into her bedroom at your grandmother's and seeing blood all over the floor. Your grandmother swore to her there wasn't any blood, that everything was okay. That she was safe now, to not talk about it anymore. If she ever had a memory of anything, it's long gone by now. I didn't get anything about the murder or fire." Sid took a deep breath and continued. "It's obvious she has psychological problems. I didn't push her too hard. She mainly told how he abused her. She knew he mistreated Emma, but didn't know of the sexual abuse."

Sid slapped her hand down on the desk, frustrated at her own delay. "We've put it off long enough. I'm going to call the police and report what you remember." She yanked up the phone.

"Not until after I leave." Jewell jumped up, grabbed her bag and headed for the door. "I don't want to hear it." She walked out then stuck her head back in. "But don't give him our names. Remember?"

How could she forget?

Sid scanned the phone book, then stuck her finger down on a page and dialed.

On-the-job-training sucked. She felt as inept as she did that first day wrapping gifts in a department store. She was sixteen and had never seen a nicely wrapped gift before. Her mother's teaching—lecture points—focused on being slim, pretty, and to not let some ole boy get in her pants.

"Chief Burns here," the gruff voice answered.

❧   ❧   ❧

"Jesus Christ." Police Chief Quade Burns meant no irrev-

erence, but the call had awakened the bloodhound in him. He
hung up the phone. A murder and arson, thirty years ago? Talk
about a cold case.

He allowed his mind to wander. Where the heck did he start?
He'd had cold cases before, but this case was from the deep freez-
er. Old newspapers and inquest reports, that'd be the best place
to start. If he found nothing there, then…he eased his long legs
off of his desk and plopped his hat on his head.

"I'll be back in a few." He threw the words over his shoulder,
to the office in general, and hoofed it out the door and in the direction of Thibodeaux Funeral Home. He hoped Marty wasn't in
the embalming room. That place gave him the creeps.

👁   👁   👁

Quade walked through double doors, as directed by person-
nel up front, and saw Marty Thibodeaux at the embalming table
wearing mask and gloves. A body lay on the table beside him. He
motioned Marty out of the room. Dead people bothered Quade,
and the sharp odor of formaldehyde made it worse. He didn't
dare own up to it, though. He'd never live it down.

"Marty, you've been coroner and funeral home owner here
for what? Twenty years? I figure if anyone knows anything about
this, it'd be you. I got a call from a private detective with a story
of a house fire and a murder—get this—thirty years ago. It seems
a woman's remains were found in the ashes of a house out toward
Hartburg. Do you remember a case like that?" Quade twirled his
hat in his hands.

Marty shook his head and hitched up his pants, but they
slid back down over narrow hips. He pulled them up again and
adjusted his suspender straps. "Man, thirty years ago, you say?
That's a little before my time." He rubbed his chin. The stubble
made a scratchy sound.

Quade nodded.

"Nothing comes to mind, Quade, but I'll check through
some old files. I'm just about finished here—I'll get right on it.

You think there's anything to the guy's story?"

"I don't know, Marty, but it's not a guy. It's a woman. Warren Chadwick's sister. Seems she's taking over his business.

"The woman said she'd found a picture of the fire. She offered to show me her copy of the newspaper article, but that's not good enough for me. The only thing I trust is my own eye. A few years in law enforcement makes a person skeptical, I guess."

"That it does," Marty agreed. "If I find anything, I'll track you down."

Quade trotted outside and took a deep breath of fresh air.

👁   👁   👁

Sid's conversation with the Chief of Police had taken longer than she'd expected. She grabbed her wallet and keys and headed to Hassie's House of Beauty.

She had a problem with beauty shops, avowing they were anything but. She'd never left one that she hadn't redone the mess when she got home. She made a mental note to cut hers again. Where had she packed the pinking shears?

A bell jangled as she stepped inside.

A conglomeration of odors assaulted her senses. Bleach, hair color, coconut-scented conditioners, and overwhelming vapors from permanent wave solution, created an unholy odor inside the bright pink walls. But no garlic.

Sid scanned the low-ceilinged room crammed full of shampoo bowls, floor stand hairdryers and Formica-topped work stations, each encapsulated by a sticky fog bank of hairspray. Orange, red, and yellow artificial flowers shoved into brass colored urns added a plethora of contrasting hues. At the far end, a six-foot, fake-marble Aphrodite stood inside a dry water fountain.

Hopefully Annie was dyed, dried and ready to go. Sid no longer took breathing for granted, and she sure couldn't hold her breath much longer.

Her heart dropped when she spied Annie, encased in a black plastic cape, sitting under a dryer with plastic wrapped around her head, a ladies magazine held at arms length, and henna running down her temples.

Sid figured a seat near the front door afforded the freshest air. She found a chair there and picked up *Short Hair Styles of the Rich and Famous.* When she looked up, Annie had moved to the shampoo bowl.

A tiny gray mouse that made a mad dash for a hole in the baseboard made Sid think of Tom Huff, a deacon in Sam's church, and his secretary's husband. Tom's pointy nose and beady eyes always reminded Sid of a mouse.

She didn't like mice.

She replayed the arsenic-laden-smoke encounter. Who wanted to kill her? Or was she the target? The logs were stacked in the fireplace that first day she'd arrived, so if they'd been soaked earlier, it wasn't her they were after, but Warren. Or had someone come in and soaked logs already there? The policeman said the rags had been there for awhile. An eye for an eye, the postcard read. Perhaps Warren had been the target, and perhaps they were successful—just using a different method.

She shuddered, pulled her thoughts away from smoke to shop patrons.

In the first chair, a bleached blonde stared in the mirror while the stylist alternately sopped up purple-looking bleach, swiped a section of hair, and then stuck the brush back down into the small plastic bowl, repeating the process, all the while talking and chomping on gum.

Pausing from the chit chat, but nary from the process, the stylist blew large, pale-pink bubbles until they popped above the blonde's head.

Sid wondered what pink on blonde would look like, but before the thought left her head, she knew.

A bubble reached such mammoth proportions that teeth and tongue lost control of the wad. The force behind it propelled the bubble out the stylist's mouth like a projectile released from a rubber band. The over-inflated bubble landed right on top of the bleach-saturated head and exploded.

Time stopped.

Then, the blonde screamed, the stylist ran, and Annie walked up to Sid done and ready to go just when things got interesting.

👁   👁   👁

The inside of Quade's eyelids felt like sandpaper. He rubbed them, hoping for tears. How many rolls of microfilm had he gone through? So far, nothing.

A hand on his shoulder jerked him back to time and place.

"Oops, sorry about that, didn't mean to startle you buddy. I'm glad you're still here." Marty stuck a piece of water-stained paper under Quade's nose. "Here man, look at this. It's an inquest from 1971. I found it in an old cardboard box stored in the basement over at the funeral home. Looks like a woman did die mysteriously in a fire that year." A grin stretched across Marty's narrow face.

Quade grabbed the paper, and scanned the inquest. "That woman is on to something. I knew it!" He tapped the page corner on his chin. "Okay, let's check out this date." He ran the machine wheel forward and stopped on the front page of the Orange Leader, a few months shy of thirty years ago. There it was. *Volunteer firemen sift through ashes of mysterious fire occurring recently at Millersfield farm, near Hartburg,* the caption under the photo read.

"This is it!" He tapped the back of his fingers against the tattered piece of paper.

"You're right. That's the same fire." Marty said, reading over Quade's shoulder.

"Oh, Marty, I love ya, buddy." Quade bounded out of the chair, eyes sparkling. "Nothing like a cold case gone hot to get my blood boiling."

He ordered a copy of the newspaper article and the inquest then walked outside with Marty. They parted at the sidewalk, and Quade pulled out his cell phone and dialed.

"Well, it looks like we have a fire and we have a body, Ms. Smart." Quade didn't bother with greeting or preamble. "I need names, and I need them now. I can't go any further without your client's name. Are you located at Warren's old place?"

Sid said yes.

"I'll be right there."

      👁   👁   👁

Sid put the phone down and tucked away the remains of the sandwich she'd picked up on the way back from the beauty parlor. Before she finished tidying up she heard the squeal of tires and brakes, and the slam of a car door. Then a man in a police uniform stood in her doorway blocking the sunlight. He bent his head as he walked in and took off his hat.

"Chief Burns, ma'am," he stuck his hand out to her. "Just call me Quade, everybody else does."

"Sid Smart." She flinched in his grip. Wet-fish handshakes turned her off, but this guy's felt like a vise. When he let go, her hand ached.

"So you're Warren's sister? I heard he'd left you the Third Eye, but I didn't know you planned to run it."

"I didn't plan to. Just taking one day at the time."

His smile lifted only one side of his mouth, giving the look of innocence. "Welcome to Orange anyway. I think it's the best little town in southeast Texas." He rolled his hat in his hand. "Mind if I sit a few minutes?"

Sid poured them coffee. It didn't pay to do too much visiting in this town or you spent the rest of the day stretched out on caffeine.

Quade ran his hand through his sandy blonde hair. "You were right—a house at Millersfield Farm burned to the ground."

He read from his copy of the old news article. "The report came in at 6:50 A.M. They identified the victim as an Ethel Elaine Perry from Melvin, Florida. A man by the name of Edward Pigeon said he'd been with her in the house that morning." Quade handed the article to Sid.

"Marty Thibodeaux, the coroner, found a copy of the original inquest in an old cardboard box in his basement. There wasn't much left to go on, some teeth, a piece of bone, and the testimony of Pigeon. They didn't have enough to make a positive ID, and with no other evidence of foul play, they had no choice but to go with Pigeon's word."

Quade took a big swig of coffee and swallowed. "Of course, if this happened today, we'd run a DNA check on the remains and tie it down real nice and tight. But right now, I need your client's name. You said her father was involved?"

"Can't go there yet." Sid felt the Taurus in her duck its head and dig in its heels. "My client has requested confidentiality. There's lots of fear in this family." She stirred sugar into her coffee and realized she felt embattled. "The father is feared. Seems he made a threat against my client's sister a few years ago, she hides from him in another country." And across an ocean, she thought.

"Well, ma'am, I can't do anything without a name." Quade leaned forward and placed his forearms on his knees.

"I understand. If I get permission from my client, I'll give the names to you." Sid felt Quade's aggravation radiate her way.

"You're a detective—not a psychiatrist." Quade's voice went a pitch higher and louder. "Why do you need her permission?"

Sid didn't tell him she wasn't even a detective. "Because I promised her…I had to find out if there was any truth to her memories. No sense in getting everybody riled up if you didn't have a body."

Quade sucked air through his teeth. "Okay, I'll be patient a little longer. It ain't easy, but I'll try." He stood and walked toward the door. "I'm heading over to Beaumont to the Regional Crime Lab. Any records from this long ago would be kept there. You want to drive over with me?"

"Are you kidding?" Adrenalin bounced her out of the chair. So this was why Warren loved the job.

By the time they reached the crime lab, Sid had confessed

to Quade just how new she was at the private eye stuff, and he seemed to take her under his wing. She listened intently, memorizing everything he said, much as she'd done when she and Sam had counseled church members. He explained how and why old crime records were kept in a regional lab and the process to view them.

He signed them in, writing private detective after her name. She felt like a phony. Perhaps it didn't show.

Quade pulled the file, scanned it, and explained its contents to Sid as he read. "At first, the firemen thought there were no human remains from the fire, but one of the volunteers stirred the final blue flame amidst the ashes, hoping to extinguish it, and found a couple of teeth and a piece of bone, identified later as a fragment from a hip. Forensics identified the bone as that of a middle-aged female."

Sid's heart came up into her throat. "Read that again about the blue flame—"

"Volunteers stirred the final blue flame amidst the…" Quade's words rattled past the fire and ashes and kept going. "Police were suspicious and investigated the fire as a crime, but lacked hard evidence. A man named Ed Pigeon said he'd been in the house overnight with Ethel Elaine Perry and that she'd been alone in the house when he left that morning. His story completed the report. No charges were filed."

Quade lowered the report and looked at Sid, exasperation danced around his mouth. "Dammit. I hate when they do that."

Sid took the report, forcing herself to pick up where he left off, when all she wanted to do was read the damn line about the blue flame until something about it made sense. "The victim, identified as Ethel Elaine Perry, white, and forty-five years old, arrived in Orange only a couple of days earlier. Supposedly she came to town with Ed Pigeon. He said he'd seen her at the house at six or six-fifteen that morning without any problems. By 6:50 A.M., neighbors saw the house engulfed in flames. Pigeon walked into a store in Lake Charles, an hour's drive away, around eight thirty. Soon as he arrived someone called to tell him of the fire."

She dropped the paper on the table in front of them.

"Wouldn't they interview some relative of Ethel's? See if she'd been reported missing or something?" This whole thing didn't make sense. Sid guessed she'd watched too many television crime shows.

"You'd think so," Quade admitted. "Looks like shoddy police work to me."

Either shoddy work or Jewell hit the nail on the head about a conspiracy, Sid thought, shivering.

They finished up and headed back to Orange. Quade looked in his rear-view mirror, checked his blind spot, and then eased into the outside lane of I-10. The interstate felt like a washboard. The rhythmic thud dulled Sid's senses.

"I really need the names of your client and her father. You did say her father?"

Sid nodded. Her thoughts spun. How in the world did she get herself mixed up in a murder and arson? Oh, yes, thanks Warren.

"You know I've got to take a statement from her," Quade insisted, pushing her toward compliance.

"I'll get it for you." Sid said.

Quade turned his head briefly, glanced at her out of the corner of his eye and sighed.

"On another matter," Quade said while staring at traffic. "My lieutenant brought me the lab report on the remains from the fire in your office. It looks like it wasn't just the wood that had been soaked with arsenic, but it had been sprinkled inside the firebox. Know anyone who might have been after your brother?"

Sid shook her head. "No, not a clue."

"My guess is, Warren had stacked the fire, and someone else just took advantage of it and soaked it good. Then, when you lit the fire, the arsenic sublimed, turning from a solid to a gas."

Sid took George's advice and pulled up the web site of Orange County Tax Appraisal, and then sat there with her mouth open. The sole owner of Good Neighbor Junkyard was Tom Huff, the beady-eyed, pointed-nose deacon in Sam's church. She knew the man owned a used car lot in Houston, but why would he own a junkyard, in Orange, of all places. Was there that much money to be made in junk?

"Annie," Sid called out to her aunt. "Come look at this."

Annie walked into Sid's office and leaned over her shoulder. "What'd you find?"

"Would you believe the owner of the junkyard where Warren's car got towed is a deacon at Sam's church? His wife is Sam's secretary."

"You don't say." Annie tapped Sid on the shoulder. "Why would he want to own a business like that over here? It's a long way from where he lives. That don't make no sense."

"It sure doesn't." Sid longed to correct her aunt's grammar, but didn't.

"You said something spooked you when you visited the junkyard."

"I don't know if spooked is the right word, but I sure smelled a skunk in a woodpile somewhere. Couldn't put my finger on it, though."

"But you will, Siddie honey. I always said—you're just like your brother."

"I am?"

"Well, you never knew you were, but I seen things. I always told Husband that if you ever got out of the clutches of that preacher-husband who only thought of his self, you'd recognize it."

Wow, Sid thought, slumping back in her chair, arms flopped in her lap. She'd never seen Annie as having an insightful thought. The idea blew her away.

After recovering from the jolt, she straightened her back and said, "Okay, let's think about this. What would Warren do if he were here?"

"He'd do something, I guarandurntee ya!" Annie said, grinning at Sid.

"And so will I." Sid smiled right back at her aunt.

"You mean we're gonna do a stake out?" Lights on a Christmas tree couldn't be any brighter than Annie's face.

Sid laughed. "We? You pregnant?"

"You ain't gonna do a stake out all by yourself, young lady. Your daddy'd never forgive me."

"But a stake out? I'd feel like a kid playing grownup."

"When we going? Tonight?"

"Don't rush me, Annie. I've got to think about this."

"Promise me you won't go without me."

"Well—I…"

"Let's go tonight." Excitement danced in Annie's eyes. "Nighttime is best, don't you think? I'll pack us sandwiches and coffee, like they do in the movies."

Twelve

Near midnight on the third night of Sid and Annie's stake out of the junkyard, Sid pooh-poohed her insight, ready to give up the watch. The tuna sandwiches were long gone, the thermos of coffee drained dry, and Annie's head lay against the head rest, drool running out the corners of her mouth. She'd been asleep for the last half hour.

Sid rolled down the car window—she'd toss out the last dregs of coffee, wake up Annie, and they'd head home—when a dark sedan and a silver SUV rolled out of the fog and stopped at the cyclone fence surrounding the junkyard.

She hunkered down in the car seat. The realization hit her. She and Annie were on a bonafide stake out, their lives at risk. She'd never felt so alive. Or scared.

She glanced at Annie, eyes closed and mouth open. "Annie, wake up," she whispered, and Annie's eyes flew open.

"What? Somethin' happenin'?"

"Shh, yeah I think so."

Annie's attention followed Sid's pointing index finger.

A tall man stepped out of the dark car, glanced around then headed to the gate. He pulled a key out of his pocket, opened the padlock, and swung the gate wide, motioning the SUV driver inside the fence.

They parked first one car and then the other inside the fence.

"What they gonna do now?" Annie whispered to Sid.

"I don't know. Wait, I think they're going after the car tags."

Once the men unscrewed the car tags, they crammed them down in backpacks they each carried, and then walked out. The same tall man locked the gate and the two leaned against the fence and lit cigarettes. The smoke curled and mingled with the fog, creating a scene from a Humphrey Bogart movie. Sid could hear them talking softly, but couldn't make out what they said.

Soon, a third car pulled up, the men got in the backseat, and the car drove away.

Only then did Sid realize every muscle in her body felt like concrete. Slow-like she let go, first her scalp and face, then her fists and arms, then down her back. She signed with relief.

So did Annie, then, "What you make of that?"

"Beats the hell out of me. Between the two us, we've got the blind leading the sightless," Sid said. "Sure looks suspicious, though, doesn't it? Why would two perfectly good cars—expensive cars—be dropped off at a junkyard in the middle of the night? Maybe we should hang around a little longer and see. You okay with that?"

"Darn tootin'. I come for action. Besides, I'm wide awake now."

Ten minutes later Annie snored.

Sid didn't realize she'd done the same until her head dropped. When she looked up, she saw the sun just at the edge of the horizon and two different cars pulled up to the fence, both with Front Chih—Front Chihuahua—license plates. The drivers repeated the process Sid and Annie had witnessed earlier, except this time in reverse. They hitched the two cars dropped off earlier to the rear of their own vehicles and drove away.

Sid dropped Annie off at her house just as a cold front rolled in, plummeting temperatures, obliterating the sun.

"Take a nap, sweetheart, and don't bother coming in today. You've done your job," Sid said as Annie closed the car door.

Instead of driving back to Houston, Sid had packed an overnight bag. She headed to the Holiday Inn, got a room, and took a short nap. After a quick shower and breakfast, she felt halfway decent again.

And for the first time, felt like a PI. She guessed stakeouts did that to a person.

᭎   ᭎   ᭎

"I'm afraid to know," Jewell sputtered when Sid told her she'd found information on a fire at Millersfield farm. "It's not good is it?" She slid to the edge of the sofa, cocked and ready to blast out of the room.

"We found records of a fire and a body. Actually," Sid corrected herself, "there wasn't a body at all, just a couple of teeth and piece of a hip bone. They identified the woman as Ethel Elaine Perry. She'd arrived in town the night before. The Chief of Police is pushing for names. I'm withholding evidence if I don't give them to him. Besides, he can't go further without them."

Jewell's mouth dropped open and she fell back against the seat.

"I'm overwhelmed at the similarities in your story and the events I've found." Sid softened her voice, but then wondered if Jewell had even heard her. She almost couldn't hear herself.

Jewell slid back up to the edge of the seat, eyebrows raised. "What did you say about the farm? Millersfield? Did you say Millersfield? My aunt was a Millersfield, remember, I told you about her. Was it her house?" Jewell's voice quivered as she spoke.

"I don't know yet."

"We have to do it, Jewell. We have to give them your name and your father's name. We can't get this far and stop." Sid walked over to the window and stared out at the street. "But you're in control." With her fingernail, she flicked a speck of paint off of the windowsill. "If you say stop, I'll walk away from it." Like hell she would. She'd come this far, no turning back now.

"I'm scared, Sid," Jewell's words startled Sid and she jumped, roused back from her thoughts, "but if I stop now, I could never live with myself. I don't know how this is going to turn out—but go ahead and give him my name."

❧   ❧   ❧

Quade sat at his desk with the newspaper clipping in front of him. A frown marched across his brow. Sid stepped further into the room and spoke. "Okay, we're ready to talk names." Quade looked up, saw her, then grinned and pushed a chair her way.

"My client's name is Jewell Stone, maiden name Manly. Her father—Roy Manly."

"Manly, yes, I know him," he replied, standing and picking up his hat, "by reputation—and not a good one."

❧   ❧   ❧

The bronze cannon, a 12-pounder Model 1857, called the 'Napoleon', sat on the courthouse lawn, cemented in concrete. An inscription on the muzzle read '1863, 1200 pounds, T.J.R., No. 315, Revere Copper Company'. The gun had been the workhorse of the Union artillery. Whenever Quade strode down the sidewalk in front of the building, he always stopped near the howitzer. He never tired of the gun's history, told to him by old-timers who sat under the shade of the big oak, across from Farmer's Mercantile, playing dominoes until dinner time.

Union occupation troops brought the cannon to Houston at the conclusion of the Civil War and transferred ownership to the Texas State Militia. The Jeff Davis Rifles, a new militia company used it in reenactment battles held in different towns. On July 4, 1906 the Davis Rifles planned the sham battle for Orange and the troops transported the cannon from Houston to Anderson Park, the site of the reenactment. When the cannon accidentally exploded, driving a ramrod through the hand of one of the participants, the forces were so upset they left town, abandoning the cannon. Eventually the cannon found its way to the courthouse square.

Quade took out his handkerchief and ran it down the length of the metal, wiping it clean of dust. Just at that moment he looked up and spotted Ben crossing the street. He couldn't believe his luck. Pushing against the winter wind, he pulled his jacket tighter, hastened his step, and reached Ben just as he got to the curb.

"Hey, Ben, got a minute?"

"Sure, Quade, what's up?"

Quade admired Ben, tall, reserved, and dignified. All the things Quade wasn't. Ben was older, getting close to sixty, Quade guessed, and gave a laid back impression, but Quade had watched him work. Ben thought out every word in advance. A local boy, Ben made a good district attorney because he knew everybody in the county. Quade, still in his thirties, had a lot to learn from him.

"I got this case I'm working on and I need to interview a woman, thought you might be interested." Quade extended his stride to keep up with Ben's.

His curiosity piqued, Ben motioned Quade to follow. "You look like you just won the lottery, old buddy, come fill me in." Side by side, they trotted up the marble steps, through the lobby, and up the polished oak staircase, its wooden steps worn thin in the middle. They turned left into Ben's office. Ben walked behind his desk and sat, motioning Quade to one of two solid-wood chairs at the front of the desk.

"What've you got? Want some coffee?"

Quade nodded. Ben strolled out of the room and returned with two mugs full to overflowing. Quade watched the coffee, took a big swig, and then shifted his gaze to Ben. "Thanks, just the way I like it, hot and strong." He leaned back in his chair and propped a khaki-clad ankle on top of the other knee. "I had this strange phone call a couple of days ago from Warren Chadwick's sister. She took over his PI business here in town. Did you know that?"

"I'd heard rumors a sister had inherited it, that's all." He shrugged and leaned back in his chair. His hands busied with the knot of his tie.

"Her name's Sid Smart. She's been working with a woman who has memories of a fire and possibly a murder here in Orange. Get this." He paused for effect. "It happened thirty years ago."

Quade had him, just as Sid's phone call had hooked him. Ben spun his chair and faced Quade straight on. "You've got to be kidding. Shoot."

Quade brought him up to date on his research.

"What's the name?" Ben went right to the heart of the matter.

"Get this, Manly—Roy Manly. He's her client's father."

Ben shook his head. "Yeah, I know him—well. I can fully see him involved in something like that." He walked around to the front of the desk and sat on the corner. "Tell you what. Let me see if I can get the time. I'd like to go with you to question the woman. Think she'll talk to us?"

"I think so," Quade answered. "I'll call Sid and see if she can set it up."

"Oh, so you're already on a first-name basis with Warren's sister, huh? Sid, is it?"

"Now don't go getting your panties in a ruffle, Ben. It's business, strictly business. You know Rachel would kill me if I messed around." He chuckled under his breath. "But she is a good-looking woman."

"Yeah, yeah." Ben waved his hand at Quade.

"She's been my only contact so far. I haven't talked with the client yet, or the sister who lives on this island in the Caribbean." Quade stood and pulled on the waist of his khaki pants. "Boy, now there's where I'd like to go." He grinned. "I'll tell you what, I'll go question her." His chances of permission to fly to the Caribbean were about as great as a pig had at flying there. They both laughed. Ben threw a book at him as Quade slipped out of the office and yanked the door closed behind him.

∞   ∞   ∞

Move-out day was upon Sid. As much as she dreaded it, she figured she better find a place to live in Orange. Warren's place was out; too many memories. Besides, his lawyer had called and said he had an offer on the house.

Definitely not with Annie. Move in there and she'd lose all privacy. But if Annie found out she was looking…

Right now, she needed to live alone. After marrying Sam straight out of high school, she'd gone from being taken care of by parents, to being taken care of by Sam. She'd never slept in a bed alone until after she'd left Sam. Never not shared a bathroom, or not had someone else telling her what she should do.

No, she'd keep this search under wraps until after she found a place and moved in. Then pay hell afterwards. Sid had driven by an old white, two-story house with an 'apartment for rent' sign in the front yard. Sid loved old neighborhoods and this turn-of-the-century house had grabbed her attention. She cruised through the neighborhood like a Sunday driver. After a couple of wrong turns, frustration grew. She found retracing her path more difficult than she'd expected. She backtracked, turned a corner, and there it stood, proud of its years.

She parked in front and got out.

A broken, mildewed sidewalk led her up tall steps to a wide front porch. Two wicker rocking chairs and a small square table perched in the corner, dust covered and forlorn in the dreary winter morning. The metal chains of a porch swing creaked in the slight breeze. Sid banged on the door and listened to footsteps pad across what sounded like hardwood floors. A juicy crone opened the door a crack and peeked out. The old woman's wrinkled eyes and toothless smile captured Sid's interest.

"Yes?" The old woman drawled three syllables out of the word.

"I'm interested in the room you have for rent." Sid smiled

and motioned to the sign in the yard.

The old woman unlatched and opened the screen door, "Come in child," she said, and put her arm around Sid's shoulder.

The parlor, decorated with furniture from the same period as the house, welcomed Sid with equal warmth as its owner. Sid wondered if the old woman had dusted the tables after she'd knocked on the door. They glistened in the glow of lamplight. Thick velvet curtains, now faded, clung to rods stretched across tall windows. Sid sat in the Queen Anne chair offered her.

"My name is Sophia," she said, and excused herself to make tea. She returned with a tray covered with a lacy napkin, dainty cups, and a pot of herb tea. Sid suppressed a grin and wondered if she'd put a magical potion in the pot before serving.

Sophia's eyes, dry a few minutes ago, now sparkled with moisture. She flitted around the room, fluffing pillows and opening curtains as if starved for visitors. "My late husband and I lived in this house for over sixty years—until he died last year." She picked up a picture from the mantel, wiped her hand across the man's face, smiled at it, then sat the frame down again. "We used the room upstairs as a guest apartment, but no one visits anymore." Besides, the extra income helps me keep the place a little longer."

After they finished their tea, Sophia led Sid through a kitchen as spotless as the parlor, out the back door, and up the outside stairs to the apartment, holding her long, print skirt in her hands.

Sid pushed to keep up with Sophia. If the stairs didn't slow Sophia, she'd be damned if they slowed her.

"Is there a place nearby where I can work out, a gym or something?"

Sophia nodded and pointed west. "There's a gym over on Green Avenue. Life Styles, I think is the name."

"Thanks, I'll check it out." Sid followed Sophia through the door.

The apartment consisted of one large room. The double bed

sat at one end and identified the bedroom merely by its presence. A faded red sofa squatted beneath a picture window on the other side, flanked by two laminate-topped end tables with lamps. Sophia switched on the lamps and the room brightened to a cheery glow. Tucked in the corner, an old porcelain sink, apartment-sized gas stove, and a tiny refrigerator designated the kitchen. To the rear, Sid caught a glimpse of a claw-footed bathtub through an open door. At least the bathroom was separate. Okay, the place was quaint.

Sophia and Sid agreed on a month-to-month rent, and Sid paid the deposit. They hugged as Sid left. The apartment might be lacking in charm, but the landlady made up for it.

Sid drove back to Houston, arranged for a mover to collect and store those things she wasn't ready to move, and then loaded up enough dishes to sustain her for a while. She collected the boxes where she'd packed bed sheets, towels, and a few of her clothes and toiletries and shoved them into the trunk. When that was full, she filled the backseat, and finally the passenger seat.

One last go through of the house and she'd be on her way. She flipped out the lights, adjusted the thermostat, checked to insure all the windows and doors were locked. Satisfied, she pushed aside nostalgic feelings about leaving the parsonage for the last time and opened the front door

The smell of lighter fluid alerted her a half second before she stepped into a small, but ominous-looking fire just outside the door. For an instant, panic rose in her throat, a thick liquid terror that threatened her ability to breathe. For there on the porch lay her Thompson Study Bible burning as if caught in the flames of hell. Immobilized, she watched the fire scorch the gilded edges of parchment and dance across the black leather binding. Within seconds the gold-engraved Mrs. Samuel T. Smart melted into oblivion.

Then she laughed.

She saw the wicked intent for what it was. The perfect preacher's wife who had never made enemies, had suddenly joined the ranks of the imperfect. Someone was horribly angry with her, and she'd gotten the message—she'd divorced her preacher-husband, thereby ruining a *Man of God*, and now she was on someone's shit list. Whoever did this, had also destroyed her kitchen, made the threatening phone call.

She headed back inside, collected a pitcher of water and doused the fire.

Relieved she was moving out of town, her car full of boxes, she struck out toward her new life, unconcerned about the things she'd left behind. Worrying about that tomorrow—or never—seemed like a good idea.

As she drove, she felt a huge blue orb lift off her shoulders and float away. She rolled down all the windows, opened the moon roof and cranked up the stereo. Shania Twain sang, *She's Not Just a Pretty Face.*

Late that night, exhausted after carrying all the boxes upstairs and unpacking, she'd crawled into the strange bed, surrounded by the unfamiliar. She lay awake, staring at the ceiling, and pondered life events, burning Bibles, choices. Did coincidence bring her here, now embroiled in Jewell and Emma's pain? Pain so great she would forget hers?

Thirteen

The light on the answering machine blinked at Sid when she unlocked the office door the next morning. She switched on the lights and dropped her handbag to the floor. "I'm coming," she said to the nagging machine, and punched the message button.

"Sid, this is Quade," the tape played. "I talked to the District Attorney, and he wants to meet with us when I talk to your client. He knows Manly, has for years. Said he has no trouble believing Manly could've done such a thing. He sees Manly all the time, walking the streets. Call me when you get in. Bye."

Surprised at the message, she picked up the phone and called Quade.

A dog barked somewhere outside, and then a child called the dog to him.

When Quade came on the line he continued. "Hey, Sid, you got my message, huh? I forgot to tell you the District Attorney's name. It's Hillerman, Ben Hillerman. Boy, I'd love to solve a thirty-year-old case." His voice betrayed excitement.

"Hillerman? Any kin to Tony?"

"Who's Tony?"

"Writes detective novels, one of my favorite authors."

"Never heard of him."

She shrugged. "It's not important. When do you want to meet with Jewell?" Sid's pulse sounded like a sump pump inside her ears.

"Ben's hoping we can meet with you and your client on Tuesday. If you can, try to keep your schedule open."

As if she had a schedule.

When Annie arrived a few minutes later, Sid sucked in her gut and blurted out, "I moved into an apartment over the weekend. I've got a new phone number," she handed Annie a slip of paper with numbers, "but it won't be hooked up for a couple of days. In the meantime, you can use my cell number."

Pain lined Annie's face, and for an instant, guilt threatened to swallow Sid into submission, but he'd had the foresight to sign the rent agreement before the confession.

"Why don't you want to move in with me? It'd be fun." Then, twisting the knife, "Guess you don't want an old woman nosing into your business when you bring men home to spend the night," she spat the words and the accompanying spittle, then swiped her mouth with the back of her hand and brushed it off on her bright orange pantsuit. Sid turned, went into her office and closed the door, refusing to feel guilty—or at least trying to.

☙   ☙   ☙

Ben's tall, slender frame leaned over his desk as he shuffled papers. At least the piles of paper hid the burns and scratch marks on the old desk. With ten million things going at once, he'd have to shift his schedule to meet with Quade, the detective, and her client. But a thirty-year-old unsolved murder sounded like too much to hope for—or resist. The thought of it lit a fire under Quade. He'd never seen the man so excited.

Ben pulled a heavy volume off the bookshelf and rubbed his hand across the cover. The soft leather binding, worn around the edges, added a reverence to the book.

A memory—pre-law school—nudged inside his thoughts. How old had he been? Ten maybe, when his uncle handed him a law book like this. He'd been too awestruck to open it. Now, the pages felt comfortable between his fingers, like home. Ben walked over to the window behind his desk, twisted the blinds open, and then raised them halfway, hoping for a better light in which to read. Grimacing at the dark wood paneling, he wished for a brighter office. He stared out the window at the sign across the street. The ludicrous giant eye stared back at him.

👁   👁   👁

The phone rang just as Sid pulled a now-cold bacon-and-egg croissant from a white paper bag. She put the phone to her ear and held it with her shoulder while she finished unwrapping the sandwich.

"This is Ben Hillerman." The warm, resonant voice caused a flutter in Sid's chest. "Chief Burns told me about the case he's been working on with you."

The tightness in her shoulders loosened. An unexpected confidence crept inside.

"I know Roy Manly, the father of your client. Let's see…" Sid heard papers shuffling then, "Jewell Stone, right?"

"Correct."

"Manly's personality and character matches what you reported to Burns. I have no problem whatsoever believing him capable of the crime. You know he's a commissioner."

"He's a what?"

"That's right; he's county commissioner for Precinct Two. He moved to Deweyville, a small community outside Orange, a couple of years ago, so he'd qualify to run in that precinct. He got himself elected last year on the coattail of his deceased stepfather, Dick Strong. Dick owned a lot of property in that area and served a few terms on the school board, ran a few head of cattle. Besides, it's a small rural precinct. I don't think anyone else wanted the job. But he won't hold onto it for a full term. People are already talking recall."

"I never cease to be amazed." Sid drummed her fingernails on the desk. What people wouldn't buy from politicians and preachers.

Ben continued. "Over the years, I've worked on several cases against him. One was a rape case then a child-support case for Jewell's mother many years ago and later, other legal matters with his second wife. After she divorced him, she moved away and changed her name so he couldn't find her."

"Sounds like a smart lady."

"For sure." Ben brought the subject back to setting a date. "Okay, let's see—today is Friday, Tuesday okay with you? Say, four o'clock?"

Sid looked at her calendar, Tuesday, and every other day next week, gaped open. "Jewell has an appointment with me this afternoon. I'll get it set up with her."

"Do you think there is any way the sister might meet with us? I'd sure like to talk to her."

"I doubt it. Trinidad is a long way, and I don't imagine they have the money for that kind of expense. They're just average-income type folks." She paused. "I also got the impression Emma will never set foot in Texas again."

"I understand. Quade and I'll be there early. We'd like to talk to you first."

Sid's teeth chattered.

☍   ☍   ☍

With Quade and Ben coming on Tuesday, the house drew Sid like a magnet draws iron. Finnell Street, 204, Jewell had said, right next door to an old brick building that had housed a chicken hatchery.

She'd driven down Green Avenue, turned left at Sixteenth, and left again on Finnell. Near the bayou now, cypress trees stood in swamp along the roadside, their knees poked up above the water.

She stopped the car across the street, and stared. The house didn't look at all like Jewell's description. It wasn't even green anymore; someone had painted it red. The color of innocence lost, she thought. But she knew she'd never see the house as any color but green. A second floor and mansard roof had been added, which disguised the house even more.

Two trees in the front yard, bare now, would provide shade from the hot, muggy coastal summers. A chinaberry tree stood to the left. The other one, a sycamore, still stood smack-dab in front of the door, only inches away from the first step, just as Jewell and Emma had described. The sidewalk simply accommodated the tree, taking visitors around the obstacle, to concrete steps at the front door. Someone else lived here now.

"So this is where it all happened," she whispered to no one.

Across the alley to the right, the deserted chicken hatchery languished in tall weeds. The old red brick building had its own sycamore tree guarding the front entrance. A screen door dangled by its hinges. The tin-roofed building had two stories in front and one in the back. The rear section, she decided, looked like an afterthought.

Her shoes crunched in the gravel as she walked across the alley to the hatchery and peered through broken, dirty windows. Piles of junk lay scattered throughout the building. A broken-down, pink child's bicycle lay on its side over in the corner. Had it been Jewell's? Odd pipes and lights drooped down from the rafters. A mixture of dark and light wood paneling barely clung to the walls.

Emma had said that she'd panicked late one night when she'd gone out behind a building and heard her dad and other men arguing. Was this the building? It had been next door to her house, and she had run back inside and jumped in bed, crawling under Jewell.

Sid turned and walked down the alley to the back of the building. Useless padlocks hung in corroded locks. The side of the hatchery facing the house had barn-type doors. Were these the doors Emma listened through?

Weeds grew outside and inside the building while the old brick walls and the dangling iron trim added to the forsaken look of the place.

Why had no one ever torn the stupid place down?

An unpleasant feeling crawled across her skin. The hatchery

had waited for her. A coarse laugh rippled up her throat. "That's a scary thought!" She said, and brushed the itchy sensation off her arms.

Sid walked to her car and pulled out a camera.

Jewell, Emma, and their mother had fled this house more than three decades ago. Even though she hadn't witnessed it, Sid felt the horror quiver up the insides of her bones like a cancer eating away the marrow.

Her eyes on the camera, she hadn't seen a man walking her way until a movement caught in the corner of her vision. She turned fast, and almost bumped into a tall, slender man, with close-cropped brown hair and a scruffy beard.

"Hello?" Startled by the stranger, she felt relief for broad daylight.

"You must be Sidra Smart."

"Yes, I am," she raised the edge of her hand between her eyes and the glare of the sun, directly overhead. "Do I know you?"

He stuck his hand out. "Ben Hillerman. I talked with you earlier today, I believe."

Why in hell was her heart racing? "Have we met before? I mean, besides over the telephone? You look familiar."

"Warren and I were friends. I saw you at his funeral. I didn't get a chance to introduce myself."

"Oh, yes, now I remember." The familiar looking dark-haired man who'd smiled at her.

Gesturing at the house and hatchery she said, "I guess this is where it all happened, huh?"

"This is it."

"The girls told me how they tried to forget what happened inside here, and how the memories followed them like apparitions." Sid snapped another picture. "Their grandmother kept telling them to put it behind them," she was running on at the mouth, "and to not talk about that anymore, but she really had no idea what happened."

A car drove by.

The female driver waved at Ben and he waved back.

Sid kept talking. "The doctors treat the mother's symptoms as cause. Mentally unstable, 'diagnosable and treatable,' they say. Her mother says she'd scream that her bedroom was covered with blood, when none existed. Nancy described how, when she lived with Roy, he'd push his face against the window at night, to scare her." Sid remembered her own fear when Nancy had described Roy's attempt to frighten her. Drive her crazy, Nancy had said. Perhaps it had worked—that and the heavy drugs.

Sid grew quiet. She'd talked too much.

Ben stood there, saying nothing, but not leaving, either.

"Do you live around here?" Sid changed the subject.

He pointed to an old colonial across the street, catty-corner from the green house. "That one there, lived there for twenty years, I guess," he held out his hand. "I'm headed home for lunch. Would you like to tour the house? It's been restored. My wife did the research and the planning." Warmth resonated in his voice when he mentioned his wife.

Sid hesitated, and mentally drew a line through his name on a list she didn't even know she kept until that moment.

"Come on, we'll make it a quick walk-through. I know you have a lot on your plate right now, but I think you'll enjoy it—if you like American history, that is." He fidgeted with his tie.

She nodded.

"The house is from the Jeffersonian era." He took her arm as they crossed the street. Just before they reached the front door, a memory of an unexpected visitor and an unappreciative wife flashed in her head. She stopped, mid stride, and turned to Ben.

"Don't you think your wife might mind me coming in without any warning?" Sam had done that to her lots of times, and she hated it. Without fail, the children were sick, the house a mess, and she, a frump.

Ben looked at her, blank-eyed then explained. "My wife died a year ago this month."

She erased the line she'd drawn on the list and hoped she hadn't smiled. "I'm so sorry. I had no idea." The irony hit her like a glass of cold water thrown in the face. There was that feigned grief. She'd just indulged herself, what she resented in others.

"Thanks, but I should be the one apologizing. There's no way you could have known." He put his hand on her arm as he spoke. The warmth of it penetrated her sweater.

Ben took his time, guiding her through the house room by room. Pride showed as he described the effort spent in the restoration. Sid walked into the master bathroom and saw herself reflected back in dozens of antique hand mirrors hung artfully around the room. Some of the mirrors were ornate and polished; others showed evidence of wear from unknown owners…women, Sid felt, whose reflections still occupied the essence of each mirror.

The tour completed, Ben led her downstairs. At the bottom of the steps he put his hand on her shoulder. "How about a sandwich? It won't take me long to fix one."

"No, I really need to go. I've taken up too much of your time. Your house is lovely, by the way. Thanks for showing it to me." Sid stuck her hand out, but instead of shaking it, he held her hand in both of his.

"Anytime, fair lady. I hope this won't be the last time." He looked her in the eyes, smiling.

Pulling her hand out of his, she stuttered something unintelligible, even to herself, cleared her throat. "I don't know much about antiques, but yours fit the period beautifully."

As she turned and walked through the living room, heels clipping on the hardwood floor, she felt the man near her, strong, hot. Half-expecting him to spin her around, relief and disappointment came when he reached around and opened the front door instead.

Idle chatter filled the space between his house and her car, still parked across the street from the green house.

Ben reached around her for the door handle, opened the car

door and Sid slid in. He gave the door a solid shut, placed both hands on the window ledge, leaned over, and looked her in the eye.

"Care to join me for dinner tonight? Seven o'clock?"

Sid hadn't noticed before how straight and white his teeth were.

Fourteen

Jewell stomped into The Third Eye and plopped onto the sofa. Her anger blistered Sid from across the room. "I just talked with my grandmother," Jewell fumed, "and it ended as usual, me losing control and screaming at her. I feel awful when I do that, but she never supports me, she's never there for me. Why can't she be there when I need her? She always makes me feel like everything is my fault!"

Sid closed her eyes and wondered how to break the news to Jewell—that they had an appointment with the Chief of Police and the District Attorney.

A loop of frigid air circled around her ankles as a voice in her head whispered. *Sid, this is your assignment.* The hair on her arms stood at attention.

After Sid told Jewell of the appointment she'd made for them next week, Jewell said, "I want Emma here with me for this meeting. I need her support. I think I'll call her right now and see if she'll come if I buy her ticket. I'll take the money out of my savings. I don't have a lot, but I can afford that." Panic crept into her voice, raising the pitch. "I really need my family's support. Emma is the only one who would come."

"Sure." Sid said, astonished at the possibility and the rapidity. "Feel free to use my phone."

Jewell got up, stepped across the room to the telephone on Sid's desk. Dialing her travel agent she found affordable, available seats on the flight leaving Piarco International Airport at ten o'clock that night. Requesting permission again, this time for a transatlantic call, she dialed her sister.

In a strange twist of events, after Jewell explained her request, Emma said yes, she'd come tell her story.

⬤ ⬤ ⬤

Emma hung up the receiver and stared at the floor.

She needed a cigarette, bad. The familiar pack of Slims lay on the table, her lifeline to sanity. Fingers, nails chewed to the quick, pinched a cigarette out of the pack and stuck it in her mouth. The lighter flame danced in front of her as she focused her eyes, first on the flame and then on the cigarette. Finally the two came together and she sucked in a big drag.

"God, what am I doing?" The ghosts she'd buried long ago rattled their chains. Shooting pains charged into her stomach, and then lurched toward her throat. She flopped down on the sofa and stared back to another place and time.

⬤ ⬤ ⬤

Emma didn't remember how old she was, but she knew they lived in the green house. With a blanket, she and Jewell had built a house over the clothesline in the side yard. Their children were their dolls and their dog, Penny, was their baby. They'd even made a doll bed out of a cardboard box and tried to get the dog to lie down in it. Just playing like kids do. She smiled. Penny must have preferred lying on the porch, but she put up with them.

After playing a while she needed to use the bathroom. "I have to go potty," Emma heard herself say; "I'll be right back."

She ran up the front steps and pulled on the screen door— locked. She banged on it, and did the pee-pee dance.

"What do you want?" he yelled. Even in her memory, his voice sounded mean.

"I have to go potty! Can I come in and go?"

"No," he bellowed at her. He always bellowed when he spoke to her. "Stay out and play."

"I really have to go!"

"No, you just stay out and hold yourself. I'll let you know when you can go. Now get."

She saw herself go back into the blanket-house, holding herself all the way. What in hell had he been doing that day that he didn't want her to come in?

Her stomach hurt so bad. She needed to go, now! She'd glanced over at Jewell, not wanting to upset her. She tried to hold it, really she did.

It seemed like hours passed. The pain grew worse. "I'm going to make a bathroom in our blanket house," she said to Jewell, and dug a small hole, pulled down her panties and peed. Covering the hole with dirt, she yanked some grass and put it on top of the dirt. No one would know. Relieved, she forgot about him.

A short while later he came outside, "Emma, you can go to the bathroom now."

"That's okay, Daddy, I already went. I made my own bathroom in our blanket house. Everything's okay now."

He reached inside the tent and grabbed her by the arm and yelled.

As he dragged her up the steps and into the house, she looked back for Jewell. Her little sister stood in front of the blanket house, holding the doll, tears rolling down her face. Just go back in the blanket house and be safe, Emma wanted to tell her.

She must have shivered. Hell, she shivered now. When they got inside, he shoved her hard. She bounced off the corner of the television and landed on her butt. She wanted to run, and started to, but he grabbed her arm. "Where do you think you're going?" he bellowed. "Lean over!" He grabbed her panties and yanked them down around her ankles.

She heard the unbuckling of his belt and soon the blows began.

That started it all, what she called Potty-No-More. It went on for what seemed like weeks. He made her hold her bowel movements for days at a time. Every 'accident' meant the belt.

She learned that lesson. Now, at thirty-five, she only went to the bathroom every two or three days. The control he still had over her bowel movements! She stubbed the cigarette into the ashtray as if it were a forest fire. He may have won that battle, but she planned to win the fucking war! By healing herself—someday.

Children ran in and out the front screen door, banging it behind them. Hot on their trail were two other children. Another bang. "You kids are driving me crazy," she yelled, shooing them outside. All the neighbors hung out at her house. Not just the kids, their moms did, too. The balmy weather encouraged it, with windows and doors wide open to catch the trade winds. Emma's caretaking sealed it. Emma, although an American, had bonded with the local women. They all came to her with their questions and problems, hoping to get advice. They never failed to get it, regardless of the day or hour.

She took off running next door to one of her friends. "I need to go to Texas and I need to leave tonight." She felt breathless, almost hysterical. "Can you help me work out arrangements for Alice and the baby?" Alice attended school during the day. Emma had Rahim to help at night, but the baby, a handful, required care all day long. The women rallied around and volunteered to care for her children.

That taken care of, Emma ran home, called Rahim and brought him up to date on her plans. "No problem, Sweetheart, you do what you need to do," he said. "The kids and I will be fine. Do you need me to take some time off from work?"

"Patsy and Floris offered to take care of the kids—get Alice to school and all—until you get home from work."

"Great, well, when I get home this evening the kids and I will run you to the airport. Your flight leaves at ten you say? We can grab dinner at Valpark Chinese Restaurant on the way."

After she hung up, she threw open the closet door and grabbed a dress, her hands shaking. No, the colors were too loud, another—no—too casual. Panic rose as she rummaged through the closet. After three or four more rejections, she found something she thought suitable. What she didn't want was to come across like some crazy woman, but she doubted her ability to pull it off.

Never mind. Just do what you have to do right now. You can think about that later. She pushed the purpose of her trip into her suitcase along with her clothes.

👁   👁   👁

Jewell drove her metallic blue-gray Nissan truck down I-10 to the Mont Belvieu exit and turned east on Highway 146, headed to her apartment. Her mind sped faster than the truck, and it exceeded the limit. Soon she reached the bay bridge. The tall expansion bridge stretching over the bay had been built a few years ago to replace the tunnel connecting Houston to Galveston. Normally she loved driving into the clouds, watching the boats journey out to sea carrying their cargo, but today the high wind required her to focus on the traffic.

Her family seldom came to visit. That one time her mother came, after Jewell had surgery, had been a disaster. Jewell ended up taking care of her mother rather than the other way around.

A pinpoint of anxiety crept in and began to grow, blending with the excitement, until the two became inseparable.

👁   👁   👁

The Stud was home alone. He'd downed a few beers and walked to town looking for his buddies, but instead, ran into that no good police chief, asking him if he knew anything about Millersfield farm. What's it to him? He'd given him the finger and gone back home and plopped on the sofa. Drinking and thinking. He hadn't thought about that place in a long time. Didn't want to think about it now, neither.

Yeah, he lost his temper easy, and yeah, he fought a lot, but never with anybody what didn't deserve it. Black people he couldn't stand. Them six what worked for him over in Louisiana? Weren't like they was black, they was really Cajun. Besides, no one knew him there.

Not black like that old Push Cart Susie, years ago. The girls always called her Minnie Trombone. How she stood that old coat with its fur collar all summer, he never knew. Bobby Joe Burch said he got some from her for only a quarter. How'd Bobby stand the smell? That's what he wanted to know.

Roy looked at the cold beer bottle in his hand. Condensation wet his fingers, and he wiped them on his pants. People said he drank a lot. Bullshit. Yeah, he put away a case a beer most nights, but he'd never touched the hard stuff, except sometimes a little whisky in his beer.

Any man'd drink, if they'd lived his life. Crazy Nancy—hadn't thought of her in years. Why she'd drive any man to drink. She'd even throwed that shoe at him while he drove the car down the road that time. Jumped out and run screaming down the road. Stupid woman. He remembered like it were yesterday. Them at the hospital said he'd drove her wacky. Hell, he'd a straightened her out right fast if they'd just a given him ten minutes with her. Would have, too, except for Mama. He didn't mess with her. He put his moist fingers up to his forehead and rubbed the scar she left the time she'd hit him with a broom handle. Couple of times she'd hit him with a beer bottle, too.

He wished he'd a killed Crazy Nancy when he had a chance, all them years ago. If'n he had, he'd put her out of her misery. Didn't know right where she lived now—with her ma and pa, he guessed, but hell, he could find out. Found out everything else he wanted to.

A box of old photographs sat on the coffee table. Reaching in, he scrambled through a stack and picked up one of himself, Nancy and the girls.

Must've been taken at Easter time, he guessed, 'cause they only got him in a candy wrapper at Easter. Mama had made him dress up. The same stupid coat he wore at his wedding. Big mistake there. By God, you didn't catch him dressed up in that monkey suit anymore. He stared at the picture, at the deep V wrinkle on his forehead. His eyes looked like gashes across both sides of his face. His mouth looked like somebody had taken a pen and drew a straight line. He threw the picture back in the box, leaned back on the sofa and ran his hands over the scratchy gold threads in the fabric. Living with that damn lunatic-woman sure aged a man.

His real daddy cut out early, so early Roy didn't even remember him. Smart man. Didn't matter none. He didn't need no pa. Didn't need no ma either, but for years it'd been just him and Mama. *Miss Maybelle,* he mocked. Mama'd been mean. She'd nag him about working, but at that age, he saw no sense in most of it. A roof over his head and a place for him and his buddies to gang-bang, that were enough.

Mama never could sit down with housework still to do. If he'd heard her say it once, he'd heard it a million times. "Any job worth doing is a worth doing right." Made him want to puke. Hell, he thought she'd made up that saying till he got nearly grown. And he hated how she towered over him, and him a man. Her friends always bragged how tall and thin she was, and how she stood up straight like she had a broom handle stuck down the back of her dress. Hell, if you asked him, she had the broomstick stuck up her ass.

She loved that hair of hers. The Stud walked over to the mirror and ran his pocket comb through his own. Her *prized possession* she'd always say. Never let a gray hair show. Many a day he'd sat and watched her tease and spray that mop till not a hair on her head moved. When she didn't use them underdrawers, she'd wrap toilet paper around her head at night. He'd snicker and point at her when she did, but she paid him no never mind. She'd wake up with one side of her hair flattened against her head. But it weren't mussed up! Once she got that hair sprayed it weren't going nowhere!

He chuckled at the memory.

The beer bottle empty, he staggered into the kitchen and opened another one with the church key and walked out on the back stoop.

The sun almost down, the neighborhood lay spooky still.

Boy, that woman liked clean. Drove him crazy, always try-ing to get him to clean this or scrub that. She'd taken a switch to him many a time. Always bossed him. He hated how she used to grab him by the ear and tell him what to do.

He sat down on the side of a broken down icebox he'd pitched in the back yard. It still lay where he'd thrown it, on its side, the door hanging open.

Things probably woulda been okay if Mama hadn't gone and married that jerk Dick Strong. He'd been twelve; he could a taken care of the both of them. But no, she wanted Dick, that bastard. Roy snickered at his secret name for him. "Dick-head," he said out loud.

Always teasing Roy, Dick-head got his kicks making fun of him in front of other people. Called Roy a sissy just because he was short and skinny. Said he'd toughen him up.

He'd toughened him up all right.

Nobody ever guessed Dick-head's brother, Uncle Mike fucked The Stud 'till finally he'd gotten big enough to make him quit. Never told no one, neither.

A pain slammed up his rear like it used to when Uncle Mike shoved it in. He shuddered and clinched his buttocks. The pain was always there—except when he found relief with someone weaker than him.

Stud walked back up the steps, piddled around in the kitchen, and went back into the living room. He tried to get his mind on something else, but Uncle Mike, revisited, refused to budge.

One day the bastard really hurt him, bad, and The Stud's under shorts got all bloody. He'd throwed them in the trash can outside the kitchen, went in and tried to tell Mama.

"You're lying! Your uncle wouldn't never do that to you!" Mama yelled at him, and reached across the table and boxed him up side the head. "You ought a be 'shamed of yourself, always try-ing to make trouble for somebody.

"You ungrateful bastard!" she squalled, then turned and walked out of the room. The subject never came up again.

He'd sworn then—nobody'd ever hurt him again.

Fifteen

After Jewell left, Sid headed to Bealls. Since she'd given away almost all her clothes, she had nothing suitable for a date with Ben.

Was it a date?

After thirty years, she wasn't sure she'd recognize one anymore.

Inside, the one thing she did recognize was a slinky black dress unbefitting a preacher's wife. She grabbed it off the rack and located the nearest dressing room. By the time she slipped into the dress and smoothed it over her hips, she felt like a nervous teenager.

Preening in front of the mirror, she didn't recognize herself. Hey, not half bad.

She paid for the dress and new underwear and headed home.

Giddy, she showered, dried, rubbed in lotion, and sprayed Gaia cologne. How long had it been since she'd felt this way? She towel-dried her hair and glanced at the clock. Hair to do, makeup to apply, dress to press—sheesh, she'd never make it by seven.

A soft knock on the door startled her. "Damn, he's early!" Before she finished the tie on her robe, Sophia stuck her wrinkled face around the door.

"You need some help, Missy?" she asked as she eased into the room. Her own white hair slipped out of pins and formed a curly halo around her face.

"Sophia! If you'd press this dress and clip the tags. You're an angel."

Sophia glided across the room, set up the ironing board, fetched scissors from the drawer. "Got a hot date, huh?" She stuck the tip of her finger in her mouth for spittle and tapped the iron. It sizzled. She adjusted the dial lower.

From the bathroom, Sid called out. "How'd you know I needed help?"

Sophia paused her chore and looked up from the ironing board. "Woman's intuition, I guess." She bent over her task. "Besides," she grinned sheepishly, "I saw you running up the stairs with a black dress over your arm, and I didn't think you were going to a funeral." Her eyes twinkled. "He must be someone special."

"I'm scared, Sophia. I'm still trying to find me."

"Trust yourself, Sid. Trust the process." She clipped the tags, pressed the dress, hung it on a hanger and slipped out the door.

Sid slipped into the dress and glanced at the clock. Five minutes before seven.

One last check in the mirror—Sid sucked in her stomach and smoothed down the dress. Satisfied with the outfit, she checked her hair and then her makeup. The eyes of a scared, vulnerable woman glared back at her.

Oh God, she couldn't wear this dress; despite Sophia's suggestions, she didn't trust herself, or the damn process.

Knees weak, heart pounding, she unzipped the dress and tossed it on the bed. A quick selection at the closet, and she stepped into black slacks and fumbled-buttoned a black and white blouse just as Ben knocked on the door.

Straight up seven o'clock. Had he stood outside the door and waited for the second hand to reach the designated hour? If so, maybe he glanced in the window and witnessed her last minute outfit change.

Mustering decorum she didn't feel, she threw back her shoulders, fluffed her hair and turned the knob.

He stood there, grinning, wearing a brown suit, dark tie, and smelling of Eternity cologne.

His eyes wandered over Sid. "You look mahvelous!" he said as he took her hand and led her downstairs. He opened the car door, tucked her in, and walked around to the driver's side.

They drove out to Esther's Seafood Restaurant where, inside, a host ushered them to a candle lit table overlooking the Neches River.

Shit. She couldn't do this.

Soon, Ben swirled red wine around in his glass, inhaled the aroma, and then touched the rim to his lips.

She had no idea classy men lived in Orange, Texas.

While they waited for the main course, their conversation touched on the case and the private eye business, and what in the world she wanted to do with her future. Only briefly did she mention her divorce. She didn't go anywhere near the fact that she'd been a preacher's wife for a hundred and ten years.

The wine warmed her insides, and she relaxed into the occasion.

From out of nowhere, and without warning from her inward critic, a wave of anger surfaced. Before she could bring it under control, she'd slapped her open palm down on the table, hard. The dishes rattled and the wine sloshed against the sides of the glasses. A vague picture of Ben grabbing wine glasses stored itself in her memory. She heard words come out her mouth, words she hadn't prepared and passed through her old screening mechanism of what-will-other-people-think. "I haven't admitted it to myself, but I really want to work on this case with Jewell and Emma."

She saw other guests staring at her, but they seemed far away—behind amorphous curtains.

"Whoa, Sid." Ben stabilized their glasses. "Hey, I'm on your side, okay?"

"It's not just the intrigue." She grappled with the feeling jabbing her in the chest. "It's more than that. It's...it's anger. You've seen pictures of a building when it is imploded by a—what do you call them? A demolition expert, I guess."

He nodded. "The weight of the building falls in on itself." His eyes followed her, wary.

She nodded. "Yes, but it's not the weight, it's the pain. Of injustice. Anguish, because violent men keep violating women."

His hands held hers. "Look at me," he said, his voice soft.

She saw herself, reflected in his eyes.

"Hang onto the fact that not all men are like that. There are plenty of us that support and defend women's rights."

"It's like it hurts me, right here." She pulled her hand loose from his and dropped her fist onto her chest.

"Like the old voodoo doll thing?"

"Exactly! A pin stuck in there, and I hurt, here." She leaned forward, her fist still on her heart.

The waiter brought their dinner, poured each another glass of wine, then set the bottle back in the bucket.

A creepy sensation crawled up the back of her neck when she glanced at the couple across from them. The man's pores radiated lust. Sid watched the woman, dressed in a red, low-cut dress, sashay to the powder room. Her hips swung wide. The man watched her walk away, a shit eating grin on his face. Drooling, probably.

They ate in silence a few minutes, but while she ate, the wine eased in between temptations she'd always kept in check. Soon, the deep purple liquid loosened the fetters. A tingling sensation crawled up the insides of her thighs.

She shook her head. "Sorry for getting so deep earlier. Can we talk about something other than the case?"

Like you, she almost said, biting her giddy tongue.

He snickered and started to say something but stopped.

"What?"

"Never mind, you might be offended."

"Try me." On impulse she laid a hand on the table toward his.

He put his hand on top of hers. "I was just going to say, that's okay; I like a woman with passion, regardless of where it occurs." He grinned, shifting his shoulders. "But of course my favorite place is in the bedroom."

That worked.

Sid took another bite of the baked salmon in lemon sauce. The tart sweetness jangled her taste buds, making the next glass of wine taste even better.

"Would you believe that until recently I'd never drunk alcohol?"

The wine sparkled in the candlelight. Un-categorize-able, that's what she was now, and she wasn't going back in a box ever again. The wine danced on her tongue and twirled inside her thoughts.

"You better watch that stuff, young lady. It's getting to you," Ben warned, laughing. "But now that I have you slightly tipsy, there's one question I've been dying to ask." He leaned forward and raised his eyebrows as if waiting for the signal to proceed.

She held out her glass and he refilled it. "Go for it, what do you want to know?" Right now she'd tell him most anything. Even that she was wearing fancy red underwear.

"Okay, here goes." He took a deep breath of air and expelled it. "Is your hair naturally that white?"

Strangling on the bread she had just bitten into, she forced herself to swallow, and then laughed, her hand at her throat. "That's what you've been dying to know? No earth-shaking question in the offing? Like will you have sex with me tonight or something?"

"It's the whitest, prettiest hair I've ever seen," he admitted, looking her in the eye. "It's a shining halo around your head, but I sure as hell hope you're no angel." Both his hands rested on top of hers now, stretched across the table.

"It's mine, all right. It's been this color for years. Colored it awhile, got tired doing that, and said to heck with it." She shrugged her shoulders and held his gaze. What would he say if he saw her pubic hair? She snickered. Oh boy, she really was tipsy.

The waiter brought their desserts; baked meringue shells filled with vanilla ice cream, topped with strawberries and whipped cream. Sid hadn't eaten this well or felt this good in a long time. As a matter of fact, she doubted she'd ever felt this good before.

By the time they left the restaurant, the temperature had dropped to an unseasonable low. "I'm taking you by my house to sober you up, young lady," Ben said after he'd gotten behind the wheel. "No way am I taking you home in this condition, it's not good for my reputation—let alone, yours!"

The cold penetrated her clothes, chattering her teeth, by the time they got inside Ben's house.

He brought logs in from the woodpile and soon a warm fire blazed in the fireplace. Perched on the edge of the sofa, she watched him sweep up tiny pieces of kindling that had fallen on the hearth. Eagle Scout, she thought, wondering whether he'd been one, too, like Warren. A light blanket lay folded at the end of the sofa. He unfolded it and spread it across her lap, and she snuggled into the softness.

"I'll go put on the coffee." He kissed the top of her head as he walked behind the sofa.

Slipping off her shoes, she nestled down, mesmerized by the flames flickering around the room, plus a remnant of help from the wine. Thickened eyelids batted then surrendered to the invitation for closure.

She didn't know how long she dozed, but she roused, feeling him, from way off in the distance, when he sat down next to her. An aroma of coffee penetrated her senses and brought her back from wherever she'd gone.

He'd taken off his coat and tie, unbuttoned the neck of his dress shirt and rolled up his sleeves. God, he looked inviting.

His hand came toward her with the cup of hot, black liquid, but he changed his mind and set it on the table in front of them. His eyes on hers, his hand, still warm from the coffee, found her knee and explored up the length of her thigh, the fingertips memorizing every inch. Each indentation of cellulite, she thought.

A smile twitched the edges of her mouth.

Moving closer, he leaned over, lips parted. She saw just the tips of his white teeth. Animal feelings she'd thought extinct, beckoned dormant memories. She'd promised herself she'd never get this close to raw emotion again, yet here it was, playing havoc with her senses. His lips touched hers. Their softness startled her. Breathless, she pushed him back and sucked in a deep gulp of air, willing a halt to the cacophony in her head.

"Whoa, I can't do this." Tears welled up and trickled down the side of her nose. "You're moving way too fast."

"My apologies nice lady." His breath forced itself through tight lips.

The clock in the hall chimed twelve times. A car drove by, headlights glaring in the window for an instant.

"No, it was nice, too nice, actually. It scared me. I scared me," she mumbled under her breath and snatched her handbag from the floor, the strap, a lifeline.

"I sorry. I guess I misunderstood your signals at the restaurant." He smiled, picked up a coffee cup and handed one to her. "It's still hot. Sip it, and let's talk." He scooted down to the other end of the sofa.

"I guess I'd had too much to drink." She perched on the edge of the sofa, knees together. "I'd heard alcohol loosened inhibitions, but that's my first experience with it."

The cup and saucer he'd handed her was Lenox; the pattern, one of her favorites, *Autumn*. She studied the gold trim around the top edges, the blue-gray, paisley-swirled borders, and tiny fruit baskets in relief on the inside of the cup. She dipped her fingers into the coffee and slid them over the orange, the lemon, and the grapes. Had he picked them out, or had his wife?

He shifted in his seat, and the motion roused her. Shaking her head, she lifted the cup to her lips and let the hot, bitter liquid slide over her tongue and down her throat. She caught a glimpse of him, the sentinel, from the corner of her eye. She felt his eyes memorizing her jaw line, her neck. She forced a lump down her throat and forbade salty tears. "I need to go home," she said. "Will you take me, or shall I call a cab?"

"What? Why? I promised I'd slow down."

"That would be a waste of your time." She stood and moved away from the sofa. "I can't do this—I won't do this."

"Do what?"

"Get involved in a relationship."

"It was just dinner, for Christ's sake!"

She pulled out her cell phone and started dialing information.

"Wait, hell, I'll take you home, you don't have to call a cab."

They rode back to her apartment in silence, and when he stopped in front of Sophia's house, Sid snatched her things, opened the door and fled up the walk. By the time she'd climbed the stairs, the sound of his car had dissolved into the night air.

She went in, dropped her things on the floor and fell across the bed. No way in hell could she do this—absolutely no way. She'd sworn off men after her divorce. Marriage stole a woman's identify, made her less than a whole person. Someone had to give in a marriage, and it was always the woman—always her, at least, but never again. Sure, she could have sex with Ben, but that would change things. He'd think he owned her. Would want to tell her what she could and couldn't do. What to believe, what political party to vote for. She turned onto her stomach and groaned.

Monday morning found Quade Burns at the police station early, as usual. He loved his job. He'd been police chief for almost two years, and it excited him as much as it had the day he started. Most towns looked for an older, more experienced man as chief. He guessed he was lucky. He'd done a good job, though. Or at least he'd sure tried.

For a small town he and his staff stayed plenty busy. The recent building renovation had helped. He liked the nice new coat of white paint, trimmed in police blue. Kind of crazy, the way the building sat at an angle on the corner lot, but he liked the quiet, older part of town.

Quade patted his stomach and resolved to lose those last ten pounds. His family raised and sold cattle, so he'd grown up a meat-and-potatoes man. Boredom, his biggest enemy, didn't run up against him very often. He'd been accused that *watchful* was his by-word. Not much happened around town that he missed, that he'd admit. When anyone wanted to know something, they came to him first—and usually he had their answer. He liked being in the know, and he liked his town, did his best to keep it safe. Also accused of having the tenacity of a bulldog, he loved a challenge, got fired up by it.

👁   👁   👁

Home late, exhausted after a day in court, Ben walked into the kitchen and opened the near-empty refrigerator. The jury had found the guy guilty and sentenced him to life, which wouldn't be too long, given his physical condition. But they'd gotten the child-molester off the streets.

He decided on toast and eggs, scrambled with fresh herbs from the garden. That decision over, he took off his coat and tie and wandered into the living room, over to the wet bar, and began his daily ritual of two vodka martinis, extra olives.

Warmth spread in his veins even before he sipped the martini. Nothing like a cold case revisited to heat up a guy's blood. He'd love to get a conviction on a case that old. Every district attorney he knew would. They all waited for just such a chance and pounced on it when one came. The martini complete, he cleaned up and walked into the family room, sipping it.

Irene had taken all his time, what with the cancer and all. He missed her, terribly. It'd been tough. But what is—is. Lately, he'd felt himself coming alive again. After what Irene went through, he'd thought pleasure out of his reach. But he guessed happiness came, in its turn, just like sadness.

Sid was a good-looking woman. A rare breed, it seemed. He liked the way she talked. Made him feel relaxed—or something. How was she going to handle him being at the meeting with her client? He'd left a voice message on her phone, thanking her for dinner the other evening, relieved she hadn't been home. He regretted the kiss. Scare the poor woman away, did you? He'd step back some—wait for her. Hell, how would he handle being that close to her?

Just as he sat down and put his feet up, the phone jangled. Reaching over, he pulled it towards him.

"Hey, Ben, Quade. Just double-checking with you on our meeting tomorrow at The Third Eye. Still interested?"

"You must be psychic," Ben laughed. "No, I won't get cold feet; as a matter of fact my whole body is tingling, just thinking about it." He didn't tell Quade he wouldn't miss the meeting for anything. Nor did he report the arousal he felt just remembering how Sid smelled the other night.

Sixteen

Sid wished she could say that she'd intentionally blocked off the day for the meeting, but honesty prevented her from doing so. Hell, she had nothing else to do but go through Warren's case files and try to figure out which cases were still open and which ones he'd closed. Annie could help her compile a list and then she'd contact all the people with open cases and get an update on their issues.

That and study the material George had loaned her. She thumbed through *The Complete Idiot's Guide to Private Investigating.* She'd never felt like such an idiot.

Quade and Ben walked in the door at three-thirty. Ben wore a navy blue suit, and Quade, a police uniform. Stiffly, Ben stuck out his hand and introduced himself as if they'd never met.

Fine, that worked for her.

Ben spoke first, explaining their early arrival. "We came a little before our appointment so we could talk with you before your client arrives. But if we're intruding, just say so."

Sid shook her head. "No, that's fine." She delivered coffee, and then sat across from them.

"Jewell arrives what time?" Quade asked.

She felt comfortable with Quade and liked his unassuming style. His down-home manner and speech declared him a country boy.

"She's coming straight from work, four or four-thirty, and she's eager to tell you her story."

She paused for effect, and then continued. "But you'll have both sisters to interview."

"What?" Quade and Ben spoke in unison.

"Emma flew in from Trinidad over the weekend."

Both men looked at each other and smiled.

"She did?" Excitement colored Ben's voice.

She recounted the intercontinental phone call and hastily made airline reservations but made no attempt to explain why she hadn't told Ben on Friday night. She could keep secrets just as well as Mr. Hillerman.

"Wow," Ben said. Quade nodded.

They reminded her of two wind-up toys, coiled and ready, but still clenched in a child's hand. Ready to go, but not yet time.

"So, do you like the private detective business now that you've been working in it for a few weeks?" Quade asked, making small talk. "What type of work did you do before this?"

Her fingers gripped the coffee cup. She hoped they didn't see the white knuckles or her stiffened back. This wasn't where she'd expected they'd begin.

She didn't have to tell them that she married at 17, before she even knew who she was. How she'd lost sight of that young woman, and instead, molded herself into the wife her husband, and her world, thought she should be. She didn't have to tell them the real reason she was reluctant to take on the PI business—that she'd left a long marriage because she had no idea who she was, or what she believed, or how to get on with her life.

No, she didn't have to say any of that.

She wondered how long the pause had been, hoping they weren't mind readers. "I don't know if I like it yet," she choked out. "I'm just taking it one day at the time." The rest of the question she ignored, and hoped for an end to that topic of conversation.

Ben changed the subject. "Now, tell me again how all this got started. Jewell just came to you and started telling you all this, or what?"

Ben's questioning appeared casual, but Sid suspected that was his intention. Lawyers, after all, knew how to interrogate.

"How did you know what to do?" he continued.

Although Ben wore no rumpled trench coat and smoked no cigar, she decided his friendly nature camouflaged the shrewd wisdom of Detective Columbo.

"I watched a lot of Columbo," she said, and chuckled. "Seriously, I looked for story consistency. When you tell the truth, you just recite it like it happened, no need to make up anything or twist something else."

Sid continued where she'd left off, and recounted, again, the events that led her to call Quade. The men sat and listened, their eyes focused on her.

"Is it possible for a three-year-old child to remember such detail?" Ben looked puzzled.

"I didn't think so. That's why I was so dubious at first. But everything Jewell told me panned out. That's why I went to see Emma. Everything one told me, the other confirmed, over and over again. Blew me out of the water! I don't, for the life of me, see how two women, so far apart geographically, who seldom talk to each other, can describe similar memories, unless those memories were either well-rehearsed or real. These didn't seem rehearsed."

A car drove up, and Sid glanced out the window. "They're here." She stood and walked toward the door. The three of them watched out the window as the sisters got out of the car, and then stopped outside the front door. Emma turned and headed back toward the car. Jewell didn't move.

"Oh, no!" Sid stepped toward the window. "She's backing out. She's leaving."

Both men moved forward in their seats, but neither of them said a word while they watched Emma walk over to the curb, throw down a cigarette, scrunch it with her foot, and head to the door.

An aura of timelessness hovered in the room as Sid watched

the women enter. The image of Warren slipped into her head, and it seemed like she'd stepped into a thirty-year-old plan.

Jewell and Emma, stiff, stoic even, greeted the two strange men. They each seemed to bring invisible walls of protection with them.

"Nice to meet you," they both said half under their breath, and extended limp palms.

They crammed themselves in the middle of the love seat, side by side, thigh touching thigh, hands clenched in their laps.

The room grew silent.

After the introductions, Sid had expected the men to begin the questioning, but they didn't. Tension ricocheted off the walls and across the floor. Everyone, she felt, waited for her. She'd just wing it.

She looked at Jewell, then Emma. "It's important for both of you to know these men are not here to prove you right or to prove you wrong. They're here to learn from you." She looked each woman in the eye. "Yes, they have fancy titles and, yes, they are dressed in business suit and uniform, but they're just plain folk, like you and me." From the corner of her eye she saw Ben nod.

Both young women relaxed a little, allowing a wisplike space to appear between them.

Ben spoke next, his voice friendly and encouraging. "Thank you for meeting with us, ladies. Chief Burns and I want to hear your memories. It's important to us, though, to hear you one at a time. You know how it is. Sometimes I only remember something when someone else reminds me of something similar." Jewell and Emma nodded. "So would it be okay if we talk with each of you separately? Sid, is there a room we can use as a waiting area, while we talk with the first one?"

Emma shot off the sofa as if in response to a cattle prod. She snatched her cigarettes and the ashtray from the table. "I'll go second, I'll go second," she laughed in itchy, high-pitched notes. Ben, Quade, and Sid glanced at each other. Emma bolted toward a door at the back of the office. She'd never been in the building before, so Sid knew Emma walked blindly into the unknown. She followed, not keeping up with Emma's sprint, and settled her in a room at the back of the building. Magazines lay on the table, but somehow Sid doubted Emma even saw them. No need to worry. Emma wouldn't eavesdrop. She wanted nowhere near the story.

Ben shifted to a more comfortable position as Sid walked back into the room and retook her seat.

Jewell leaned forward on the sofa and tugged at her dress. "Sid, do you still have the floor plans Emma and I drew of the green house?"

"Yes, they're right here." Sid thumbed through the case file in her lap and handed the drawings to Ben.

His eyes widened as he compared the two drawings. "I've been in that house many times. I'd know it anywhere. Except for very minor things, that's exactly the floor plan." He paused. "It's changed now. It isn't green anymore, and a second floor's been added, and a mansard roof, but that's the floor plan of that house." He looked at Jewell. "When were you last inside the house?"

"Not since I left as a small child. I don't remember leaving, but I couldn't have been more than four."

"This is incredible." He held the pages out in front of him, dumbstruck. "How could a three or four year old remember such detail? And how old was Emma when she left?"

"Around five, I guess. Five or six."

"Actually, Jewell, yours is more accurate than Emma's, yet you were the younger."

He opened his briefcase and pulled out a copy of a yellowed piece of newsprint and handed it to Jewell.

"Is that the fire you saw?"

"Yeah," Jewell replied, "it looks familiar, but where are the horses? I remember horses there, I think."

Quade leaned forward, "We haven't found information on horses there, not yet at least."

"He did have horses, though, I remember them." Ben said as he handed her another piece of paper.

"What about this picture?"

"Is this her?" Jewell asked and watched for confirmation from Ben. Getting it, she said, "It could be. I'm not sure." She handed the picture back to Ben. "I remember the police coming up to our house to arrest him one time. They took him away, but he came back."

"They arrested Roy Manly once for rape, but he paid the family money and the charges were dropped," Ben said.

"He got off by paying money?" Jewell's voice came out in a screech. "How could he get off from rape by paying the family money? Something's not right in our system of justice if a man can rape a woman, a girl, and pay money and get off!"

No one in the room voiced disagreement.

"Okay, Jewell," Ben said, "start at the beginning. Tell me what you remember."

"I have a lot of memories from living in this town. At first, I didn't know I did, but as I started describing them I remembered much more than I realized. One of them stands out above the rest. I'm alone, I think, no one is watching me. I'm sitting on the floor playing with some balls. I couldn't have been more than three years old. My father walks in with this woman, and they were laughing and carrying on. She sits down on the sofa. He goes into the kitchen gets them both a beer and sits with her. They drink and talk. He decides to go to the bedroom. Now, in this house we lived in, there's no door that you can close to the bedroom. So, they go in and start to make out. At first, she seemed to go willingly. I remember her reaching up and taking something out of her hair.

"Then, all of a sudden he hits her and throws her down on the bed and hits her a couple more times, even butts his head up against hers. Then he uses the backside of his hand. He climbs on top of her and rapes her.

"Did he know you were there?" Quade asked.

"Of course he knew. That made no difference to him. In a few minutes, he gets up and goes to the kitchen and gets another beer. I remember looking into the bedroom and seeing her sitting up on the side of the bed. She looks kind of dazed, but she begins pulling her clothes back on."

"Do you remember what she wore?" Quade asked.

"Yeah, a yellow top, sort of flowery, and a blue skirt. Denim, maybe."

"Good, continue."

"He walks back in, and its like 'you're not done yet,' and he drags her into the kitchen and pushes her into a chair. By now she's come to her senses and wants to leave, but he won't let her. Shortly after that two men come in through the back door."

"Could you describe the two men?" Quade asked.

"One's a tall black man. He's older, and I picture him wearing like—it's not an army jacket but it's green and heavy. He's wearing bib overalls and brown boots. He's big, and quiet.

"And the other is white, shorter than my father. Jeans and a T-shirt, that's what I see him wearing. It doesn't seem like my father is surprised that they walk in—like he expected them or something."

"What do you mean?" Ben asked.

"Well, it wasn't like, 'Oh, hi, how you doing?' It was more like 'Okay, you're here now.'

After a few minutes they all went out the back door, I thought they'd left me there alone.

Eventually, Emma comes home from school and I want to show her something out on the back porch. She's not in her school clothes, so she must have had time to change. I pull her out there and point to something, I don't remember what, but when I looked over at her, she wasn't looking where I pointed. She stared straight ahead, her mouth open, and she had this horrible look on her face.

The woman who'd been in my house earlier hung with her hands tied above her head. She had something stuffed in her mouth and her hair had come loose. She didn't have any clothes on. Her feet didn't touch the ground." Jewell went on to describe the scene she'd recounted to Sid days before. "My father seems to be looking for something. I thought he saw us, but he looked right through us. The black man stood behind her facing sideways and the other man—I could hear him throwing tools or doing something in the back, but I couldn't see him. I remember my father looked up but I don't remember if he said 'get out of here,' or what. I knew I needed to go. I remember looking in the woman's eyes, and she just looked like—you know, please go get some help and stuff. I had on a T-shirt and underwear. My father had always told us the neighbors ate children, so I was afraid to run next door.

I grabbed Emma's hand and dragged her into the front closet in the living room. I tried to talk to her, I wanted her to hold me, but she wouldn't respond."

"Emma's the oldest?" Ben asked.

Jewell nodded. "Yes, a year and half. She always took care of me, but this time, I took care of her."

Jewell stopped for air, and then continued. "We stayed in the closet for a long time, I don't know how long. I only came out when I heard my mother get home. I remember she took off her coat and threw it on the sofa, saying, 'I'm home.' I remember thinking, Mom's home, everything will be okay now. I followed her into the kitchen and I saw this woman's body lying on the table, kind of spread out with no clothes on.

The black man is standing behind her with a sickle in his hand. Her body lay cut open, from here all the way down." Jewell pointed to her chest and then ran her hand down her torso.

"The impression I have is that they are taking parts out and laying them on the counter onto some kind of paper, white, I think. My father kneeled by her head and washed off something bloody."

Jewell shook her head and ran her hand through her hair. Then she picked up a glass of water and swigged. "I don't know why. I don't know why," she repeated.

"The other man stood between her legs. My mother screams,

'What have you done?' My dad just yells something to her and throws his shirt at her. 'Wash it,' he orders. I could tell my mother was scared. She did what he told her to do."

Jewell paused.

"I think I must've gone back to the closet then. I don't remember coming out of it again."

"What's the next thing you remember, Jewell?" Ben shifted in his chair.

"Standing in the back yard with my coat on, looking down at the ground. A woman's head and shoulders—one arm, flung out to the side—stuck out from under a piece of tin. She looked so peaceful. Her eyes were closed. She was ghost white. I knew she was dead—and I didn't even know what dead was! I remember thinking I wished I was her."

The room grew silent after that last remark.

Sid swallowed hard. She'd heard the story several times by now, but her chest ached thinking what kind of life a three year old led to make her wish that she were dead.

Quade broke the silence. "What happens next?"

"He comes to the back door—"

"He?" Ben asked.

"My father. He had his cigarette pack rolled up in his sleeve. White socks. He goes, 'Get away from there.' So I walked to the other side of the yard and watched."

"What happened next?" Quade asked, his face white now, too.

"Two men came in a large truck with a bed and sides on it, wooden sides. They took some carpeting and rolled something up in it. I couldn't really see what, their backs were to me, then they put the carpet on the truck. I didn't see the woman anymore. I thought that was the end of that."

"Was it?"

"I saw the rolled-up green carpet again when my dad put me and my sister in a white pickup truck. We drove to a farm. I thought we were going to go see the horses or something. But when we got there he told us to stay down. He told me to sit under a gunnysack, but I peeked out and saw him carrying the carpet into this old house. I knew the woman was in the carpet. He laid her down in the house and when he came back toward the truck I saw smoke and fire coming out of the windows of the house. I got down and hid."

Ben squirmed in his chair, picked up his coffee mug and took a swig. The coffee must have been stone cold, Sid realized, and almost offered to reheat it, but he was a big boy, if he wanted it reheated, he'd ask. She thought he might, when he swallowed and frowned, but he just sat the cup down and continued.

"We're going to need to talk to your mother. Nancy, is it?"

Jewell's brows knitted together. "My grandparents are leaving for a vacation in New Mexico, and I don't want to mess up their trip. They need it badly, and my mother couldn't handle the interview by herself."

"That's no problem," Ben assured her. "We can wait until your grandparents get back from their trip. Just let us know when it's a good time."

Seventeen

Emma paced in the back room, the ashtray laden with cigarette butts. Sid wondered if she'd sat down at all during the two-
hour wait, but didn't ask.

The sisters traded places, but Jewell's presence lingered in
the room.

Slipping out of her shoes, Emma sat on the love seat and
curled her feet up under her yoga style, for insulation—protection, maybe. Then she reached for a cigarette, apologizing for the
habit. "But I couldn't do this without my cigarettes." She looked
like she might make a run for it at any minute. No one in the
room asked her not to smoke.

Her hands took on a life of their own. She jerkily struck the
match and then attempted, unsuccessfully, to land it on the end.
She fidgeted in her seat; when she spoke, her voice was shrill. "I
want you to know this is not easy for me. Not easy at all. I even
can't believe I'm here talking to you. I told Sid, I don't want to
read this in the newspaper or see myself on TV."

She paused, struck another match, and clasped shaking
hands around the flame and the cigarette. Successful at last, she
tossed the burnt match into the emptied ashtray. Smoke twirled
around her head.

"I understand, Emma." Ben shifted his body and uncrossed
his legs. "Maybe it won't come to that. Would you tell us what
you remember?" Sid noticed Ben gave no premature reassurances
and tucked away the technique for future use.

Emma began. Story after story tumbled out, events she'd never forgotten and some she said she'd forgotten for years. No, she didn't remember seeing a woman hanging in the storeroom. Yes, she did hide in the closet—often—from him. Yes, she did remember the house fire and described it for them. No, she'd never forgotten it. Yes, her father had raped her, but that wasn't the worst thing he'd done to her.

Sid wondered what a father could do, worse than raping his own daughter, but she didn't ask. Neither did Quade or Ben. Already spooked, one small push might send Emma right over the edge.

Emma's description of the house and the neighborhood hit dead-on. She told how she'd run behind the mosquito truck, about the icehouse, the railroad and the river. She described the alligator that lived in the park and the kindergarten she attended, the Dairy Queen and the Laundromat, Minnie Trombone and the egg hatchery, detail after detail. The two men sat quietly, listening, only occasionally asking a question. They alternated between leaning back in their seats and sitting on the edge of the sofa. At times, Sid saw their mouths drop open. At other times, their eyes stretched wide.

"Emma," Ben said when she paused to light another cigarette, "I grew up in Orange, and I want to tell you your recollections are right on target." Emma sat up straighter and stubbed out the cigarette.

On and on the meeting went. The sky darkened outside, the hands on the clock moved to midnight. After they finished talking to Emma, Sid brought Jewell back into the room.

"Now is it our turn?" Jewell asked. Once again, the sisters expressed their fears for their mother, for themselves. They searched for assurance the results were predictable, that they'd be safe. Quade and Ben listened patiently, but made no promises of an outcome, committing only to walk through the process with them.

After the meeting, Sid called Quade aside.

"Something's been bugging me and I wanted to ask your opinion—this is on another matter." Out of the corner of her eye, she saw Ben engage the girls in conversation.

"Sure, what you got?"

"What would you think if you saw cars with a Mexican license plate haul off, in tandem, perfectly good cars with U.S. license plates? Would you be suspicious of something illegal going on?"

"First thing in my mind would be someone was involved in transporting stolen vehicles down into Mexico for resale. Why? You know someone doing that?"

"I might. Give me a little time, though, and I'll get back with you."

"I'll be around—working on this case. This one's a doozy, Sid." He turned and stepped outside.

Ben finished with the girls, walked to the door and stood with his hand on the doorknob, glancing her way. He hesitated, and then stepped her direction. Anticipating an invitation that she couldn't accept, she stiffened and turned to Jewell and Emma, "Ladies, how about I take you out for a bite to eat, you must be starved."

The door snapped shut.

❧   ❧   ❧

Jewell dragged herself out of bed the next morning and forced herself to dress for work. She didn't want to. She wanted to stay right there with her sister, right in the midst of the memories that had been locked away so long, but she rejected the idea.

The drive to Clear Creek Regional Hospital seemed short. Her eyes watched the road, but her mind reverberated conversation from the evening before.

❧   ❧   ❧

Alone in her sister's apartment for the day, at least Emma could smoke without Jewell bugging her. That girl's tolerance for cigarette smoke was nil. Emma paced the room, her mind cannonballing. Images, memories she thought she'd squashed long ago, refused to lie down on command. She tried to put up the roadblock again, but the memories squirmed around it.

A dark man in overalls. His name was Bubble. No. Bubble? That's a stupid name for a man. Bubba? Yeah. No? The elusive name flitted around in her memory, refusing to squarely land. She could see him standing in the living room, tall, her neck arching up, still not seeing much above his chest. Light filtered through the window of the green house, and dust floated in the sunbeams. Cigarette smoke swirled, making fancy patterns in the sunlight and dust particles. He took her hand and led her toward the bedroom.

Emma stopped pacing. She stuck the cigarette between quivering lips and used the free hand to dial the number for Sid's office.

"Hi, Emma, how are you this morning? After yesterday, I'm surprised you haven't fled the country."

No. Emma was not quite ready to tell what she most feared had happened to her. So she just told of the black man and the overalls and the name that wasn't a name. Images, feelings long stamped down, ignored, denied.

"Wait a minute." Emma dropped the phone and ran to the bathroom and threw up. When she returned, Sid said, "Good, Emma, throw it up, throw it all up. You don't need to keep it anymore."

"You mean its okay to throw up? I always felt that a bad thing," Emma admitted. She stood at the window and stared out at the parking lot below. A car drove up, stopped, and a woman and child got out and walked together into the building.

"Absolutely not. Throwing up is your body's way of ridding itself of all the stuff you've held onto all these years. It's like a metaphor. It's okay to get rid of it."

"But will I ever be able to stop?"

"Sure you will. You'll stop when you're finished. Trust your-self. Trust your body."

They hung up. Emma went back to the bathroom.

Within an hour, she dialed Sid again.

"It's me." She took a deep breath, hoping to still the tremor in her voice, then jumped right to the point. "There was a metal building behind the green house. It was old, with red paint that had started to peel." Her voice heightened. "I'm scared of that building, but I don't know why." She paused to catch her breath. Her mind bolted backwards. Thoughts and memories tumbled over each other, eager; it seemed, to tell their story.

"My grandmother should remember a phone call from me to their friend, Don. I was a teenager. I called and asked the op-erator to put the charges on Grandma's bill. One summer, we had to go visit my father and his wife Rose. It had something to do with child support my mother tried to get from him. I knew I was in trouble and I wanted to go home.

"My grandmother also witnessed Roy dragging me around on the carpet by my hair when I was younger, claiming I was his property and he could do whatever he wanted to do to me. But I don't know what it is about the red building.

"About testifying, I know I should; I want to, but I don't know if I can. I go back and forth with it." She knew she jumped around from one subject to another, but didn't know how to stop. "I think my Mom worked at a bag factory. I tried to picture her in that house, and it's just—I don't know if—" Lost in her own patchwork of thoughts, she grew quiet.

Emma hung up and continued pacing, but within minutes she dialed again. After a while, she stopped counting the times she called Sid that day.

Heat and crowds filled the Houston Bush International Air-port. Emma inched along in the impatient line of flyers waiting to board the flight to Trinidad. Suddenly she felt menacing, frigid air on her back. When she looked around to locate the source, her eyes locked onto a passenger dressed all in black. A black-metallic medallion dangled from a chain around his neck. His dark eyes latched on Emma's. She bolted onto the plane, pushing aside passengers ahead of her. She grabbed a seat up front and watched for him as others boarded. Relief washed over her when the attendant slammed shut the large door without him. Guess he wasn't flying after all, at least not on this plane.

Suspended in the time warp over the Gulf of Mexico, her emotions clawed at her gut. Scrambling in her bag, she resurrected pen and paper. The pen skimmed across the page as she hastened to catch her thoughts.

I'm scared. I feel like I can't breathe. I want all this pain to stop! Please, if there is a God, make it stop! I hate my mind and my body; they betray me. Every time. They want to talk, but my soul says NO! Just make it all go away. Please, just let me die! I can't relive this again.

In spite of her prayers, she'd taken her finger out of the hole in the dike. The pressure behind the trickle tore through barriers erected over a lifetime.

The dark man paid her dad money. He sold her body—for change! If that's love, she didn't have any to give. Her head sunk on her chest, tears pelted, unheeded, off her chin into her lap. God help her. She was crazy, just like her mother!

The flight seemed endless. Memories shuffled in and out of reach. Emma closed her eyes, begging sleep to visit. Instead, a building showed up, the red one.

What had awakened me in the middle of the night? Voices? I couldn't sleep. I'm standing by the back door. The house is here, she motioned in her mind, *kind of towards the alley but not quite. Right here on the stones, like an old cement foundation kind of thing, but no, that doesn't seem right. I have on a dark, crabby green something or the other, it reminds me of a peacock, teardrops, crazy things, paisley, I guess. I'm listening to noises, yelling, like they're having a disagreement. The biggest thing seems who can yell louder, or angrier at each other. How many of them? Three, maybe? Yes, three voices. It's dark outside. I know he's there because I can hear his voice. I'm not sure if they're inside the building or not, maybe they're on the side, or behind.*

Screams, they're screaming. I shouldn't be here. It's dark. I'm feeling really yucky, like my cupcake is going to come right back at me.

If they were smart they'd have gone down the street to the parking lot of the VFW. They're angry, somebody didn't do something right, they're babbling about this, babbling about that, screaming. They're mad at each other. Angry. Anxious. Desperate.

I'm scared, and run back to the house, falling on my knees as I run into the house, not looking left, not looking right. Get back in bed fast. I talked to my feet. Stupid, who talks to their feet? Run. Just go. I'll put band-aids on you later. Just get me where I'm going.

I crawl in bed beside Jewell, trying hard to get up underneath her, and get kicked right in the chops. If I could just get underneath her I wouldn't exist anymore.

Emma's thoughts surfaced when the flight attendant brought a meal. Emma's stomach rejected the idea of eating, so she sent the tray away with the attendant.

You know how it is when you can't see in the dark and you just kind of get out of bed and there is the dresser, there is the door jamb, there is the other wall—sidestepping everything, just slide one foot at the time. The noise draws me. I can hear it from inside the house. The streetlight is shining through the living room window.

There was perfume. I don't know what that is. That's the smell that drives me crazy. Her mind leapt back to the elevator and Rahim.

Where am I now? I'm in the house, in the kitchen. I'm in the kitchen and I smell the smell. Sleep finally showed up. What happened next? Morning, oh, okay, morning. I made it through the night. Guess I didn't get caught and he isn't mad at me. That's all I care about anyway. As long as he stays in a good mood, nothing matters.

Where's Mom? I don't see her. I never see her. I don't know where the hell that woman is and I sure would like to know.

👁   👁   👁

Quade's comments about stolen vehicles transported into Mexico kept battling for air time in Sid's head. If Tom Huff owned the junkyard, and through it, stolen vehicles were transported into Mexico, either it was going on under his nose, or it was a part of his operation. She wasn't ready to take her suspicions to Quade, however. Even a novice like her knew she'd need proof.

Could Tom have had anything to do with Warren's death—or the arsenic in the fireplace? Oh God, the thought sickened her stomach, made her knees weak.

Shoving her mind off that thought and onto Jewell, Sid knew she still missed a piece to the puzzle regarding Manly and the fire. It bugged her like a splinter beneath her fingernail. Nothing new had surfaced yesterday in the meeting with Ben and Quade and the girls. She hadn't expected it to. But there must be more, somewhere. That afternoon she headed back to the state crime lab and combed through the records of the fire, this time, without Quade. She wanted to dig for herself, now that she knew the ropes.

Signing in at the front desk, she showed her identification, explained what she wanted and an assistant ushered her to a small room at the rear of the building. She waited while the clerk searched for the box of records. When she gave them to her, Sid poured over the inquest, the police investigation, the coroner's report and the statements of several men, including Edward Pigeon. According to him, he'd said he and Ethel Elaine were planning to marry, and had driven over from Florida for him to do a job for his boss, Big Daddy.

Surely the man had another name, Sid thought.

They'd moved into the old farmhouse the day before.

Electricity wasn't turned on. The coroner described the fire as the hottest he'd ever seen. The intensity of the heat either melted or burned everything.

"If the house had been vacant for years what was the source of the fire?" Sid puzzled out loud. "The only possible source for a fire that hot must have been gas, or some other type of propellant. The house had an old cook stove in it, the records said, but she saw no evidence in the coroner's report that he had questioned whether there had been butane in the tank. Unlikely there'd be enough to cause that hot a fire, especially after years of vacancy.

Pigeon reported he'd gotten up early that morning and Ethel cooked him breakfast. With what? The house had no butane in the tank or electricity. Supposedly she'd waved to him out the kitchen window as he left. He drove fifty miles to pick up furniture, he'd said, and had just walked into the store when he got a call telling him the house was burning. Who knew where he was? People didn't have cell phones like they do today.

Dammit, someone knew something—it didn't add up.

The answer didn't sit in a pot at the end of the rainbow, but she knew it squatted somewhere.

Quade's patrol car sat parked outside Sid's office as she drove up. She saw him sprint toward the door leaving the car door hanging open and the motor running. "Say, Sid," he called, as she crawled out of her car, "I've just talked with a deputy present at the fire. Thought you might want to know what he said."

"You're damned right I do." It felt good, this newfound freedom to use words that expressed the intensity of her feelings.

"He lives in Austin now, and works for a state legislator. I asked him if he remembered the fire, and he did. Then I asked him if he saw anything strange or unusual there. Here, I took notes; let me read you what he said." He raised his clipboard, "'Yes, there was something strange about it. I've never forgotten. I walked around the yard, checking for anything we might have missed—you know how you do—and there was this doll head stuck on the fence post. The red hair stood straight up on end, like it was scared or something. I remember wondering who in the world put that there.'"

"One more confirmation," Sid said. "I guess Jewell did see a doll's head in the newspaper clipping. I wasn't sure—it could've been anything. Well, now we know for sure."

Quade's phone, clipped to his belt, sputtered at him and he walked out to the car's two-way radio. A couple of minutes later, he poked his head out. "I've got to go, Sid, talk to you later," he called out. His car sped out of the parking space, siren wailing.

Eighteen

Sid didn't want to go see the bastard. The legal system says innocent until proven guilty, and she had proof enough already. She knew he was guilty. But Jewell had shown Sid a picture of Roy Manly when he was in his late twenties. He looked like a creep then. She couldn't imagine he'd look any less like one now.

But she had to see for herself.

She called Roy and bluffed her way to an appointment. She wanted to catch him by surprise, his guard down, so she made up some story to flatter a fragile ego.

The precinct two commissioner's office consisted of a small, square, yellow-brick building next to the Water Utilities office. Rainwater had splashed mud up a foot or more on the brick. Above that, mildew and mold grew rampant. The grass stood tall, the mushy ground under Sid's feet oozed into the seams of her shoes. A man operated a ditch-witch behind the building, cleaning out a drainage ditch overgrown with elephant ears, weeds, and trash. A nasty wet pile of muck stretched itself down the length of the trench, getting higher as the machine progressed.

"Hello," she walked into his office and offered her hand to Roy. "My name is Sidra Smart. Thank you for seeing me." She added an extra teaspoon of sugar to her smile. "As I said over the phone, I'm writing a feature article for News Day Magazine on county commissioners. Your reputation is such I wanted to include you in the article."

Might as well make it something good.

"May I impose upon you to answer a few questions for me?" She counted on her white hair and a few wrinkles to factor in her favor. She figured wrong.

He perched one leg over the corner of a desk and indicated a chair for her. His weak-blue eyes sparkled and she swore his chest grew six inches. He looked less a politician than he did a creep.

"Welcome, Mrs. Smart. It is Mrs., I presume."

Patriarchal son of a bitch, she thought, surprised he even knew a word like presume.

"No, as a matter of fact it's Ms., thank you." With a smile as sweet as sugar, she looked him square in the eye, expecting him to catch the reprimand.

He sputtered, his face red, but he recovered quickly. "How can I help you, Mrs. Smart?" His voice italicized the Mrs.

The air grew colder, but she'd be damned if she'd shiver.

"Tell me how long you've been commissioner."

"I'm in my first term. Next month'll be a year."

"What did you do that got you elected?"

"Ran the best damn campaign ever's been run, that's what. I got elected because this county needed a man that knows roads. I was that man and everybody knew it."

"What do you think your chances are for re-election?"

"Sweetie, I'm in this for the long haul. I don't mean to brag, but ain't no one around who can touch me. I know roads better'n anybody in this county. Years of experience."

"Have any women working on the roads?" Sid moved the conversation her way.

Roy stuttered. "Women? Well, I don't rightly think so." He yanked on the waist of his pants, slung low on bony hips. "This work needs a man. It's no place for a woman, Mrs. Smart." Sid heard derision in his voice.

"I can see that," she fed his ego. "You know, I had an aunt that burned in a house fire in this area a long time ago—must have been thirty years now, out at a place called Millersfield farm." For effect, she thumbed through the notebook in her hand. "Near Hartburg,

I believe." She hoped she sounded doubtful, innocent.

Roy looked granite-faced. Only the slightest twitch of his lips gave him away.

A mosquito buzzed around Sid's ear and she swatted at it. "Her name was Ethel Elaine Perry." She stared him in the eyes.

He bounded up and shoved his shoulders back. The motion yanked the last little bit of shirttail out of his pants. The bottom buttons of the shirt were missing, and Sid caught a glimpse of dingy underwear above his belt before he hastily tucked the shirt back in.

"I understand you were friends with an Edward Pigeon, who said he'd brought Ms. Perry with him from Florida." She italicized Ms. herself this time.

"Never heard of 'em." He picked up a cigar from the ashtray on his desk and relit it. "Who the hell did you say you were?" His voice wasn't political now.

She pushed a little harder.

"Mr. Manly, is it true that your daughters are both afraid of you? So afraid in fact, that one of them has actually left the U.S. and refuses to allow you to know where she lives, and that—"

"Honey, I don't know where you're going with these questions, but you better get there fast."

"—and that you actually impregnated her when she was a teenager?"

Roy hoofed toward her. His eyes shot fire-arrows her way. He snatched at her arm but, outguessing him, she yanked it away just as he grabbed.

"I know who you are now," he sneered. "You work at that PI place with the eye out front. I saw my daughter's car parked there t'other day right next to yours. I figured the two of you were up to something."

"Thank you. You've answered my questions." Sid turned and with brisk steps, headed to the door.

Just as she closed the door she heard glass shatter against the other side.

❦   ❦   ❦

"Dammit, Sid, so much for having surprise on our side." Quade struggled for composure. Ben stood over to the side, watching. She guessed he figured someone needed to maintain composure. "Manly stormed into the police station demanding I arrest that blankety-blank bitch for threats and intimidation. What the hell did you do?"

She chuckled. "So he called me a bitch, huh? Well, sometimes being a bitch is all a woman has to hang onto," she quoted her favorite line by Kathy Bates from the movie *Dolores Claiborne*. "I wanted to see his reaction when I brought up his daughters and the murder." She thought better of telling them the real reason—the pleasure in seeing him sweat.

"What did you tell him?" Quade asked, accusingly. "Give him too much information and you arm him. The less he knows the better. And you stay away from him, Sid, he's bad medicine," Quade warned.

She didn't make any promises.

"Don't go off half-cocked. Coordinate with me or Ben, otherwise you might get hurt."

She knew he really meant she might screw up the investigation, but she let it ride.

❦   ❦   ❦

Ben walked out of Sid's office, his knees like rubber. He'd not told Quade why he'd said nothing. Why he'd let Quade do all the talking. He'd walked in ahead of Quade, and bumped into Sid, coming out the door. They'd both grabbed each other for balance, and he'd been surprised to see that her soft features camouflaged a strong aura he'd missed before now.

Her gentleness ran alongside a strength that shrouded her in mystery. He loved a mystery. But she pissed the hell out of him.

Soon as Quade and Ben left Annie stuck her head around the door of Sid's office. "Siddie, you have a call on line one. She's been holding a while."

Sid reached for the phone. "Oh, Annie, I've been meaning to ask. I need to know which of Warren's cases are still open. Would you go through these file drawers and compile a list for me?"

Annie marched in with Chesterfield stretched across her shoulder. "How will I know which case is open and which one's closed?"

"I haven't a clue. You'll probably have to go through them all." She put the phone to her ear and punched the button. "Hello. Sid Smart."

"Sid? This is Nancy Manly." The weak voice sounded uncertain.

Straightening her back and swinging her chair around to her desk, Sid tightened her grip on the phone. "Hi, Nancy, are you okay? You don't sound like it."

"I need to talk to you." The woman barely spoke above a whisper.

Easy, Sid. "Okay. Want me to come see you?"

"No. Yes. No, maybe you better not."

"What do you want to tell me, Nancy?"

"There are some things I didn't tell you the other day, things I didn't remember, but I do now. I'm not crazy, you know."

"I believe you."

"And if I am, it's because he drove me there. Said I was loony."

The talking stopped, but Sid heard quick, shallow breaths.

"I wanted to get out of the marriage from the very first day. He was cruel."

Still is, Sid thought.

"But when you're young and dumb you're easily swayed. I thought he and his Mama knew what was best for me."

"I can understand that." Sid didn't add that she'd done the same thing.

"When I first met him, I thought he was great. He rebelled at everything, and I had rebelled at nothing. I felt heady, going against my parents, powerful, on top of the world."

Hell, Sid had never rebelled at anything—and hadn't even been inclined to, until recently.

"As I told you when you were here, sometimes I still see blood all over the floor, but everyone tells me it's in my mind, not on the floor. But I smell it. I saw it, too. I know I did, that night in the kitchen."

Sid waited, fearful of pushing Nancy too fast.

"You know, I've always worried about my girls." Nancy changed subjects. "I knew they weren't safe around him. My parents helped me raise them, but you probably already know that. I used to walk through the house at night, checking on them, making sure they were safe. Emma always slept with me. She was too scared to sleep by herself. Jewell slept alone in her own room. I remember one night I couldn't sleep and went to check on Jewell. I cracked the door open, so's not to wake her, and I saw this blue flame hovering over her bed."

Sid froze rock solid. She trusted her own senses. What she could see, touch, taste, hear or smell.

"Funny though, it didn't scare me. It seemed like it was there to protect Jewell." A hoarse laugh erupted.

"May I come see you again, Nancy? I really would like to."

"Okay. Come tomorrow. Just make sure he doesn't follow you."

Sid hung up. She had no doubt who *he* was. Seemed like his whole family referred to him by the pronoun. Nancy must remember something about the woman, else why would she call?

"Who was that?" Annie asked as she lifted a stack of folders from the top of the file cabinet and headed out of Sid's office, the cat trailing along behind.

"Jewell and Emma's mother. She didn't sound well, and I'm getting spooked."

☞ ☞ ☞

The dog in the neighbor's yard flinched and looked up, then shrugged and went back to sleep.

Sneakiness guided him through the locked door and down the half-lit entryway. The unfamiliar house caused momentary panic, but he stood stock still for a moment, sucked in a couple of deep breaths, then inched down the hall.

Her room was dark. The first-quarter moon hung low outside her window. Light filtered through bare branches swaying in the cool night. Her face looked skeletal in the moonlight and a twinge of guilt fluttered in his heart, but he captured it in the net he reserved for such occasions.

Her pillow was the weapon he'd planned to use, easy and untraceable. He held his breath and tugged on it, but he couldn't get it free. With his heart pounding, he steadied himself and tugged again. He'd practiced this at home with a buddy, and he'd gotten it loose without breaking a sweat. But now it lay twisted under her neck. He squatted beside her, his nose just inches from her face, and eased the pillow out an inch at a time.

A smile creased his face as her head finally released the cushion and it slid off the bed. He'd been waiting to do this for so long. Delight warmed his cheeks and a fine bead of perspiration popped out on his upper lip.

With little fight left, the sheet covering her body barely shifted with the struggle.

Out the door, down the hall, and into the crisp darkness he slid, like a specter making his nightly rounds. The neighbor's dog waited for him in the shadows and barked a warning to the neighborhood. He gave one swift kick to the head. The dog yelped once and lay still.

The phone jangled on the bedside table. Sid's flailing arm banged the water glass on the nightstand and it fell to floor. Cobwebs of dreams entangled her brain as she lifted the receiver to her ear.

"He killed her. I know he did!"

Sobs racked the voice. "Jewell? Is that you?"

"My mom's dead. My grandparents called early this morning. She didn't come for breakfast and they went to check on her. They said she just died in her sleep. But I know she didn't. He killed her. I don't know how, but he did it."

Sid tried to comfort Jewell, despite a nagging guilt behind her words, and agreed to meet later that morning. After she hung up, she dressed and headed to her office.

Think, Sid, think! How in the world did he know her plan to go see Nancy this morning? Guilt crashed into her like a tidal wave, and pulled her down in its undertow. Keys, thrown on the desk, slid across the top when the first book hit the floor. After emptying the bookcases with no sign of invasion there, she tore into desks and ran her hands underneath the edge of tables and looked under lampshades and inside wastebaskets. "Of course, the phone." She tore open the mouth and earpieces. Nothing.

Roy had tracked that phone call from Nancy. How? Think! Standing in the middle of the office she swiveled, her eyes scanning the room inch by inch. If he'd planted a bug, it had to be in the front office. That's where she'd been when Nancy called. Okay, regroup. How would you bug an office?

This time, she scanned with smaller sweeps. Her vision passed the doorway, the coffee pot, the restroom door, the bookshelf, and the pot of mint in the window. Wait. She stopped the sweep and swung her eyes back to the mint. What's that? Warren had one just like it in his closet. A video transmitter, Wave COM Senior, she'd seen the ads when they popped up on her computer, hating their interruption. But this one, spying on her, pissed her off royally. A shaky hand grabbed the camera and slung it across the room. "Goddamned son of a bitch." The camera shattered against the wall.

Time to go see George.

She sat in George's waiting room, white-faced, dwarfed by the sequence of events she'd unleashed.

"Where the hell do I go from here?" she cried, after his client left and she'd been ushered into his office. "My bungling of this case has now caused a death.”

“Dammit, Sid, you haven’t bungled anything.” Not a hint of a Cajun accent this time. “Nothing you did made him kill her. Hell, he’s wanted to for years, never made any bones about it. Why, I heard him say that if he’d ever wanted to kill anyone he’d have killed his first wife. Every regular at Sparkles Paradise has heard it. He just had a little more investment this time.”

“What do you mean?”

“I figure he feared she’d eventually remember what he’d done. Not that any jury would have taken stock in her testimony. She’s been on psychotropic drugs too long.”

“Okay. What do I do next?”

“Sid, I can’t tell you what to do. You’re the only one who knows that. But I can tell you this.” He leaned against the front of his desk again, with his arms crossed against his chest. “You do know what to do, but you’re not listening to yourself. We each have this almost silent bell of inner knowing and it dongs loudly, somewhere deep inside of us. The problem is, we charge right over it, time after time. After awhile, we don’t even recognize it anymore. It’s time you started listening to your own sense of inner knowing.”

“How the hell do I hear a silent bell? What a bunch of bullshit.”

“Sid, Sid, Sid. Listen to me. It isn’t a sound, as we think of sound; you don’t hear it with your ears. You feel it, that little quiet voice in your head. Honor it. Follow it.”

“I thought you didn’t follow your intuition, George!”

“I never said I didn’t follow it,” he said, giving a belly laugh. I just said I work with facts. Intuition can lead you to facts.”

Nineteen

Sid packed an overnight bag, ate a quick bite and headed to the office. As soon as she opened the office door, she smelt litter box, walked straight to Annie's desk and wrote a sticky note that read 'change litter box today,' with a couple of exclamation points after the words. She stuck it on Annie's telephone just as her aunt walked in wearing a floppy-brimmed black hat, gold-colored leggings, black sandals, and a baggy, mesh shirt.

Sid grabbed her bag and car keys.

"Good morning, Siddie. Have a good weekend?" She held the cat over one arm, and rubbed his back with the other.

Chesterfield stared at Sid, disinterested, bored. Sid swore the dang cat felt himself superior to the whole world. Reminded her of Sam.

Annie walked to her desk, snatched up Sid's note, read it, dropped it in the trashcan. "Chesterfield and I brought back fresh yard eggs, and home-smoked bacon and sausage. Come by tonight, and we'll have them for supper. I'll bake some of my homemade yeast rolls."

"Sounds good, but I'm heading out of town for a couple of days. Just came by to check the messages."

"You have your cell phone, huh?" Annie called after her.

Sid waved it in the air. No need to tell Annie to call, if need be, she would.

👁   👁   👁

"Okay George, I'm listening to your stupid silent bell," she mocked. It nudged her east in search of Ethel Elaine Perry's sister, a woman named Beatrice Watkins, last reported to live along the Louisiana coast near Morgan City.

Hours later, Sid parked her car in the driveway of an old clapboard cottage and marched up the sidewalk. A screened-in front porch ran the width of the house. The screen door wasn't locked, so she let herself in and knocked on the inside door. While she waited, she wiped sand from her shoes onto a straw doormat that had *Welcome* written in big green letters. She hoped the greeting included her.

An older woman opened the door a crack and peeked out at Sid. "What do you want?" she barked.

"Are you Beatrice Watkins?"

"I am, but you pronounced it wrong—like most people who ain't from these parts. It's Bee-attress—like mattress, 'cept with no M and add a B." She waved her hand as if she figured Sid wouldn't get it, anyway. "Just call me Bea. Most people do."

Her face looked sad. It sagged a little. But the skin, thinned with age, revealed a survivor, Sid decided. Chapped hands clenched the door, the fingernails short.

Sid hitched her bag on her shoulder and attempted to look like a professional, certain her amateur rank showed through. "Bea. My name is Sid Smart. I'm a private detective." She still felt phony, calling herself that. "I'm looking into the death of an Ethel Elaine Perry who died almost thirty years ago. I believe you were her sister. May I talk with you?"

The door slammed in Sid's face. Displaced dust filtered down into her nose and eyes, and she sneezed. *Okay, I guess I didn't handle that very well.* She stepped off the porch and walked to the car. Throwing her bag into the back seat, she climbed in the driver's side and waited. Just as she expected, a face peeked out from behind a gap in the lace curtains. "Okay, Bea, or Bee-attress, you'll get another chance."

A few inquires that afternoon and Sid learned Bea and her

brother owned and ran a fresh seafood shop just under the big bridge.

The next morning, Sid made her way to the shop. It sat at water's edge, where boats came in with their daily catch. The fishy smell made her toes tingle, like they'd grow webs between them if she stayed long enough. Not-so-fond memories flicked behind her eyes like crabs entangled in a fish net.

It was 1964. They'd been married just a couple of months and Sam had accepted the pastorate of First Baptist Church of High Island, down the Gulf Coast of Texas. Not yet out of high school and barely seventeen, she'd accepted the feeling of inadequacy without question. She was inferior. Sam said God had called him there, so who was she, an insecure teenager, to question God? She just wished God would've told her about the call. She hated it. She hated the feeling of being in over her head, the feeling of a child playing grown-up. Acting like she had a faith, when what she had wasn't hers at all.

This morning, the crushed shell walkway shifted under Sid's feet, she adjusted her pace, feeling the pull on her calves. She'd missed her last couple of workouts and the tug reminded her to stop by the gym on the way home.

She looked up just in time to see Bea peer through the front window, then disappear in a back room as Sid opened the door and walked in. So much for catching her by surprise.

After yesterday, Sid expected Bea to hide, but sooner or later, Bea had to come out. She had a business to run, customers in the store.

Sid wandered down rows of old white freezer-chests, the bottoms rusted out, perched in the middle of the store. The doors slid open to an array of frozen crabmeat in pint and or quart-sized plastic containers. De-headed jumbo shrimp sat frozen in big blocks of ice. Or they could be bought, the sign said, fresh, heads on, by the pound. Crabs, alive for the moment, scratched frantically against the sides of galvanized washtubs. Fresh fish, cleaned and dressed, were piled up in neat rows behind the glass doors of a refrigerated display case.

Classifying shrimp seemed a good way to pass the time. Their smell reminded her of her dad. He'd gone shrimping almost every weekend and taught her the difference between the whites, and the browns, and the pinks. Said he preferred the sweet taste and firm, almost crunchy, meat of the free-range whites. Lots of them—heads still on, sat piled on mounds of ice on a table with built up sides. Beady eyes, like tiny obsidian marbles stuck on each side of pointy heads, stared at nothing.

Sid suppressed a smirk when Bea skulked through the door a few minutes later. Customers, piled up like the shrimp, expected a salesperson. One by one she took their orders, loaded piles of shrimp on white butcher paper, weighed and priced them, and collected the money. The customers chatted easily at first. Regulars, Sid figured.

A puzzled look creased their foreheads when Beatrice didn't return the idle chitchat. A sense of uneasiness eventually permeated the room. Finally, the last customer completed her transaction and left.

The store empty, Bea turned the lock on the front door and flipped over the *Open* sign.

Sid looked at her watch. She'd been there an hour and a half. Bea walked toward Sid and sighed, fanning the air with her hands. "I give up. What do you want?"

"Is there somewhere we can talk?"

"Well certainly not here, else wise folks will just knock on the door wanting me to open up just for them. There's a café down the street, half a mile or so. Ruth's. You go on ahead, I'll meet you there."

Sid wheezed. "You're not trying to pull a fast one on me, are you?"

"No." Bea pushed salt-and-pepper hair off of her face and wiped her brow with her apron. "No, I give up. Might's well get this over with. I'll be there directly. Order me a cup of coffee and a piece of Ruth's chocolate pie. I'm coming."

Thirty long minutes later, Bea slid into the booth across from Sid who'd done as she was told and ordered extra pie and coffee, cold by now. Bea couldn't wait. The woman pulled the saucer over, stuck her fork into the pie, and wrapped her lips around a big bite of the milk chocolate seduction. Swallowing, she looked up at Sid and smiled. "Ruth makes a mean chocolate pie. Did you try a piece?"

Sid nodded. "You're right. It is good, but—"

Bea shook her head and closed her eyes. For a minute, Sid wondered if the woman was having a seizure—but no, the whole world just had to wait until she finished the pie. Sid sat stiff-shouldered, with her hands clenched on the table in front of her. Just hold on and wait, she told herself.

The busboy cleared the booth next to them, clanging the dishes as he plunked them into a brown plastic pan. Then he pulled a rag out of his back pocket and wiped the table clean, rearranged the salt and pepper shakers, and refilled the sugar bowl. He collected a few packets of Sweet and Low left on the table, and stuck them in his apron.

"I'll give you this," Bea said, after almost licking the plate clean, "you sure are stubborn."

"Sorry. I didn't mean to bug you. There's a lot at stake here."

"'Sthat right? Actually, I always thought someone would come. Just didn't think it'd take this long." Bea raised the tiny metal cover on the sugar jar and thumped some of the white granules into her teaspoon. She eyed the contents, shook the jar again, evaluated the contents of the spoon, sprinkled the sugar over her coffee, stuck her spoon into the cup and made a beating motion with the spoon.

What the hell's she doing, mixing a cake? "Bea, I need information regarding your sister. It's important." The stirring slackened and stopped. In slow motion, Bea lifted the spoon out of the dark brown liquid and tapped it on the edge of the cup, her eyes veiled. Sid's irritation grew.

"Ethel." Sadness coated Bea's voice as she set aside her spoon and stared at a fly walking across the red laminate table top. "My half-sister, actually."

Sid listened to Bea's breathing, heavy, labored.

"We shared the same mother. She didn't know her father. I did mine, for all the good that did me."

An uncomfortable feeling crept over Sid's shoulders, like she'd just seen inside a person without their permission.

"She was older than me by ten years."

"Where did she live before she died?"

"The last I knew, she worked at this motel in Melvin, Florida and lived in a trailer parked behind it."

"What kind of work did she do?"

"I don't know for sure. Maid work, I guess. I hope."

"What do you mean, you hope?"

Bea held her answer while the waitress warmed up their coffee. A noisy young couple and a baby came in and sat on the other side of the room. "Something seemed awfully fishy about the whole thing."

Sid sniffled and rubbed her nose. The salty odor of Bea's sea-food market lingered in the soft tissues of her nostrils. Pulling a tissue out of her bag she blew into it and then tucked the tissue back inside her pocket. "What do you mean?"

"I didn't know she'd even gone to Texas, much less died, un-til after they sent her remains home. I thought she still lived in Florida. I drove over to the motel where she worked to check on things before the funeral, just to make sure she weren't there. I couldn't believe she was dead.

There was her car, still parked behind the motel, full of gas and everything. I swear, when I walked into the lobby of that mo-tel I'd a thought I walked into a den of thieves. No," she corrected herself, "gangsters. I don't know what it was about the place, but it gave me the heebie-jeebies."

She scooted up higher in her seat, leaned her elbows on the table and put her head closer to Sid's. Glancing left then right, she looked Sid in the eye and lowered her voice. "Her trailer looked like she'd just walked outside to pick up the newspaper or something. Lights were on, but weren't nobody home, if'n you know what I mean." She leaned closer, her voice a whisper. "I found her purse there, her toothbrush, her makeup," Bea's hands covered Sid's. "Now, you got to understand. Ethel went nowhere without her makeup—maybe her purse, but not her makeup. She liked to dress up and look real purty." Her eyes checked Sid's, she smiled and leaned back.

"Okay. So then you began to get suspicious. Is that right?"

"No ma'am. Actually, I got scared. Then the funeral, oh, boy, the funeral."

"What happened at the funeral?" Sheesh, it was like pulling hen's teeth.

"We was at the cemetery, the one out from town a ways. The service ended. Most folk had left already. This big black Cadillac drives up. Creeped down the drive, it did, and around the graves until it reached us. We all just stood there and watched it come. It had a chauffeur driving it. Now I'd only seen that on the TV before—

I'm sorry, I gotta go pee, I'll be right back." Bea slid off the bench and walked to the back of the room.

Sid waved down the server and got a refill of coffee. A frozen margarita with lots of tangy salt on the rim traipsed through her mind. Her butt ached. She'd sat there an hour and a half and gotten only fifteen minutes of information.

Bea stopped and chatted with a woman on the way back to their table. Ruth, Sid decided.

"Anyways," Bea picked up where she left off even before she'd eased herself into the booth. "So this big black Cadillac stopped. The chauffeur got out, walked around the car, opened the back door, and this giant of a man crawled out." She held one hand over her head. "He towered over me. Walked right up, he did, and started talking. Didn't tell me his name or nothing. I heard the chauffeur guy call him Big Daddy, so I weren't sure if that was the guy's name or if he was the driver's daddy." She shook her head. "'You Ethel's sister?' he asked me. Don't think I even opened my mouth. I guess I nodded or something 'cause he kept talking. Ethel owed him some money, he claimed, and he was taking her trailer and everything inside it. Figured that about made them even. He also kept her brand new car. That's what I never figured out—if Ethel was moving to Texas, why didn't she take her new car?"

"Did you ever see him again?"

"Ma'am, I won't lie to you. As I said, these men scared me." Her hands, clasped on the table, were clenched so tightly the fingers turned white. "There was something way off kilter. I don't know what my sister got herself mixed up in, but I figure it weren't good, and my meddling around in it might just get me burned up myself."

Sid hardly moved, fearful of breaking the spell.

"Maybe you think I'm a bad sister, never doing nothing to find out what happened to Ethel, but I'm here to tell you, I've never been so scared." Tears welled up and ran down her face. Her chin quivered.

For just an instant Sid was sorry she'd come to talk to Bea. Not waking sleeping dogs, and that sort of thing.

"The man she went to Texas with? I forget his name. Anyway, he come up to me a few days later and wanted a copy of an insurance policy Ethel tried to take out. He thought himself the beneficiary to lots a money. He had nothing coming to him, anyway. She done put my name on the line as beneficiary, but she didn't get it approved. Failed the physical. Guess she didn't get a chance to tell him. I wonder why."

This time, Sid covered Bea's fists with her own hands. Her voice caught in her throat when she started to speak. She cleared it and started over. "Bea, I'm not here to judge you. We all do the best we can at any given moment. Fact is there was probably nothing you could have done. Ethel was gone. No sense in you being next." She forced down the lump in her throat. "I'm just a fellow traveler trying to help two young women solve a woman's murder they witnessed when they were kids."

Her voice came out dry and scratchy. She took a big swig of water, tepid now. The glass left a ring on the table and she swiped it with her hand. "I'm here because these two young women remember seeing a house burned by their father when they were only three and five years old, and they're convinced a woman's body had been thrown in the house shortly before the fire. Plus, the three-year-old saw a woman I believe was Ethel, the day before that—" She cut off her sentence. No need to go into the gruesome details, she'd find that out soon enough.

"Oh, my God, those poor little girls, are they okay now?" Bea jumped to her feet, accidentally shoving the table against Sid. Her hand flew to her mouth, eyes wide.

Sid held on to the table to keep from tumbling backwards. "No, they're not, but they will be, because I'm going to get down to the bottom of this. I promise you and I've promised them. That's why I'm here. What you've told me helps. If you remember anything else, here's my card. Call me, collect."

Sid cried for Nancy and Ethel all the way home. What is it about some men that make them abuse women and children? She'd read about a type of chimpanzee clan that when a male jumped on a female all the other females ganged up on him and chased him out of the pack, and made him stay there until he behaved himself. She liked that solution.

Twenty

She'd slept late, exhausted from the visit with Bea the day before. Sophia had awakened her at nine with a tray of buttered orange scones and a steaming pot of coffee. She'd drained the pot and licked the crumbs, then jumped in the shower. Irritated when the phone rang, she grabbed a towel and answered, dripping water on the floor.

"Sid, I met a woman yesterday. I made an appointment with her and I want you to go with me to her house."

It took a moment before voice recognition set in or water cleared out of her ears. "Jewell?"

"Oh, sorry, yes, it's me. I should have said. I'm just so nervous about this. You'll think I'm crazy."

"Hell, I'm already crazy, myself. So don't worry your head." Sid laughed, but a vague sense of something out of the ordinary snaked inside her. Perhaps Sid, too, was close to the edge of insanity, like Nancy.

"Ethel Elaine Perry haunts me. It's like she's trying to tell me something, but I can't get it."

"So who is this woman and what are we supposed to do at her house?" Sid asked. "How can she help you?"

Ethel nudged her on the shoulder, too, but she refused to admit it to Jewell. One of them had to maintain a level of sanity in this situation.

"I have no idea how she can help, or even if she can," Jewell's voice elevated at least three notches.

"Well, that makes a lot of sense," Sid laughed. Nothing made sense anymore. "What's the woman's name? Where does she live—maybe I can meet you there."

"Her name is Andrine Gilbeaux. A friend introduced us. We ran into her while shopping at the mall. Get this, she's a psychic. But, I'll pick you up. We have to take a pirogue to get there; she lives in the middle of the bayou."

"We have to go on a what? She lives where?"

Einstein's description of insanity—doing the same thing over and over again and expecting different results, certainly didn't meet the criteria for this venture.

They paddled deep into Blue Elbow Swamp, a waterway caught between the border of Texas and Louisiana. Spanish moss hung heavy in bald cypress and water tupelo trees, the moss so low it brushed the surface of the opaque water.

The old guy paddling the pirogue sat wordless. Toothless, too, Sid guessed. She feared if he talked, a spell might be broken. She was in no mood to break any spell.

Now, Sid leaned back, careful not to tip the boat, and whispered in Jewell's ear. "She's a psychic, you say?"

"Yeah, she talks to dead people. I guess she's some sort of voodoo woman or something." Jewell rattled on. "She says there's no such thing as death, really, that just our bodies die. Weird, huh?"

Holy be-Jesus. Sid had lived a long time, and she'd never talked to dead people. She wasn't sure she wanted to start now. Easing a look from one side of the boat to the other, she felt alligators stare at her from beneath the murky water. Nutria surfaced and swam to the bank and scurried into tall grasses. Scratchy moss brushed her face as they eased through tight bends in the swamp, mosquitoes buzzed her ears.

Humped down, expecting some voodoo spirit to snatch her up any minute, Sid eased air in and out her lungs with as little movement as possible. What in hell had she gotten herself into?

A mist moved in and obliterated view of everything within twelve feet of the boat. Sid felt like she sat in the doldrums, lost forever. An alligator snapping turtle eased its way up from the bottom, the three ridges on its back surfacing first. Its claw-like mouth opened at them and a little pink squiggly thing waved in its throat, almost in salute—or warning. A water moccasin slithered away, and except for the movement, seemed indistinguishable from the water.

They eased out of the swamp and into the main portion of the river past rusted-steel dry-docks, abandoned and half submerged—twenty-two of them, an eerie reminder of the last big war.

The pirogue eased into another arm of swamp. The paddling slowed and there sat an ordinary-looking house. If you can call a house sitting on stilts, smack in the middle of a bayou, ordinary.

The old man guided the pirogue up to a dock in front of the house and tied a rope around a post, motioned them out. Sid crawled onto the landing and stood motionless while Jewell got out and walked to the front door. The woman must have heard their silent approach because the door opened the instant Jewell knocked.

She didn't look at all as Sid expected, although what that was, Sid had no idea, either. The clothes were of some shade of dark, a loose fitting blouse hanging outside of a long full skirt. She wore beads around her neck, lots of beads. The color of her skin reminded Sid of the dark water, with wrinkles like the ripples left behind by the water moccasin. When she smiled, Sid expected toothless, like the pirogue man. But instead, beautiful white teeth glistened. Her dark hair hung in curly ringlets down her back.

Something about the woman drew Sid up the steps and into her arms, warm, soft, and gentle. So this was Andrine Gilbeaux.

"Welcome."

"Thank you for seeing us," Jewell said, "I brought my friend. This is Sid." They laughed at the introduction coming after the hug.

"Welcome, Sid. I like ya name, by de way." She held Sid out at arms length and looked her in the eye. "I can tell ya got a story behin' ya self."

Sid returned her smile but said nothing.

"Come in, come in." Stepping aside, Andrine waved them through the door. The cool comfort of the room surprised Sid. Candles and coal oil lamps cast dancing shadows on the walls. Their purpose, Sid decided, was illumination, rather than any dark and sinister intent. She felt her muscles relax.

After serving hot tea, Andrine led them into a small back room. A square table stood in the middle of the room, with four mismatched chairs around it. An oilcloth covered the table, a triple-wicked candle lit the room, and bookshelves lined the walls. Sid strained to read the titles, but the dim light kept them secret.

"Jewell, you sit der, 'cross from me. Sid, you sit on my left." They followed Andrine's instructions.

"Tell me, chil', why you come?"

"I saw a woman die when I was a kid. Her name was Ethel Elaine Perry. I need to know if she's okay. I keep feeling like she's trying to tell me something, and if she is, I want to know what."

"Ethel Elaine Perry. Okay." Andrine closed her eyes and leaned back in her seat. "Did she got dark hair—reddish maybe? Pull up, sort a like dis?" She demonstrated with her hands.

Jewell coughed, answering, "Yes, she did."

"She wear maybe a skirt—sky color, short-like, and a yeller top wit' blue flowers?"

"Oh, my God. Yes, that's what she had on when I saw her in my parents' bedroom."

"Okay. Don't say no more. Just say yes or no."

"Yes."

"She die untimely? Violent like?"

"Yes."

"Den dis her. She sittin' right der beside ya, my dear."

Sid strangled, and then coughed to clear her windpipe, the air grew warm. She tugged on her collar and fanned her face with her hand. Desperate for something tangible to focus on, she scanned the room and stopped at a photograph on the wall behind Andrine. A small boy, she guessed a grandson, sat in front of a fire roasting a hot dog. Blue flames licked at the wiener.

"Then she's okay?" Jewell asked.

"She okay. She jes rouse from long sleep. Took her a while to heal from dat ordeal. It do take de dead time, recoverin' from violent death. But she okay now. She smile at ya, look at you lovin' like. Yeah, she recall you from dat day."

Andrine paused, looked to the side of Jewell. "Yea, she know who you be. She say t'ank ya for tryin' to help her dat day. Dat wha' she want ta tell ya."

But I haven't helped her, Sid thought. Guilty men were still unpunished.

"Yeah, honey, but you done seen dat blue flame." Andrine whispered in Sid's ear as they walked outside. "An dat yer secret, chil', keep it dat way."

Andrine needn't worry.

The sun hung low, barely visible between the trees, as they climbed back into the flat-bottomed boat. Sid's knees were weak from their encounter with Ethel Elaine Perry. Now the ethereal swamp did nothing to ground her in reality. The only indication of a separation between earth and sky was the tiny ripples left behind as the old man slipped his paddle into the wet darkness. The pirogue skimmed across the surface of the turbid water, as silent as the world beneath it. Night critters, starting their day, chirped and squawked in the shadows while Egrets settled in the treetops. The old man just kept paddling. Sid wondered if he was as lost as she, but didn't dare ask.

As she stared, bleary-eyed, out across the narrow expanse

of water she thought at first that she had imagined the sudden bubble of light floating toward them, but then it exploded just at the water's edge. She grabbed Jewell like a lifeline. "What the hell was that?"

The old man chuckled under his breath. No longer wordless he said, "feu follet." Paddling over to the bank, he climbed out of the boat, pulled out his pocket knife and stuck the blade in the ground then climbed back into the pirogue and resumed paddling. Sid watched as the flame appeared again, danced around the blade then vaporized.

"Der, dat cut de spell. Feu follet," he explained, "some folk say, is souls escapin' purgatory, come back for prayers. Others say is bad sign, evil—sometime death. If'n I come back tomorrow to get me knife and der's blood on de blade, I knowed I broke de spell."

Sid shivered, certain she wasn't coming back tomorrow.

Finally a breeze picked up and scattered the clouds overhead. She looked up into the darkened sky where millions of stars twinkled at her, almost as if they were in on the evening's entertainment.

The magic of a Creole moon lit their way out of the swamp.

When Sid got home, Sam had left a message on her answering machine. Just hearing his voice still made her feel judged and found wanting. He made everyone feel that way. After the divorce, several friends and family told her they hadn't come around much because he always treated them like they were beneath him.

Fact is, he felt he was. Days before the divorce he'd told Sid he'd always felt superior to her, but now he didn't—he felt inferior.

When she'd learned who she was, and what she stood for—and what she wouldn't stand for—he'd fallen off his pedestal, to her, at least. Were it not for church members who reinforced his feeling of superiority, he might succeed in keeping his feet planted on solid ground. Heady business that—pedestal-standing.

His message threatened if she wanted the books she'd insisted were hers, she'd better come get them soon, or he was giving them to the Salvation Army. He didn't want them in his Study at the church.

Now he didn't want them. Before, he'd taken them there.

Collecting her books meant she'd have to face Sam's secretary, Dorcas Huff, Tom's wife. Dorcas' idea of a Christian woman so fit Sam's belief one would suspect he had shaped the mold and poured Dorcas in it. She made Sid sick to her stomach. Both Dorcas and Tom had ganged behind Sam in the divorce, convincing many parishioners of Sid's fall from grace. Certainly Dorcas wasn't beyond making threatening phone calls.

Maybe afterwards she'd go see Tom. Narrowing down the possibilities, if Tom owned a junkyard involved in grand larceny, she had no reason to believe him beyond vandalizing her kitchen. Something behind the man's eyes, when he looked at her, told her not to trust him. She'd even mentioned it to Sam before, but he'd dismissed her opinion.

She'd acted for years; this performance might well carry Oscar proportions.

The next morning she stopped by the office, hoping Warren had some type of recording device. Sinister-looking PI technology filled the closet. She took a deep breath and rummaged through various paraphernalia. Just touching equipment used to violate another person's privacy made her feel underhanded, criminal. She couldn't believe she was about to wire herself for sound. So unbecoming for a preacher's wife—ex-preacher's wife, she reminded herself.

After a brief search, she located a recorder, inserted fresh batteries, tested it, ran the wire under her shirt and tucked the recorder in her vest pocket.

☞   ☞   ☞

Sam barely looked at Sid when she walked in the door carrying empty boxes. When she saw how pale and gaunt he'd become she flashed right back into her old feeling of guilt for having left him. He mumbled something and excused himself.

Dorcas, the self-proclaimed holy woman, stuck her head around the door as Sid crammed selected books into cardboard containers.

"Hi, Sid. Just thought I'd check and see how you were doing," Dorcas said, needles prickling out of every word. Her face had that—let me show you how holy I am—look about it. Sid wanted to vomit. She'd seen right through Dorcas a long time ago. There'd been lots of women just like her, parading through her life, through Sam's life. She knew the type, outwardly humble but inwardly arrogant. Like Sam. She'd seen Dorcas hover over Pastor, tending to his every whim, kissing his feet, drying it with her hair, hanging onto his every word, defending him at every turn—feeding his ego. No wonder he wanted to stay in the pastorate.

Sid bit her tongue and smiled. "I'm doing fine, Dorcas. How are you?" Sid pushed a smile as wide, and as phony, as Dorcas'. "Just packing my books and files."

The protector of all things deemed holy, Dorcas stepped over and inspected the books in Sid's box. "I know it's none of my business, but...

"Spit it out Dorcas. Say what you want to say."

"I—I think—you should be ashamed of yourself for what you've done to Pastor." Her words came at Sid like a flaming arrow shot from a bow. "He didn't deserve that. He's such a wonderful man. I've been devastated, we all have. The other day Tom told me I shouldn't worry—that what goes around comes around. It can't come fast enough as far as I'm concerned."

Ten million responses flooded Sid's head. How Sam had sacrificed his family for his denomination. For Sam, his belief in God was the same thing as God. Anything less threatened him to the core. How he viewed a woman's role as inferior, subservient. How, from the first day of their marriage, he'd molded and sculpted

Sid into a wife who supported his values, his views, his beliefs. How threatened he'd been after she'd found her voice.

She could have said all those things—but she didn't. Dorcas would learn that for herself, and if she didn't know what her husband was up to, she soon would.

Sid tucked the flaps closed and lifted the box under her arm. Affecting a religious-sounding mew, she asked Dorcas, "Didn't you and Tom give me that Thompson Study Bible as a gift last year?"

"Bible? Why—uh—yes, I think we did." Dorcas fumbled with the papers in her hand, her face turned red. "Why?"

"Someone burned it on my doorstep the other day. Since Sam always insisted you have a key to our house in the event of an emergency, I couldn't help but wonder. You know how paranoid I can get. Oh well, one less book to pack, huh? See ya."

Eager for a breath of fresh air, Sid walked down the hall, pushed the panic bar on the door with her hip and headed to her car.

Now, on to Tom's used car lot. The half-hour drive in Houston's noon traffic gave Sid too much time to contemplate what she might be getting into.

She'd always gotten the feeling that Tom carried a smoldering libido in his pants for every woman but Dorcas. The way he looked at Sid, that sideways grin, and a look behind his eyes that carried an underlying message.

Maybe if she flirted with him.

By the time she arrived and saw him through the plate glass window of his office, her nerves couldn't be wound any tighter and still remain inside her body.

He looked up, saw her then glanced away, trying to pretend for a second that he hadn't seen her, but he couldn't make it work.

She slipped her hand into her pocket and flicked on the recorder as she walked in.

"Tom, got a minute?" Without waiting for an invitation, she sat beside his desk, crossed her legs and smiled.

He kept working with the figures on his desk. "Mrs. Smart. To what do I owe the…"

"Cut the bull, Tom. You don't have to act with me. I know you've been hoping I'd call." She forced herself to look in his eyes, hoping her aversion didn't show.

"Well—I—we—yes, I guess now that you mention it, I had wished I could help you out sometime. I know how lonely it gets…"

So—her friend had been right—men would be interested in bedding her, even the religious conservatives.

She forced her plan in motion, feeling ridiculous, feeling like a cheap actor in a B-rated porno movie when she slipped off her shoe and stuck her foot up the leg of his brown trousers. "Someone vandalized my house you know."

Tom stiffened, sat up straighter, yet kept his leg in contact with her toes. "They did?" His pitch elevated several octaves.

"They did. I thought maybe you knew who it was, even thought perhaps it was you." She packed seduction in every syllable.

His face turned as red as the tie underneath his double chin. "No, no, I don't know who would mess up your kitchen."

Sid scooted her foot higher up his leg, let it slide along his inner thigh. "I never said anything about my kitchen, sweetheart."

His body shivered, still he didn't remove her foot. "Well, uh, maybe my wife said something about her and a deacon's wife—but I had no part in it, if that's what you're getting at. I'd never…"

Her foot explored further up his leg, Tom squirmed, saying, "But I can put a stop to it. You know how Dorcas and some of the other women are about Pastor."

"No, how are they?"

"Humph. Not only do they think he and God created the moon, they think he hung it in the sky and sent it orbiting the earth. It's sickening, I tell you. Everything I do gets compared to Pastor. They've been livid with you."

Envying her courage, truth be known.

"I hope you're not going to press charges or anything. That wouldn't be good publicity for the church. I can make them come over and clean it up and all." Anxiety rose in his voice

"Sh-h-h that's okay," she whispered, running her foot up higher. "It's all cleaned. I thought it might be Dorcas' doings—the threatening phone calls and all, but I certainly hope you don't wish me ill."

In a bound, Tom reached her side and pulled her up in his arms. He smelled of cheap cologne. "But I can make it up to you," he whispered, his breath hot in her ear. "I promise. We can…"

"Sure, we can," Sid fought her revulsion and forced her hands up the back of his neck, toyed with the curls touching the collar of his white shirt. "Maybe we can meet somewhere. There's just—"

"What is it baby?"

"—something else I was wondering. It's about all that money you make off of those stolen cars you sell down in Mexico—you know—from that junkyard in Orange?"

"What about it? Don't worry, baby, that'll all be yours. My guys over there handle all that. I'll put you up in a little apartment. No one will ever have to know. Just you and me." He panted like a dog trailing a bitch in heat.

Banking on Tom's ignorance as to Sid's connection with Warren and the Third Eye, she swallowed the bile in her throat, moved her hand down to Tom's crotch, forced breathlessness in her voice. "I was just wondering, did that private detective—what's his name?—did he cause you any trouble?"

"Nah, well, this one jerk tried to, but the guys over there took care of that. Took 'em a couple of tries, but they got him. Why?"

"Just wondering." Weak-kneed, Sid forced down the lump in her throat. She'd been right. No one at church—not even Sam—knew or cared what she was up to. The church members didn't even know she had a brother, much less that he'd died since her split with Sam.

"When can I see you again," Tom asked, planting wet kisses all over her neck.

"Soon, sweetheart, soon, tonight maybe." Sid strangled on her own saliva, coughed into her fist until she caught her breath. "I've got an appointment, but I'll call you afterwards and we can set a time." She pried herself out of his arms, promising to call, and fled out the building, staggering to her car.

The admission of vandalism of her home was of no importance, but Tom's response about the junkyard and *getting* Warren confirmed her worse fear. Warren had been murdered, and Sam's fundamentalist, holier-than-thou church member was responsible.

She pulled the recorder out of her pocket and flipped the switch to Off, laid it in her lap then drove around the corner and parked out of sight from Tom's business. After she'd rewound the tape, Tom's words came back at her, feeding the horror growing in her heart—the arsenic poured in the fireplace must have been their first try.

Someone jerked open her car door, startling her. She fumbled for the switch to turn off the tape.

"Sweetheart, I forgot to…" Tom's face rammed inside the door. He heard his own words playing back at him. "Why—why you bitch!" He spit at her, snatched the recorder and stalked off.

The Stud rewarded himself with a day off from work. Hell, he got a week's work done in half a day anyway. He'd slept till noon, and then went to Sparkles Paradise.

At that hour, the place was empty. "The usual," he bellowed, then grabbed the bottle handed him and claimed his table in the corner. Didn't like the bartender none, he'd throwed him out before, saying he'd had enough. Nobody told The Stud he'd had enough. He threw his head back and downed a swig of beer and belched. A movement caught his eye. A rat skittered across the floor and out of sight.

He used to play a rat game with Emma. What was it?

Oh, yeah, Rat Trap. Emma was the trap. She whined about the game, but he knew she really liked it.

Come here, let's play a game, he'd say and Emma'd drag her feet across the kitchen linoleum like she didn't want to play.

Let's play rat trap, he'd say, and you're the trap. Then he'd pull out the roll-a-way bed and Emma'd climb up and lay in the middle. He'd fold the bed up and latch it at the top.

She looked so silly, head stuck over the edge of the mattress like that. He'd tell her to lie still, and then he'd drop pieces of bread on her face, slow and easy. She acted scared, just to make him happy, but he knew she liked it.

The Stud grinned, remembering how Emma'd squirm. Lay still, he'd say, or else he'd have to slap her. She knew he would, too. He'd reach down into a box and bring up two big rats. He could still see her eyes, wide, excited, cemented on the smelly thing. Made him horny just thinking about it. The rat's toenail's dug into Emma's cheeks while the rat nibbled on the bread.

Well, we ain't gonna catch a rat this way, he'd tease and stick his hand into the roll-a-way bed, leaving a trail of breadcrumbs from her stomach up to her neck. Then, he plopped the other rat on her. Its tail stuck right up under Emma's nose and he'd laughed when she wrinkled her nose and twitched. Then the thing crawled down inside the bed with her.

The fun all went out of the game then. Emma's eyes looked like weren't nobody home any more. Guess she'd had enough for one day.

The Stud emptied the bottle and ordered another.

👁   👁   👁

Edward Pigeon lived in Sulphur, Louisiana, just off I-10. Sid packed a small bag, tossed it in the car and headed east on the freeway. Her world seemed like dots connected by the concrete thread stretched from one side of the country to the other. Even the trip up Blue Elbow Swamp started at a boat ramp off the freeway. After the meeting with Andrine, Sid's beliefs hung in limbo. But if Ethel were there encouraging Jewell, as Andrine had said—then Sid better keep at it. Maybe Ethel waited for her, too.

The modest house sat on a corner lot in an established neighborhood. She'd given Ed Pigeon a similar story she'd given Manly. He and his wife invited her in and offered coffee. Contrary to Manly, however, they were both gracious.

Mrs. Pigeon wore a modest cotton dress and sweater. She'd pulled her light brown hair back in a chignon. Ed stood tall, over six feet, Sid guessed. Age had thickened his middle and thinned his hair.

"Mr. Pigeon, did you know a woman by the name of Ethel Elaine Perry?" Sid asked, placing the coffee cup on a table in front of her.

He stiffened. "Name sounds familiar."

She dug in her bag and pulled out a photo she'd gotten from the crime lab. "I have photos of her here."

He seemed reluctant—but he took the pictures from Sid.

A cloud crossed the path of the sun and the room darkened.

"I worked with Gette—I called her Gette—off and on for a year or so. Sometimes I left town to work on odd jobs," he explained. "We'd just moved to Orange when she died in a house fire, 1970 or '71, I believe." He shook his head and handed the picture back to Sid. "But this ain't her."

Twenty One

The sun slipped behind the horizon while she'd talked with Ed Pigeon. Now, darkness enveloped Sid as she walked to her car in a daze. But this ain't her, he'd said. What the hell's going on?

She turned on the ignition and backed out of the driveway. In the midst of confusion, hunger pains rattled her stomach. She hadn't eaten since breakfast. A neon sign advertising *The Cajun Café* blinked at her, and she pulled in and parked. Customers filled every chair, it seemed, but she found a small table in the back and eased into the seat. Plastic crawfish decorated the walls, and Louisiana Red Hot, buckets, and rolls of paper towels graced every table. A man and a woman sat next to her, each in front of large trays piled high with boiled potatoes, chunks of corn on the cob and bright-red boiled crawfish. Sold by the pound, the menu read. Sid watched as they broke off the heads of the crawfish and sucked the meat out, then pinched the meat from the tails, bit them off and threw the empty shells into the bucket. So that's what the buckets were for. Sid pushed aside the bucket on her table.

The spicy bowl of filé gumbo and rice, loaded with shrimp, crab, and fish arrived and quieted Sid's hunger, but startled her brain awake. She'd planned to stay overnight in a local motel, but after the gumbo and the revelation from Pigeon, she knew she wouldn't sleep. She circled around the underpass and headed back to Orange.

The meeting with Pigeon brought up a whole new set of questions. If it wasn't Ethel's body in the fire, whose was it? Had it been Ethel murdered in the storeroom? Were these memories false? No, they couldn't be, they'd been too accurate, too many times for it to all be made up. Okay, say it happened, who were the other men involved and why? Was Pigeon? She glanced at the clock on the dash and then at a road sign. Toomey-Starks, it read.

The driver behind her had his truck lights on bright. She peered into the rear view mirror, wishing he'd dim them.

He's awfully close—how long had he been behind her? Maybe if she braked he'd get the message and back off.

No, he's too close—he'd hit her. A highway sign announced Orange, eight miles, good.

She rolled down the window and stuck her arm out, signaling for him to pass.

He didn't.

Damn. She sped up.

He sped up.

She slowed down.

He slowed down.

Who was that, some wild-ass kid out for a thrill ride? Fear snuck up her spine.

He inched closer.

The hair on her arms stood erect. Her fingers drummed on the steering wheel. Her breath came in short bursts.

She felt a hard jolt. He'd rammed her! The car skidded and she overcorrected but with effort, wrestled it back in control.

Cell phone. She'd call 911. She reached over to her bag on the passenger seat and jammed her hand inside.

What's he doing—slowing down? No, here he comes—he's passing. He's had his kicks and grown weary of the game.

A heavy breath escaped her chest.

Who is the bastard? Get a glimpse when his car goes by.

"Oh God," she cried out loud, "he's not passing!"

Her hands gripped the wheel, knuckles white.

The truck swerved into her door and the grinding sound of

metal against metal dug into her eardrums.

Each battled for control—chariot drivers locked in mortal combat.

Why won't he stop?

He gave one last big swerve and knocked her car into a spin.

Hang on—pull it out, turn into the spin—don't brake. Lift off the floor, her brain yelled to her foot.

She'd be dead by the time it stopped.

When the car finally creaked to a halt, Sid sat motionless, dazed. She shook her head, then summed up. She wasn't hurt, but her car tilted sideways…caught on a railing!

Where is he? She spun her head around. Frantic.

Off to the side, the truck now faced her broadside. It sat motionless, catlike, a patient predator relieved that dinner waited. The truck motor gunned a little, as if the predator grew tired, anxious for nature to take its course.

Questions flashed through her mind like lighting bolts. This wasn't a teenager's stunt. Whoever it was, that driver wasn't done. Tom had been involved in Warren's death so what would stop him from killing her himself, or having someone else do it? Then there was Roy Manly. Oh God. Her sweaty hands gripped the steering wheel.

The beam from the truck's headlights reflected off the roof of her car. She sat in darkness—below the shaft of light. Maybe he couldn't see her. She looked over at the passenger door, ajar. Farther out, what little moon there was reflected off of water.

Now she knew her location. The Sabine River flowed below her. She also knew where he wanted her to go.

She heard him gun the engine, building momentum.

He wasn't done. He wouldn't stop until he finished her off; she felt it in her bones. Wiping sweat stinging her eyes, she reached across her lap, braced herself and released the seat belt. She scrunched down, ducking her head below the back of the car seat.

Minutes were gone, only seconds left, and not many of those. She snaked down the seat to the passenger door and peered into the darkness below. Unsure where solid ground lay below her, she had few options.

He released the brakes. The tires squealed on the pavement. Burning rubber choked out what little breath she had left. Slithering out head first, she stuck her hands straight out and hoped for solid ground.

Gravel tore into her palms as she slid across asphalt. She tried pulling her legs down behind her but one ankle caught on something.

Wheels screamed. Metal on metal…only seconds away.

Sid thrashed with her free foot until it contacted the door handle. One hard yank and her pants leg ripped free. She crawled to the rear of the vehicle, slipping and sliding on her belly. The gravel scraped her wrists and inner arms all the way up to her elbows. The pain registered, but she ignored it. One last leap and she'd be free from danger. For the moment.

The truck rammed her car and the cacophony of metal slamming into metal, metal across pavement, and the stench of scorched tires drove her senses into overload. The truck backed up, and then came at her car again. It rammed into the side of what had once been the driver's door, but now only a pile of crumpled metal, fiberglass, and chrome.

Her car broke free of the railing and careened over the side, snapping trees and splintering brush as it went, then swallowed up by cold water below.

Silence.

Sid forbade herself a breath or an itch.

The truck's headlights shot out over the river. She imagined her car sinking below the surface of the water. The only sound left, the sinister hum of the truck motor. Did he see her escape? She sat in shadow and tall weeds, just at the edge of the bridge, enveloped by the acrid smell of her own fear.

Could he smell her? She felt fast frozen, like someone had

pushed the pause button on a VCR.

Eventually, he shifted into reverse and backed onto the road-way, spinning wheels and spewing gravel as he accelerated. She pried back weeds and pampas grass. Red tail lights of a light-colored truck rattled down the road, bumper dragging, sparks flying.

❧   ❧   ❧

The orange sun peeked over the horizon before Sid saw a police car loop around the access road and approach her from behind, lights flashing. Her muscles ached as she limped down the side of the road. The palms of her hands bled from embed-ded gravel. Blue jean-covered knees, protected by denim, were sore and bruised.

She watched, as the police car grew larger, willing Quade into the driver's seat. Cars had passed her, as she stood on the side of the road. She didn't blame them; she wouldn't have picked her up, either. But she'd hoped that someone with a cell phone would call the police department.

The car screeched to a stop. Quade jumped out and ran toward her, stumbling, as he raced around the fender of the patrol car.

"My God, Sid...I hoped it wasn't you, but something told me—" His kept his eyes fixed on her. The look on his face led her to think he might have had some reason to think that. He grabbed her by the elbow. She flinched, and he eased his grip and slowed his pace.

After he held the door for her, he secured her seat belt, then went around the patrol car, crawled in and buckled his. The car's wheels spun on the pavement as he accelerated, then he asked, "What the hell happened?"

By the time they reached the emergency room, she'd told him about the truck and her visits with Beatrice and Ed Pigeon.

"Damn it, Sid, if you're going to survive as a private eye, you've got to buy a gun and get some small arms training."

"Where to now?" Quade asked, as they left the hospital.

"Well, I guess I better call the rental car company and tell them where their car is." Sid laughed sarcastically. "Since they probably won't rent me another one I guess you'd better drop me off at a car dealer." She pulled her wallet out of her jacket pocket, thankful it hadn't fallen out during the attack. The pain medicine kicked in and her muscles relaxed. Laying her head back against the headrest, she closed her eyes.

Quade, for once, said nothing.

"You know what" she broke the silence, "after Nancy died, I considered quitting this whole thing. Find a job in a nice air-conditioned office, in a soft chair—and be bored." Straightening up, she pushed back against the seat and sucked in a deep breath. Anger drove up her gut. "But now I'm 'het up,' as my grandmother used to say. That guy really pissed me off."

Quade stayed with her until she drove off the lot with a taxi-cab-yellow Nissan Xterra, black grill and all. Hell, to survive this new life, she might as well enjoy the ride. Besides, she'd take better caution, driving one with her name on the dotted line.

And if he wanted her, he'd damn sure see her coming!

⚜   ⚜   ⚜

"I went to see Ed Pigeon yesterday. Weird," Sid was eager to tell what she'd learned.

Ben's hands shook as he took the police report from Quade, who had just recounted the attack on Sid the night before. When he looked at her, his eyes were hard. "Oh no, you don't, you can't just waltz in here with this kind of a report and expect me to sit and listen to a story about a visit with Edward Pigeon." Ben threw the folder on his desk.

She faced Ben, impatient and resolute.

Quade leaned against the cabinet in the corner.

Both men stared at her, their faces the color of wet cigarette ash. Their lips were straight lines slashed across the lower halves of their faces.

Sid tried to ignore the burns on the inside of her arms, stuffed her bandaged hands out of sight in her coat pockets.

"Quade, did you get a description of the driver and the truck? Got any leads on that?" Ben asked, ignoring Sid.

"I'm working on it. Got an all points bulletin out on the vehicle, but the description fits half the pickup trucks in Orange County. Every Cajun or cowboy in the area drives one just like it. And she didn't get a glimpse of the driver."

"Was it Manly, you think?" Ben pushed.

"I looked when he came alongside me…but it all happened so fast. Even if it was, I'm not dropping this case, Ben. I can't. I don't care what you say." She dug her heels into her shoes. "I'm not taking the easy way out." Not anymore.

"Okay, Sid, if you insist on continuing this search, what the hell have you done to protect yourself?" He paced the floor behind his desk.

She opened her handbag and pulled out a Glock 17. "This. It can put a group of five shots inside a two-and-a-half inch circle at a range of twenty-five yards, and I did just that this morning when Quade took me for my first class." She knew she looked smug, she felt it.

Ben raised his eyebrows and looked at Quade.

"I swear, Ben, she's a natural. First time she ever fired a gun. The guys couldn't believe it when they checked her target. You should a seen their faces!"

"Beginner's luck." Ben shrugged. "You are planning on taking more lessons aren't you?"

Sid nodded. "And I bought this." She pulled out a key chain with a cylinder of mace clipped on the end.

"Now, can we talk about my visit to Edward Pigeon?" Without waiting for an answer, she began. "He confirmed everything we already knew about the fire that morning." She swallowed a lump in her throat. "But get this. He kept calling the woman Gette, short for Georgette he said. Then I pulled out this picture of Ethel that Quade gave me. He took one look at it and swore he didn't know that woman—but it wasn't Gette."

Both men raised their eyebrows this time.

"You think he lied?" Now she had Ben's attention.

"I don't know. It didn't seem so. He admitted he brought Ethel over here from Florida and said he worked for this guy they all called Big Daddy."

Quade finally spoke. "Well, if it wasn't Ethel Elaine Perry, who was it?" And what happened to Ethel?

"I think it's time we paid Roy Manly a visit." Ben said. "First thing in the morning? Let's catch him off guard."

                 ◈   ◈   ◈

"Hell, I fought my way in and out of Sparkles Paradise every Friday night. I had lots of fights," Roy answered the question thrown at him by Quade.

He and Ben had agreed Sid could come along, but they asked her to not say anything—to let them do the talking. She figured they were afraid to turn her loose on him. They weren't far off.

They'd surprised him at home early that morning. He answered the door with sleep still in his eyes and booze on his breath. When he saw Sid, his face froze. But of course that proved nothing, since she'd already pissed him off at his office. Glad she'd brought the Glock, she rubbed her hand across the outside of her handbag for reassurance.

The interrogation started with questions of little consequence. Loosening him up, Sid figured. After Roy made several racial slurs Ben said, "Seems to me you don't like black people."

"No, I don't like them at all. I had five of them what worked for me over in Louisiana once." He stopped and took a breath. When he exhaled, enough alcohol fumes blew out to light a match. "The only thing I do with 'em is fuck 'em. The bitches, I mean." He glared at Sid, his voice guttural and suggestive.

Bile burned her throat.

"I'm confused," Quade said, acting dumb. "If you don't like them, why do you sleep with them?"

Roy shrugged but said nothing.

"Still keep your cigarettes rolled up in your tee shirt sleeve?" Quade asked.

He grinned and patted his shirt pocket. "Nah, not any more. Keep 'em here now."

"Do you remember a woman called Push Cart Susie?" Ben took over the questioning.

"Yep, the kids called her Minnie Trombone. She always walked around with an old brown coat on, summer and winter, had a fur collar."

"I've been here a long time," Ben said, "I remember her, too. A young boy followed her around didn't he?" Now he played dumb.

"Yeah, probably Bobby Joe Neighbors."

"How come he hung around her, do you think?" Quade jumped in.

"Because a piece only cost him a quarter—but what I can't figure out is how he ever stood the smell."

Ben cleared his throat. "I hear you've got a couple of tattoos, is that right?"

"Yup."

"Mind if I see them?"

"Nope." He pulled up his shirtsleeves.

On one arm were the words, *Born to Lose*, on the other, a picture of the devil.

Quade asked the next question. "Did you ever kill a goat or a lamb?"

"Nope. Don't like mutton." Roy rolled his sleeves back down.

Ben stood and stretched his legs. "Did you ever kill an animal and clean it in your kitchen?"

"Nope, never did."

"Tell me about your first wife." Ben moved the conversation.

"Crazy bitch. Went off her rocker. Them doctors at the hospital told me I drove her wacky, but hell, if they'd a given me fifteen minutes with her I'd a straightened her out."

Quade and Ben both took that opportunity to inspect their shoes for any telltale speck of dust.

"Who took her to the hospital, Roy?" Ben looked him in the eye.

"Mama and the old man. I knew she didn't need to go, but you didn't mess with Mama."

"What do you mean?"

"See this here scar?"His index finger pointed to a scar on his forehead. "Mama hit me here with a mop handle once, and here, a beer bottle. Why you asking me all these here questions? I gotta get up and get dressed. Got roads to work on."

"We're almost done, hang on." Ben held the palm of his hand out toward Roy.

"We're investigating a fire that happened out at the old Millersfield Farm a few years ago," Quade said.

"Well, I never killed nobody or burned down any house. So you're barking up the wrong tree, if you get my drift."

"Did you ever fool around on your wife, Nancy?" Quade bore down on him.

"Hell yes, I did. Fooled around with a lot of women."

"Who were you fooling around with in 1971?'

"Peggy O'Dell."

Sid noticed how quickly he came up with the answer.

"Ever bring her to your house?"

"I always met her in Lake Charles. Her old man left for months at a time, what'd he expect?"

"You get laid a lot?"

"Lots of times." Roy huffed his chest out.

"Ever tied up a woman?"

"Nope. I don't do that." He sniffed. "What I got, they want."

Sid wanted to throw up.

"What is it you think I done?" he asked, his voice rising.

Ben answered. "I've learned someone died at your house and her body burned in a fire."

"Listen, I tell you, I ain't never killed nobody or hauled any dead body anywhere."

"Okay, Roy. Now," Ben switched subjects, "how many girlfriends would you say you had? And where did you take them?"

"Aw, hell, my house was a whorehouse deluxe. I threw many a wild party at that place. We always had gang bangs there. Once, I hung around with this girl, Olive Murdock her name was. I brought her to my house and when we got there the house was full of men gang-banging a girl from Mississippi. I didn't even go inside. I just told Olive let's get the hell out a Dodge."

"If you didn't go in, how did you know they gang banged?" Quade turned the screws.

"Well, I went in, but then we left. The girl was in the bedroom."

"Is this the girl you killed?"

"Well, I saw her in the living room." He hadn't answered the question, but they let that slide for now.

"Remember the color of her hair?"

"Brown, I guess, I'm not sure. The bitch was a whore anyway, sittin' around—*éjarer,* legs spread wide, just waiting for a dick. Five or six of 'em got the clap that night." A chortle crackled out of his throat, and he rubbed the back of his hand across his mouth and snorted. "So much gang banging went on in that house the sheets got so stiff I had to pitch 'em away—you know what I mean?" His grin reminded Sid of the Cheshire cat. She hated cats.

"Get drunk much?" Sid saw Quade put a check mark on his list.

"Nah, I've done that since I was kid. The stuff don't bother me none."

"How much did you drink yesterday?"

"Ah, a case of beer, I reckon."

"That's a lot of booze," Ben said.

"I can drink a case of beer and fifth of whisky in a day. You won't get drunk if you eat while you're drinking."

Ignorant bastard.

"I see where you were arrested for rape one time, Roy." Ben flipped through pages on his clipboard. Sid knew he did it more for the effect than for information.

Roy didn't hesitate. "Had to give her daddy seven hundred dollars to get out of it, too. That girl also done it with a guy from Mauriceville, but it got thrown out of court."

Ben leaned forward. The clipboard dangled between his knees. "Tell me what happened."

"I met her in this bar, and we went to the barn, out at old man Richardson's place. Had a couple of beers on the way. When we got in the barn, she pulled her pants down. Now I ask you, how in the hell can anyone call that rape?"

No one answered the question.

"Turned out she was 15. I thought she was 29," Roy continued. "Then I took her back to the bar and Randy Miller took her and kept her for four days."

"Well, that about does it for me." Ben let out a long sigh, and then looked over at Quade and Sid.

Quade shrugged his shoulders, "I think I'm done, too."

They were almost to the door when Roy called out, "I want a lie detector test."

Sid turned just in time to catch the look exchanged between Ben and Quade. They'd oblige him. Couldn't be used in a courtroom, but that didn't matter.

"Let me get it set up and I'll contact you." Quade said as he turned and walked out the door. A smile, ever so slight, played across his lips.

Twenty Two

Time to talk to Sophia. Sid parked her car and knocked on the kitchen door. She leaned on the door frame, listening to Sophia's footsteps paddle across the linoleum. Just the sound of them eased Sid's pain. When the door opened Sid held back from falling into Sophia's arms. She wanted to crawl up inside them and listen to the soft beat of the old woman's heart. Surely goodness centered itself there.

"Sid, honey! What's going on? You look terrible." They both laughed as Sid allowed Sophia to lead her to the parlor and guide her to the sofa. Release came with the deluge of tears. She'd held it in for so long, it felt good now, the letting go. Sophia asked no questions, she simply sat next to her and pulled Sid's head into her chest and let her cry.

"I thought I could do this job, Sophia. Now, I—I don't know that I can."

"Sure you can, honey."

"I always saw life as so simple, but it isn't is it?"

Sophia shook her head. "Afraid not missy. Life's full of a whole lot of ambiguity. That's where personal choice comes in. Anybody can screw up, but most folk want to blame somebody else for their problems. Don't work that way. Hold on, I'll be right back."

She slipped out of the parlor and returned shortly with a tray and a pot of tea with two cups and saucers. "I always say, nothing fixes the droopies like a good cry and a cup of hot tea."

After Sid finished, she knew Sophia was correct.

"Tell you what, missy, let's dance." Sophia turned the radio on to a soft rock station, pushed the coffee table aside and pulled Sid to her feet. "Feel the rhythm," she urged as she began to sway. "Let it touch your soul."

Sophia's aged body took on a life of its own, transformed. Sid could have sworn Sophia floated across the room.

Sid stood, stiff, in the middle of the parlor. The music touched her soul, but if she'd ever had a line of communication between soul and body she'd been trained to disconnect that years ago.

"Close your eyes, missy."

She did. The notes played on tense muscles until the tightness melted away. Sid felt connected with everything good.

👁   👁   👁

The next morning Sid beat Annie to the office and stuck the key in the lock just as the phone rang. Wrestling the ornery lock open, she stepped to the phone, getting it after the fourth ring.

"Good morning, Sid."

"Hi, Ben." She hoped her voice sounded cool, irritated that every time she heard his voice, her dang heart went on a rampage. Steadying the flutter with her hand on her chest, she sensed his smile over the phone, and that peeved her even more.

"I was watching for you out my window and saw you drive up. Hope I didn't rush you."

"Just a little." She paused and took a breath. "Couldn't get the door unlocked."

"Can you come by my office today?"

"Now?"

He hummed in the phone and she heard pages turn. Checking his calendar, she figured. She'd be glad when she needed one.

"Looks like I have an hour."

"I'll be right there."

"See you in a couple."

She forced herself to take slow steps as she crossed the street, but when she walked into his office and it smelled musky, like

Ben, her defenses went up. By the time she realized he was talking, she'd missed the first part of the sentence.

"...uncovered what we think was an interstate prostitution ring."

"A what?" Damn, what had she missed?

"Yeah, I know, preposterous, huh? You just never know, in this business."

"You mean Roy?" And then she felt silly after she'd asked. Of course he meant Roy.

"We found a connection between Roy and this Big Daddy."

"Tell me more."

"My guess is Roy played the dupe. The way I figure, Ethel Elaine found out she'd bit off more than she could chew and tried to get out of it. But deep debt bound her to Big Daddy. He just cut the rope."

Steam from the coffee tickled her face as she drank. She rubbed her nose with the heel of her hand.

"Needed a local yokel to do his dirty work," Ben continued, "and Roy fit the bill, especially with Peyton Place being reenacted at his house every day.

"But he's no yokel, now he's a county commissioner." Sid struggled to reconcile the father she'd met through the eyes of his daughters with the position the man held today.

"Still is, just got smarter as he got older. Besides, precinct two is a small rural precinct. Good folk, for the most part, but no one else wanted the job. Besides, you know how it is—tell people what they want to hear and they'll vote for you"

"And what they want to hear is?"

"Something for nothing. His campaign speeches forewarned me that the county courted trouble if they elected Roy. But, you've got to understand Sid, he'd spent years working on road construction, even oversaw a couple of work crews, so he sold himself on his knowledge of repairing roads. That's the most important thing to a lot of people in a precinct like his. Their world revolves around whether or not they can get to town.

We get lots of rain, and that tears up roads pretty quick. Manly promised them he wouldn't let the rain do that. Enough of them believed him and he got elected. Never mind the county roads are worse than when he took office a year ago. There's even talk of financial impropriety. An investigation is already in the works. Besides, his cronies made getting elected a simple matter, they hauled people in from the backwoods and swamps, most of them having never voted before.

"He almost got away with his past. He did—for close to thirty years. He took a misstep, though, when he discounted his daughters."

A blue flame danced in the middle of Sid's brain. A smile started on one side of her mouth and continued to the other. "That and a persistent blue flame."

"A what?"

"Oh, nothing."

"But we never know what a jury will do," Ben admitted. "It isn't over until it's over."

He'd made them set him up for a lie detector test. Damn snotty-nosed police officer set the appointment for the afternoon. He'd just have to limit his beer that morning, that's what he'd do. His mind had to be fresh and sharp. He'd beat this rap; he just had to play it cool. They had nothing on The Stud except the stories of his two fucking kids, and no one would believe them. They was just babies then. Who'd a thought they'd a remembered that day?

The Stud humphed down the hall, threw coffee and water in the drip-o-later, and flopped into the chrome kitchen chair.

After slurping down two cups of coffee, he clumped back down the hall and into the bedroom. His bare feet found their path through the piles of clothes, shoes, and random junk scattered throughout the room. He raised an arm and stuck his head down toward his armpit. His nose curled upward. He picked up a damp washcloth from the side of the lavatory and wiped under each arm, sprayed deodorant, and then pulled on a less-than-perfectly clean dress shirt and a narrow tie.

He knew Mack Fontenot. He'd worked on Stud's campaign for a while—until he just quit, mid-campaign. But Mack'd give him a break on the polygraph.

Risky, taking the test, but the results couldn't hang him. Besides, he'd bluffed his way this far. No reason why he couldn't keep bluffing.

❦   ❦   ❦

"I want to take this to the grand jury," Ben announced as soon as Quade and Sid settled in their chairs.

Sid's heart raced. "What about the lie detector test?"

"He flunked it. Every question." Ben thumbed through the report.

Quade leaned forward; his hands gripped the chair arms. "Let's do it."

"Before we do, let's go over everything again." Ben sat at his desk and thumbed through piles of documents. "All we really have on the murder, you know, is the testimony of Jewell. Emma's memory of him saying he'd burn her up like he did the woman in the house fire adds some credence to Jewell's memory, but she doesn't remember the woman in the storeroom. She witnessed arson, but I can't charge him with that. The statute of limitation on arson is five years. Sad thing about our law is, I can't charge him with child sexual abuse either, the statute of limitations has run out on that, too."

"What?" Texas laws didn't make sense to Sid.

"There is no limitation period if the sexual assault results in biological evidence being taken and the DNA doesn't match the victim or any other readily ascertainable person. But that law doesn't apply here. We have none."

"But what about sexual abuse of a child?"

"Ten years limitation for sexual assault without biological

evidence. Also ten years for sexual assault on a child from the eighteenth birthday of the victim."

"Do you mean to tell me, that Emma could only charge her father with rape for ten years afterwards? She was just a child?"

"Yep."

"Incredible—rape a child and after a few years you're handed a get out of jail free card?"

"Afraid so." Ben held his palms up to toward the ceiling. "Go figure." He stood and walked to the window and looked out. "Our theory of the prostitution ring is just that, theory. No hard evidence. It's been too many years ago. Most everybody's either dead or disappeared. But I think I can get an indictment on the murder based on the testimony of Jewell and, add Emma's story to that—an arson conviction."

"I sure would like to see the guy locked up," Sid said. "I know Jewell and Emma would feel safer." Not to mention herself. "What about Nancy?"

"I talked with the police there," Quade jumped in. No evidence of forced entry, no weapon. With her medical condition they found nothing to warrant an autopsy. Slick, huh?"

By the time they finished the review, Ben said "I'll present it to the next grand jury. I think I can get an indictment, but whether I can get it before a judge and jury is another matter. But we're gonna try, dammit." He pounded the table with his fist.

Sid stood just inside the door of Ben's office. He stomped around the room and ranted, "I can't believe this. The judge is treating this like a civil case instead of a criminal one. Hell, he almost let Manly out on his own recognizance! Five thousand dollar bond? Peanuts! We're talking murder. Two people came to see me and said they heard Manly swear to kill me when this is over. Tell me, does that sound like an innocent man?"

He paced, running his fingers through his hair. "The grand jury indicted Roy Manly for murder without any hesitation."

Ben stopped, looked at Sid and chuckled.

"Of course, some people say a grand jury will indict a ham sandwich."

"Why is that?"

"They only hear one side of the story. They don't hear any defense, don't even see the accused." Again, Ben paced. "I know what it takes to present a case to a jury beyond a reasonable doubt—but I can't get this one before a jury." Ben walked to his chair and sat, fidgeted, then stood and continued pacing. "The judge's tied my hands, plus, Manly's defense lawyer is out to destroy Jewell, Emma, and anyone else in his way—all for the price of fame. All circumstantial he says, except for the eyewitness testimony of two women who were three and five at the time. But he convinced the judge, regardless of the grand jury indictment, there was no hard evidence. It's been too many years for Jewell's memory to be that accurate, the judge said, and threw it out."

Sid felt heat flush her face. "No one cares about the truth, Ben. No one! It's razzle dazzle, plain and simple." Sid pointed her finger at Ben. "Right now, where this case sits? That's exactly what these two women feared. Nothing would come of it. That's why they were reluctant in the first place, why the three of us put our lives at risk. Now what the hell do I tell them?"

She knew Ben felt bad, but she didn't care. She turned and stormed out of his office.

The next morning Sid sat at the kitchen table with eggs and bacon and the morning newspaper when the headlines jumped out at her. 'Judge dismisses thirty-year-old case.' Lack of evidence, the reason given in the dismissal the day before, the article continued. She laid her arms on the table, put her head down, and sobbed. Why did she get caught up in this mess in the first place? Her skin felt prickly, numb.

The doorbell rang, but she ignored the intruder. It rang again. Damn, who ever you are, go away, she thought, as she dragged herself to the door and wrapped her robe tighter. Tears blinded her eyes and she stubbed her toe on the sofa. Cursing at the pain, she swung the door open and stared at an overweight, middle-aged man with a thick head of red hair.

"Are you Sid Smart?"

"Who wants to know?" She blasted the man, knowing she sounded rude, but was beyond caring at the moment.

"My name is Robert Murphy. I should have come by earlier, but I didn't think what I had to say, important. Now, I'm sorry I didn't." He shifted his weight and pulled his sweater down over his belly.

"Excuse me?"

"Pardon me, Ma'am. But I just talked to Chief Burns. I planned to go see him today anyway but when I read the paper this morning I knew I better get there quick. After I talked with him, he told me to talk with you. I read in the paper the judge dropped the charges against Roy Manly. I remember something that happened when I was a teenager, and the chief thought you ought to know."

"What are you talking about?" Sid wiped her nose and pushed her hair out of her face.

"I was born and raised here in Orange, and we lived just down from Finnell Street. One day, I walked home from school—I must have been around fifteen—and the little Manly girl ran out to the front yard and told me to come see the dead woman in her back-yard. I thought she was kidding me and kept walking, but she ran after me and grabbed my hand and pulled. I started to follow her, but then I freaked out and ran home. I never told anyone. I forgot it until all this news broke about the murder and the fire."

Sid mustered a weak thank you and shut the door. Too little too late.

Just as she settled into her misery, another knock. Expecting Robert again, she yanked open the door to tell him to get lost. But instead of it being him, a U.S. Postal Express Delivery envelope lay at her feet.

What now? Everybody just leave her alone, she was done with the whole shittin' mess.

She tore open the cardboard envelope, reached inside and pulled out a sheet from a legal pad. At the top someone had jotted a note listing the make and model of a car, plus the date and delivery of such, to a man in Juarez, Mexico. The date was one Sid would never forget—the day she'd been notified of her brother's death.

Below that, and in the same handwriting, Warren's name, with a black line drawn through it.

Weak-kneed, she slumped to the floor and dumped out the remainder of the envelope's contents, a micro recorder tape—the same kind her machine used. Around it someone had rubber-banded a sheet of notepad. Sid flipped open the note and read the words scrawled in blue ink.

I found these in Tom's pocket. I believe they belong to you, and signed, *Dorcas Huff.* Then, as a postscript, *I'm sorry.*

Twenty Three

Sid tossed the contents of the envelope on the table beside the half-eaten eggs and cold coffee, threw off her robe and crawled back into bed. Rain splattered against the window, making faces at her, and then rolled down the windowsill. Several times she started to get up, but then just rolled over and pulled the covers over her head, ignoring the phone that kept ringing and ringing. She looked at the caller id and saw Ben's name—calling to express his regret, but she didn't want to hear it. She felt sorry enough all by herself. After the sixth call, she stuck her fingers in her ears. "Shut up!" she yelled. Where the hell did she go from here? Her first private eye assignment and she'd failed. It had taken a woman she despised to deliver hard evidence of the transportation of stolen vehicles, and possibly to Warren's death.

Sid had stomped on piss ants while elephants stampeded.

Evidently Ben had given up. The phone hadn't rung in over half an hour. Buried under a pile of pillows, she wallowed in grief until banging on the door finally put her feet into action. She ignored the robe, and instead, grabbed the blanket from the bed and wrapped it around herself, even covering her head, trudged to the door and peered out the peephole. Damn. Ben. She turned and headed back to bed.

The banging rattled the pins in the hinges. Any minute Sophia would be out her door and up the stairs joining him, so Sid finally threw back the dead bolt and slid the safety chain off of the hook.

He walked in and stood with his hands on his hips, staring.

"What the hell do you think you're doing?" He yanked off his raincoat and dumped his umbrella into the stand by the door. "Why don't you answer your goddamned phone?" Rain splattered off of his coat onto the hardwood floor. He took it off and tossed it on top of the umbrella. She watched puddles form as water dripped off the hem of his coat. Should she take off the blanket and wipe up the floor? Or let the whole floor rot away? She decided on the rotting.

The bed beckoned and she followed, leaving Ben standing in the middle of the room dripping and yelling. He followed her and towered over the bed. Rain dripped off his hair and fell onto her face. She wiped it away, angry that she still wore her Mickey Mouse nightshirt.

Tears had run down her nose and into her mouth. He got a tissue from the bedside table and handed it to her. "Here, wipe your nose, you look ridiculous with all that snot running down your face."

"You can be a real jerk when you want to." Sid threw back the insult then stopped to blow her nose. "Why did the judge dismiss the charges? Couldn't he see? And now this Murphy guy comes by and tells me Jewell wanted him to come see a dead woman in her backyard. Doesn't that count for something?"

"Sid, we knew this was a long shot. It's been thirty years. It's not that the judge doesn't think he's guilty. He does. But judges can't go on personal opinion. Enough evidence to convince a jury must be there. We're talking murder here. Juries don't hand down murder convictions easily. Or shouldn't, at least. Convincing a grand jury is the easy part. Getting a conviction is another matter. But, sometimes, even harder, is getting it before a judge and jury. We tried, we didn't make it."

"But he's guilty, I know he is. Those girls know he is. It's like adding insult to injury."

"I don't know what to say." He sat with his head down.

"Sometimes you just have to let it go, Sid." He placed a warm hand on her thigh.

"Ben, I—"

"Hush, don't say a word." He leaned over and touched his lips to hers. They were soft and warm, just as she'd remembered from that night on his sofa.

No, she couldn't. She pushed him away.

"It's okay, Sid, you're in control." He pulled her to him and whispered the words in her mouth.

Like hell she was! Not over the case, and not over the passion he made rage inside her groin. She felt herself yield, but when his hand slipped around her back and pulled her tighter, she jerked back into resolve, stomped to the door and threw it open.

"Damn, here I go again, letting you suck me in so you can shove me away!" Ben snatched up his coat and umbrella.

Sid picked up the envelope with the tape and note from Dorcas, and shoved it into Ben's hands. "Here, give this to Quade. He'll know what to do with it."

Ben stormed out. She heard his footsteps charging down the stairs. Without a doubt, Sophia heard him, too.

Sid went into the bathroom and stared in the mirror. Embarrassed by her behavior and half-expecting God to strike her dead, she snickered and ran her hands through disheveled hair, splashed cold water on flushed nose and cheeks. She had to watch herself around that man. She couldn't be trusted.

A small silver heart lay on the floor by the front door. If must have fallen out of Ben's pocket. Sid picked it up and fingered the shiny metal then slipped it into the top pocket of her nightshirt. She felt it lying alongside the throbbing valentine that thumped in her chest. Sam had ripped out her heart and devoured it. Maybe life wanted to give it back to her. But she wasn't ready. Not yet. Maybe she'd never be.

Something moved in the mirror—behind her. She turned quickly, half-expecting to see Ben, but saw no one. Sid turned back to the mirror and saw it again. She twisted at the waist, and gradually let her hips follow. A blue flame hovered in the middle of the room. She blinked, but her vision didn't clear away the flame. It moved across the room and dipped over her briefcase, then vanished. Sid crept over to the case, lifted the lid, and there lay the tattered picture of the fire. "Okay, this is weird. I know I put that picture in the folder." She dropped the lid back in place and ran back to the safety of the bed covers. Ridiculous behavior for a woman her age. She didn't believe such nonsense. Her heart drummed like a tom-tom.

Shrouded in the bedcovers, Sid dozed then woke with a start. How long had she slept? She slipped out of bed and walked on tiptoe to the briefcase, and peeked inside. A manila folder lay on top. No picture in sight. She was now certifiable.

Deciding to go with that fact, Sid dressed and took off, drawn to Hartburg. Millersfield farm didn't exist anymore, Ben had said, but she hoped she could find where the house sat before it burned to the ground. She headed out Little Cypress Road.

Small businesses etched out of pine forests became less numerous the further she drove. The door of a dance studio opened and a swarm of small girls in yellow and black tutu's buzzed out the door and into family vehicles. A mom and pop tombstone store displayed dozens of grave markers alongside the road.

Pine trees won out, the further she drove. Only an occasional house peeked out from behind claustrophobic trees.

A highway sign announced Hartburg; she turned right onto a two-lane asphalt road. Houses again competed with pine forests. The ubiquitous Baptist Church told her she'd found Hartburg. Another right took her by King Cemetery, an old burial ground maintained by family members of the deceased. Moss hung heavy in the trees, much like she'd seen in the swamp. Andrine claimed death didn't exist. King Cemetery argued the fact.

Sid crossed the railroad track, turned right again, and drove down a narrow, overgrown gravel road laid out by a snake. As she'd suspected, thirty years of weather had not totally changed the pile of burned out remains. That was where the house must have sat, she pointed mentally. Sid turned off the car motor, eased out and walked up the weed-infested oyster-shell driveway, her eyes fixed on the burned-out ruins.

Gingerly she stepped over rusty strings of barbed wire and stood in the middle of what she guessed had been the flaming house.

Grief hit Sid in the knees. She sunk to the ground, her head in her hands. Images of a fire raged in her mind. Without warning, she saw a woman scratching against a window ledge, desperate for oxygen, desperate to escape the escalating heat. Ethel Elaine, or the leftovers of her body, burned with the carpet in the living room. A second woman? Who? Georgette Sanders? Had both of them been scapegoats—victims, too, of a male-dominant—what? Social arrangement?

Sid sat on the ground, eyes closed, and replayed the facts she'd read in the inquest. A fireman stepped through dying embers, stirring bits of what had once been a home, when a final blue flame captured his attention. He approached and poked it with a stick. Burning in the flames were pieces of human flesh clinging to a couple of teeth and a small piece of hipbone.

They found no other evidence of human remains. The result of the intensity of the fire, some said.

Perhaps.

Perhaps not.

When the smoke first belched into the early morning air, before firemen arrived, Jewell and Emma imperceptibly breathed in the smoke. They must have. They were here.

In Sid's mind she saw the particulate air join oxygen meandering through the small girls' bloodstream. Particles of truth spirited out places to hide within their small bodies, promising dormancy, awaiting the call of the NOW!

Before, Sid felt like a caterpillar demanding the chrysalis stage hurry and pass. Now she sat in the cool breeze of sweet-smelling country air, the beautiful wisdom of life's rhythms filled her.

She left the farm and headed to the library. Neither stupid nor certifiable, she knew another piece of the puzzle existed.

Settling into archived records, Sid hunkered down for a long search. She felt more comfortable this time, knowing how to start and where to look, but she didn't get there much faster.

It was almost closing time before she found what she looked for. A small article, stuck down in the corner of a three decade old Mississippi newspaper, The Sun Herald, caught her eye. *Woman Missing.* She scanned the article. Red hair, slim build, worked at a motel, but this one near Bay St. Louis, Mississippi. Her name? Georgette Sanders. Sid almost said eureka.

👁   👁   👁

She printed out trip maps on the library computer, spun out of the library parking lot and headed home. There, she packed a bag and called the office to tell Annie she was leaving town for a few days.

"I really don't like you heading out by yourself, Siddie," Annie argued over the phone. "You know what happened last time."

"I'll be careful, sweetheart, I know how you worry." Worry hell, Sid knew what Annie really wanted was to be going with her. "How's that list coming?"

"I'm just about done. I found this one file I want you to see. Looks like Warren was working to break a car theft ring and he suspected the owners of that junkyard we staked out. Remember?"

Sid's heart changed rhythm. "Good work, Annie. Make a copy of the file, call Quade and ask him to stop by and pick it up. See you in a few days."

Sophia watched her from the front porch swing as Sid threw her suitcase into the car. "Going to Bay St. Louis, I see," she called at Sid. "Here's some money, drop it in a slot machine for me, will you? A smile crinkled her eyes, almost hiding them behind folds of skin.

"How'd you know?" Sid's jaw gaped. She waved Sophia off. "Never mind. I should be used to this by now." She stuck her hand out. "Give me the money. If I get a chance I'll pull a few wheels for you." Sid grinned and dropped the money in her pocket.

Her hastily packed bag thrown in the back seat, Sid sped east past the Texas tourist center established to welcome visitors from Louisiana. She wondered if Ethel Elaine had stopped there as she entered Texas. A chill played down her backbone and her foot responded with added pressure on the accelerator when she approached the bridge where she'd been slammed off the road. Burned-rubber tire marks still gave testimony of that night.

Road signs on the interstate whizzed past Sid faster than she could read them. She wasn't surprised when she turned on the radio to a station that blared the perfect song. She sang along, broadcasting her destination through the open moon roof. "M I crooked letter, crooked letter I, crooked letter, crooked letter I, hump back, hump back I Mississippi, floating down to…"

Wow, cocky felt good. She headed for the missing puzzle piece. What she'd do when she got there, she had no idea, but when she went home, she'd take Georgette Sanders with her. Either her or her cold, dead body.

"Ben?" she announced into his cell phone message center, "I didn't get a chance to call you before I left town. I just stopped to fill up with gas and food. Hoped I'd catch you. Anyway, I'm taking some time off, don't know how long I'll be gone, but when I get back into town I'll call." No need to get his hopes up—or his fears.

👁   👁   👁

Evidently hotels in Bay St. Louis didn't come without casinos. After she dumped her bag in her room at Casino Magic, she wandered downstairs looking for food. A poster announced Shirley Jones in concert that evening. In the picture, Shirley, all decked out in a sparkling silver evening gown the same color as her hair, smiled, beautiful as ever. The concert must have ended. Droves of people poured out the auditorium doors.

Sid stuck her hand down inside her pants pocket and fingered

Sophia's money. She'd better give her money to the casino now. When the sun came up tomorrow, she'd be too busy. She didn't have the heart not to try.

A three-person group sang and played on a stage in the lobby behind the bar. A woman dressed in black, from pants to sleeveless top and black arm band, topped off with a spiked hairdo, supplied the energy of the group. She moved from cymbals to drums to sticks to shakers of some kind. The contagious beat forced rhythm into Sid's former Baptist feet.

Behind them, rows and rows of slot machines jangled with the magic of a win. Diehards sat at video poker machines, to the left. Sid selected one that announced Draw Poker and stuck in Sophia's money.

"How do you work this thing?" Sid interrupted the game of the woman who overflowed the stool next to her.

The woman nodded, but kept right on punching buttons that asked hold or draw. "Honey, you look up there at the top of the machine—there, see it tells you what wins what. You push this button to bet and that one to draw." She demonstrated for Sid and drew a jack of spades and a ten of diamonds. "Hot damn, I just missed a Royal Flush. See here, if I'd a drawn a queen of diamonds, I'd a won big." The woman's eyes sparkled with the thought.

Soon Sid enjoyed the game as much as her teacher. Her name was Thelma, she'd told Sid in between spins. When Sophia's twenty dollar bill doubled, Sid cashed out, pocketed the cash slip for safe keeping, and pulled out her own twenty.

"Child, you're getting the hang of this thing now, aren't you?" Thelma sang. "I just love to gamble." Excitement bubbled in her eyes. "I set a few bucks aside every month, come over, double my money, and go home. You have to know when to quit. That's the key. That and always play the max bet. That's the only way to win."

Sid smiled at the woman. "So, do you live near by?"

"Nearby? Child, I live right down on the corner. Have for fifty years. You?"

"Texas." Sid pulled out another twenty and put it in the machine. The game fascinated her. Always dangling hope in front of her with near misses.

"Texas? What brings you to gambling country?" Thelma glanced at Sid, and kept her momentum going, her total wins registered three hundred quarters.

"Looking for someone." Sid hesitated, but decided what the heck, and asked, "You ever hear of a Georgette Sanders living around here?"

Thelma's body stiffened. She hit the cash out button, grabbed her cash slip, and walked off without a word.

Coincidence no longer surprised Sid. She cashed out, too, and went upstairs to bed.

👁   👁   👁

Thelma said the house on the corner. Which corner? There were four of them. It was Saturday morning. After another sleepless night thinking of Thelma and synchronicity, Sid dared herself to intrude on the woman's life, like it or not. A lifetime of people-pleasing had ill-prepared her for jumping into someone's face. But Thelma knew something. Either that or she had a sudden call to the bathroom.

One house was a good as another. Sid picked one, knocked and a young man dressed in baggy shorts and a T-shirt with the sleeves cut out, came to the door.

"I'm looking for Thelma. Does she live here?" Sid looked back at the road, as if disoriented.

"Thelma?" He opened the screen door and stepped to the porch. "No ma'am, you have the wrong house. Thelma lives in that house—over there." He pointed to a neat frame house, diagonal from his. Painted yellow, with dark green shutters, someone had placed red geranium-filled pots along the edge of the porch.

As Sid crossed the street, Thelma walked out the front door

and across a thick carpet of San Augustine grass toward Sid. She threw the question at Sid. "Who are you, and what do you want?"

"My name is Sidra Smart and I'm investigating a case of arson and murder that occurred in Orange, Texas—over thirty years ago now."

"Are you a private detective or the police or something?" Thelma stared Sid in the eye.

Sid sucked in a deep breath, her hand across her midriff. "I guess you could say I'm a private detective."

"You could say? Well, ain't you or not? Which is it?"

"I am."

"So what connection does Gette have with the fire? You think she did it?"

"No, I don't. Perhaps a victim, but not the perpetrator."

"I see." The older woman ran her hand across her face and down the back of her hair. "I'm going out on a limb here—I'll tell you what, give me a couple of hours, then come back. I'll see what I can do for you."

⬤   ⬤   ⬤

Pitch black filled the sky when Sid drove back into Orange, her odometer reporting an additional two thousand miles on the Xterra. Her body complained as she pulled herself out of the car and climbed the stairs to her apartment. The first thing she did after dropping her bags on the floor was call Ben and Quade. It was late, they were probably asleep, but she didn't care. This wouldn't wait, she needed to see them first thing in the morning.

The Glock tucked under her pillow, Sid crawled into bed, eager for sleep, but the alarm clock ticking next to her pillow sounded more like a train whistle warning cows to get off the tracks. The damp sheets stuck to her skin. The moon came up bright and full, piercing into her room like a floodlight determined to wipe out all darkness. She hoped her guest, bedded down on the living room sofa, slept better than she. Flipping to her right side she scrunched a pillow between her arms and snuggled into it. Cobwebs clouded her thoughts. Her body began to relax. With a start, Sid woke to the eerie feel of a strange bed. She lay awake, but where?

The bed felt hard and lumpy, not like her pillow-top mattress. Her mind raced to catch fleeting memories of the night. She sniffed the dark air; nothing smelled familiar.

So many beds in so little time, where was she now? Her mind grappled and clawed at pieces of memory, no longer able to track where she'd last laid her head. She forced the cotton out of her thoughts and flipped groggily to her side. Where am I? Panic crept into the unknown quarters of her mind as amnesia clouded brain cells. She forced herself bolt upright in the bed and peered through the darkness. Moonlight made ghostly shadows against buckled paint peeling off the walls.

Sophia, she thought, all's well with the world. Sid turned over, straightened the twisted blanket beneath her, and went back to sleep.

👁   👁   👁

Sid pranced into Ben's office like a prize show horse. Quade sat, dipping a doughnut into a cup of coffee. "Ben, Quade, I want to introduce you to Sadora Thomas," Sid turned and motioned forward the bottled red-head standing behind her. The men shook hands with the woman, but kept their questioning look.

"Thirty years ago, Sadora went by the name Georgette Sanders." Sid paused and waited for comprehension to sink in. "Sadora," Sid clasped the woman's arm, "or Georgette, moved to Las Cruces, New Mexico, where she's lived as Sadora Thomas since the mid 1970s. We've driven for two days, just got home last night."

Both men, who had been standing, dropped in their chairs, speechless and wide-eyed. "You mean—Gette?" Ben found his voice before Quade.

"Yes, Gette." The woman smiled and stuck her hand out to Ben again. This time he clasped her hand in both of his.

Sid recounted her discovery of the news article regarding the woman from Bay St. Louis who disappeared during the same time period as Ethel Elaine Perry. "I drove to Bay St. Louis, and my first night there, I ran into a woman, quite by coincidence, who knew Sadora's aunt." Sid was no longer sure there was such a thing as a coincidence, but to keep conversation flowing, she stayed with the traditional word.

"Thelma, the woman I met, and Sadora's aunt have been friends since high school," Sid explained, enjoying the shocked look on the men's faces. "Gold Dust Twins, one of their dads called them. They kept nothing from each other, so it was natural Thelma be brought in on the family secret, the charade of Georgette's disappearance. It served as a protective cover, not only for her, but for the whole family.

"You mean there never was a missing woman?"

"Oh, there was one all right, until after the fire—and then again afterwards—until Gette felt safe enough to contact her family and tell them of her new identity, but they held the secret close."

"Okay, I'm confused. Start at the beginning." Ben stood and paced.

"Putting the pieces together, this is how I figure it all happened," Sid pulled up chairs for herself and Sadora and both sat.

"Ethel Elaine" Sid explained, "was a good-looking woman and Big Daddy saw a way to get more from her than clean motel rooms. So he brought her across state lines as a part of his prostitution ring. Manly and his cronies were always willing to chip in for a gang bang, which elevated the profit for Big Daddy. Ethel fell victim to them, and things got out of hand. Before they finished with her she had been subjected to brutal sexual assault. The guys got scared, so to cover the crime, they strung her up, killed her, and then hid her body under a piece of tin in Roy's backyard.

"That night, they met in the old red barn behind the house

and argued over how to dispose of the body. One of them, Roy I figure, suggested downsizing. The next day they dragged her body into the kitchen and dismembered her. Big Daddy got wind of it and wanted to make sure the police didn't find out about the murder for fear of losing business. So he sent Ed Pigeon, his handyman, literally, down to Orange with Georgette, who worked at the motel too. Pigeon introduced her to everyone as Ethel, under the pretext of a marriage, when in fact they set the scene to dispose of Ethel's body without raising suspicion."

Sadora leaned forward in her chair and spoke for the first time. Her brown eyes tense, her mouth tight. "I went along with what Big Daddy told me to do, but I didn't know about the murder. All he told me was to go to Orange with Ed and tell everyone we were engaged. After things cooled down, I could come back home. That I was disposable—and if I didn't go along with the scheme, I'd be sorry. I knew what he meant. I'd worked for him for years. Tried to quit several times, but he always found me and dragged me back. He was mean."

"Who is this Big Daddy?" Quade leaned forward and rested his forearms on his knees, the doughnut still in his hand.

"His real name is Pat Butchard. He hates the name Pat, said it sounded like a girl's name. Always insisted we call him Big Daddy.

"Do you know if he's still alive?"

"Oh, yes, he's alive all right." Sadora snorted. "Lives in Jasper, my family tracks him for me. He's old now, went out of the motel–prostitution business years ago. But still dangerous, I assume."

"And Ed Pigeon?" Quade asked.

"Just like me. He did what Big Daddy told us to do. I figured he must have gotten suspicious after the house burned down, but I don't know."

"It seems," Sid said, "both women were near the same size and coloring, red hair, brown eyes, and all. So it would have been an easy switch."

Ben jumped in, "So Pigeon conveniently drives out of town in search of furniture while Manly takes Ethel's body and dumps it, then sets the house on fire. What happened then?"

"I was in the house. I'd gotten up and fixed us some breakfast, and then Ed left. I didn't know where he was going." Sadora stood and paced the floor, her head down. "I'd walked back to the bedroom to dress when I heard a noise in the front part of the house. I looked through the crack of the door and I see this man, I guess Roy, but I hadn't ever seen him before then, pouring gasoline on everything."

A far-off look covered Sadora's face as she told her story. Sid knew Sadora lived it all over again.

"I don't claim to have been very smart in those days, but I wasn't a fool, either. Big Daddy might have instructed them to burn me up, too, I didn't know. So I grabbed a chair and threw it through the bedroom window. I heard a whoosh as I climbed out and ran fast as I could. I had a chance for freedom, I figured. So I high-tailed it out of town, ran for days, hitched a ride when someone stopped—walked the rest of the way—then settled in Las Cruces, New Mexico. I've been there ever since."

"Well, I guess that takes care of Big Daddy." Ben nodded at Quade.

"Think we'll ever find out who the other men were?" Quade asked.

"I think I know who they were. If so, both of them are dead now. But we'll try. Where can we reach you?"

Sadora left her phone number and address with Ben. "After I sign a statement, Sid is taking me to the bus station, but just give me a call. I'll help you all I can. I'm tired of hiding and it's been a long time since I've been home."

👁   👁   👁

Sid stopped by her office to touch base with Annie before heading home. She'd been mighty neglectful of her aunt, and promised herself she'd do better. After what she'd been through, Annie's fingers-down-a-chalkboard voice didn't seem nearly as bad.

"Hey! I'm glad you're back. You okay?" Annie held Sid at arms length, gave her the once-over.

"You're a sight for sore eyes," Sid said, and gave Annie a hug.

"Okay, catch me up, what happened? Did you get everything figured out?"

"Looks like we've got enough to take Manly to trial now," Sid said, grinning. "Quade's getting a search warrant right now, and then he's heading to Manly's house to arrest him. We did good, Annie, we're a good team."

"Shoot, I didn't do much. You figured this one out all by yourself. But don't you think you're gonna make that a pattern, young lady. I was just telling Chesterfield that I'm just getting started learning the detective business and all. You know what I mean?"

"I sure do sweetheart, I'm still figuring it out myself."

"Now, tell me everything. Where've you been, what'd you find out?"

"Can I go home, clean up and take a rest first? I'm bushed."

"'Course you can. I'll tell you what. You go home, take a shower, rest up then come by the house for dinner. I'll cook us up a pot of chicken and dumplings. They always was your favorite. Besides, you ain't even seen my new digs yet."

"That's a deal. See you what time? About seven?"

"Sounds perfect. That'll give me time to stop by the store."

Twenty Four

Sid opened her front door and felt something amiss. The threadbare Victorian red-velvet chair lay on its side, her favorite white ginger jar lamp—shattered—on the floor. She knew better than to attempt to retrieve the Glock, still under her pillow, but the cell phone in her car? She turned to retrace her steps but a movement flashed off to her side and instinctively she swung toward it.

👁   👁   👁

She awoke to darkness, the way a nightmare wakes a child in the night. Only this nightmare didn't go away. Hands bound over her head; she dangled from creaking rafters like a pig ready for slaughter.

Sid lowered her head and closed her eyes. But even that slight movement sent a searing pain down her neck. *Where the hell am I?* She tried to look around, but her head throbbed with the effort. The room looked small and built of rough-hewn wood. Dark, except for the sliver of light from a street lamp that struggled to penetrate a filthy window. The bulb in the streetlight shone dimly on the fender of a familiar-looking pink child's bike on the floor. The back room of the chicken hatchery, that's where she was.

A macabre stillness imbued the room. How long had she been unconscious? Cool air rippled against her breasts, and she felt her nipples harden. Only then did she notice that she'd been stripped naked, from the waist up. Blood—hers, she realized in a panic—had trickled down her chest and dried. The stark contrast of ruby-red webbing against her white skin triggered a memory, but the elusive link fizzled with the pounding in her head.

She twisted around and the movement, even breathing, goaded the rope deeper into her flesh. It wasn't just the hemp that cut into her wrists. The specter of raw fear paralyzed her soul and blocked any rational thought of escape.

She'd seen this whole thing before. Hanging—naked, tied, but where?

Oh my God! She hadn't seen it, Jewell had—thirty years ago! And she knew the outcome of that. Someone was coming back, and she'd have to face her captor and whatever madness a person of his nature and caliber devised. Who was it—Manly? It had to be.

She tried not to breathe, hoping she'd die first, wondering how many breaths it took to do so, and what it felt like to die.

A voice floated into her head, unbidden. Words she'd heard before. *Sid, you are undoubtedly the bravest woman I've ever known.* She raised her head to see who had spoken, but saw no one. The words were familiar though…a friend had said them to her after the divorce—that's when it had been. After she'd walked away from a past that had bound her soul.

And just what do you propose to do now, Ms. Sidra Smart? The words continued. *Just hang there and take this? You've gotten out of tough times before. Do something.*

"What the hell am I supposed to do?" she screamed, then winced as the ropes dug deeper.

You're smarter than he is, the voice echoed back at her. *You have to lower yourself to his level. Get inside his head. Think the way he thinks, whoever he is, whatever he is.*

If it was Roy Manly, like she figured, she wasn't sure she could get that low.

She heard the doorknob rattle and peered over her shoulder just as Roy Manly stepped inside the room. The kerosene lantern he carried cast weird shadows across his face, making him look anything but human, and when he spoke, his thin, reedy voice didn't change her opinion. "Hey, girly-girl, so you finally woke up, eh?" He turned the small brass knob on the lamp and the flame shot higher.

She struggled to swing herself around, ignoring the pain. "So it was you. I figured as much." She strangled on her words and coughed. "You could've at least left my clothes on." She pitched and twisted, willing the movement itself to cover her.

"Aw, that takes all the fun out of it," he taunted. "I didn't leave any clothes on her, why should I leave any on you? Don't worry your pretty little head none, the blue jeans are next."

A surge of anger balled up in her gut. She shocked herself when she heard her own thoughts pop out of her mouth. "Yeah, that's what I thought. It's a power trip for you, isn't it? That's why you killed her!"

"Well, hell, we'd fucked the life out of her anyway. Your pussy is so old it probably don't have any fuck left."

Sweat beaded on the surface of her skin. "So you thought you'd burn her up in an old deserted house and no one would ever know, is that it?"

"They wouldn't have, neither, if it hadn't been for those damn kids of mine. Always like their Mama. I knew I shoulda never taken them with me that day. But my goddamn mama called and said not to bring them over to her place. She had to go get her hair done." His voice went up an octave on the word hair.

"Did you kill Nancy, too?" She'd never rest in peace without knowing for sure. Neither could she face her or Ethel Elaine on the other side.

"Shoulda done that one a long time ago. Crazy bitch." He paced back and forth in front of Sid. "She weren't supposed to come home early that day," he shouted, holding his hands out in front of him, palms up. "It was her fault, seeing all that blood on the floor."

"Okay, now that we're confessing, how about the sexual abuse of Emma?" She pushed the envelope, she knew, but hell, dead was dead.

He snorted and walked around behind her and slapped her on the butt as he passed. She twisted to see him, but couldn't. When he came back in front of her he held a long-handled propane lighter.

"Killing you is too easy," he said, running the back of his hand across his mouth. "Let's have some fun first." His eyes gleamed like a madman's. Holding the lighter up to her face, he taunted, flipping it on and off.

Blood, hotter than the fire at the tip of the lighter, raced across her skin and flushed her face and neck. "Now why do you want to mess up a perfectly good body?" *Play along, Sid—you're smarter than he is.* "Wouldn't it be better to keep it like it is," she said, trying to make her voice sound seductive, "at least until after you get a good fuck?" The word, still unfamiliar on her tongue, came out easier the second time. "Then you can torch it later, like you did Ethel's."

"All in good time, is that it?" He leered at her from top to bottom.

"All in good time." Sid felt like she'd sold her soul to Satan for a few more minutes of air.

The flame arched between her breasts now. She sucked in her breath and forced her ribs together as the heat blistered her skin. Look him in the eyes, she told herself, but instead, she bit her lip and tasted blood. He pulled the flame away from her. She stared at it, mesmerized. Light blue at the base, where it jutted out from the round hole, it flickered to a darker shade, then licked up to a golden-yellow tip before vaporizing into air at the tip of the flame. It came closer. The stench of singed hair penetrated her nostrils.

"Okay, you've made your point." Her voice had turned raspy, forced. She writhed away from the flame. Her lungs held on to all the air they could.

"I ain't even started making my point." He snickered again and released the trigger—the hot blue flame extinguished itself.

Get inside his head. "I don't understand you, Roy. Do you hate women or something?"

He'd turned his back to her, but she saw the question stop him in his tracks. Did his shoulders stiffen? He opened his fingers like they held nothing but air, and let the lighter fall to the floor like a death rattle. "What's it to you?"

"I don't know," she forced casual into her voice, "I'm just a student of people, I guess." A car drove by outside. The lights slashed through the windows in the front of the hatchery and reflected off the wall in back. Probably Ben, going home from work.

"Women are good for just one thing," Roy spat out. "Anyone ever tell you different, he's a fool."

He rummaged in a black canvas bag and came up with a bone-handled hunting knife. He held it up.

What's he going to do with that? Despite herself, a warm liquid dribbled down the inside of her thigh. The smell of urine reached her nostrils. Oh, god, he'd reduced her to an infant. How much longer did she have?

In one quick step he lunged towards her, rammed the knife up her blue-jean clad leg and tore open the denim to the top of her thigh. He grinned. "Nice leg. You do work out. He shook his head. "Short—but nice."

Before now, she'd thought Roy either crazy or just flat mean. He was. But more than that, he believed men had the right—he had the right—to treat women any way he wanted. She'd been trapped in that world before. She still was.

Okay, use his beliefs against him. Feed it. Use it. Work him, that same voice she'd heard before whispered in her head. "You're right. Women should know their place."

He rammed the knife up her other pants leg and slashed it open all the way to her waist, scraping her skin as the knife cut through underwear and denim, then he yanked the mess all off and threw it on the floor. She hung before him, totally exposed. "I know what you're trying to do, bitch." He banged the knife against the wall.

Careful, Sid. "I'm sorry. I didn't mean to offend you." She hoped she at least sounded respectful.

"You bitches are all alike. All you want to do is break men's balls."

Where did she go from here? She watched him, head bent, as he fumbled through piles of debris—junk left over through years of abandonment. His shoulders sagged, but he pushed them back with a shrug.

Keep him talking.

"Why did you bring me here? What do you want from me? What did you want from her?" She figured he knew who she was.

He did. "Ethel? I didn't have a problem with her. A good enough fuck. We'd about used her up, though, ready for the trash heap." Roy turned from the junk pile. "I'd a let her go, but Big Daddy wanted her dead. 'Dead women don't talk,' he said."

"Talk about what? What did she know?" Sid asked. *It's safer, talking about Ethel instead of him.*

"He had several things going on." Confidence marched across his face as he talked.

"Like what?"

"You don't want to know."

"So, is she the only one you killed or where there others?"

"Not till now. Been waitin' a long time." Wickedness crept across his lips as they curled up into a grin.

What a schmuck. She wanted anger, but fear forced its way to the top.

After a deep breath she tried another tack. "It's fascinating, seeing how you men work. I wish I were a man. Your power turns me on. Did you have someone help you tie me and pull me up like this?"

"Nah, I didn't need no help."

"That takes a lot of strength in those arms." Her body swung like a carcass in a meat locker. Hoping to steady herself, she grasped the ropes above her wrists with her fingers. "I like power, but I've never had any. Pisses me off, too. I couldn't have done what you did—this—without help."

He shrugged and pulled an old milk crate over, straddled it in front of Sid and stared at her crotch. His lips twitched. Just below the surface of her skin, it felt like an army of ants crawled. Her arm sockets ached, but her hands were numb. If she didn't get some reprieve soon, they'd never have any feeling in them again. But if she didn't get out of this mess...

Sid cleared her throat. "I don't mean to bother you, Roy, but could you stick one of those crates under my feet? Just for a little while? My arms hurt." She knew better than to whine or demand. Instead, she spoke matter-of-fact, reasonable.

To her surprise, he kicked a crate her way. It banged against her feet and landed behind her. She swung herself just enough to catch the edge of the molded plastic with her big toe and inch it under her feet. Only her toes and the balls of her feet supported her. She couldn't stand this way for long.

"Good catch," he sneered.

"Thanks."

He pulled a pack of Camels out of his shirt pocket, knocked it against his index finger and wrapped his lips around a cigarette. He retrieved a book of matches from between the cellophane wrapper and the cigarette pack and flipped open the cover, pulled out a match, and lit the cigarette. Smoke curled up his nostrils and he hacked.

Maybe he has lung cancer. One could always hope. Not that it would do her any good. Her own rational thoughts amazed her.

"Big Daddy had less use for women than me," he said, returning to their earlier conversation, "but he learned how to make money off of them. Lots of women trying to get out of the mountains of Arkansas and the backwoods of Florida and Louisiana, and for the price of a trip out, they sold their pussies. Man, did he have a way of finding 'em."

"He ran a prostitution ring?"

He took a deep drag and blew a smoke ring her way. "I guess you could say that." He raised his other hand, stared at it, and then rubbed the edge of his fingernails across his shirt.

She'd love to wipe that cocky smirk off of his face, but instead said, "He gave women what they wanted. What they deserved."

"I guess you could say that, too."

"What they were created for."

He pitched the cigarette butt to the floor and stumped it out with his foot. "Now you got it."

"And you were in the white truck that night."

A gravelly laugh choked him. "I sure thought I'd got you," he said, snorting. "Shoulda seen my face that day you showed up at my door with Burns and that Hillerman guy. How in the hell'd you do it?"

Instead of answering, she asked, "You know anything about arsenic?" Not that it mattered now, but she still wasn't certain who put the poison-soaked wood in her office. If it wasn't him, then she knew who it was; the same ones who made the phone call, messed up her kitchen, and burned her Bible—and she knew who did that—the couple who'd given it to her last year for Christmas—Dorcas and Tom Huff.

"Arsenic? What for you asking me that? You're not in any condition to be poisoning me, or anyone else."

"Humor me, okay?"

"Stuff's used in rat poison." He spat on the floor. "Hell, I never killed them little buggers, had too much fun using 'em on Emma."

So, it wasn't him.

A ringing cell startled them both. He dug in his pants pocket, pulled one out and flipped it open.

"Yo. Unh huh, I got her here."

Pause.

"No, not yet. Takin' my own sweet time. She ain't goin' nowhere."

The vernacular of his childhood fit him, like a glove.

"Okay," he nodded. "Okay. I'll finish her and be right there." He slapped the cover back down on the phone and laid it on the table next to the wall, exchanging it for the knife. "Gotta get this over with, bitch, but it's a damn shame. I looked forward to a little life in my pussy, but hey, I can take it either way."

"Can't you come back later?" she asked, sprinkling as much sugar into her voice as she dared. "I hoped we could have some time, too." She steeled the nerves out of her voice and adamantly refused to shiver. Beads of perspiration covered her top lip.

He caressed her throat with the knife, and inched it down to her breasts. "So—you're getting all hot and bothered, huh? I knew you wanted me. I can always tell what you women want. You say no, but you always mean yes." He ogled her again, from neck to thighs. She recoiled under his gaze, but he didn't seem to notice. Instead, he looked at his watch. Then he paced the floor, head down.

"Hell, I can do whatever I damn well please," he boasted, pushing his shoulders back.

"Can you?" Her brain refused to let her lungs either take in oxygen or to let any air out.

Roy lifted his free hand and examined his nails again, then ran the knife blade beneath one. Perspiration glistened on his upper lip.

"Here, I'll give you just a little taste of what you can look forward to." He toyed with her, a cat after a mouse, running the tip of the blade down the middle of her chest until he reached her navel, stuck it in and twisted.

Sid writhed; her heart beating double time, the pain seared itself into the realization this was a twinge compared to what was coming. She felt a trickle of blood run down her belly and into her pubic hair.

"Don't go anywhere. There's more where that came from. A lot more." He flung the knife onto the table. It clattered and stopped, the blade glistening.

Sid's ragged breath pierced the stillness.

Finally, he looked up at her and grinned. "I'll be back in a few minutes." He stalked out the door.

He's coming back, and it won't be pretty. What the hell did she do now? Sid eased her body lower on the milk crate and allowed her toes to relax, but her shoulder blades seared in pain. For the first time ever, she gave thanks for her weekly workouts, the ab extensions and the pull-ups.

Standing on tiptoe, she worked her fingers up the rope. Sweat dripped into her eyes and stung them closed. She turned her head sideways and wiped her face on her forearm.

He'd simply strung another rope between her tied hands and then slung it over the rafters and tied it. Sloppy work, she thought, relieved. Leaning her head back, she strained to see overhead as her fingers pried and pulled on the knots. Her bloody hands slipped off the rope several times, but she steadied herself and tugged again. Finally, the knot slipped, and she fell under the weight of the release. Hitting the floor hard, her hip slammed the edge of the milk crate.

How long had that taken? Ten minutes? Fifteen?

Reassess. Her hands and feet were both still bound. Which should she free first? The urge to run won out. She pulled her legs up to her chest and spread her knees, stretching her tied hands between her legs. Frantic fingers yanked on tight, wet ropes. Her breath came faster now.

Dammit, loosen! She banged the sides of her hands against the knots. A room scan revealed a rusty screwdriver in the corner. On her hands and knees, she slid her legs across the floor and then skidded forward on the heels of her hands. Slide, skid. One more time. Then she'd have it. There. She grabbed the tool but it slipped out of her hands and rattled to the floor. Gently— wind the fingers around the handle. Yes. She switched over on her butt, stuck the screwdriver blade in the knot and jerked. Did it loosen? Do it again. Hurry. Pull.

A car drove by outside. Breath froze in her chest until it drove out of earshot. A mouse skittered across the floor. Its tiny feet scratched against the dry wood, and escaped into a small hole near the floor. Lucky rat.

The first knot came loose. She sighed. Pull the next one, harder, faster. Her fingers slipped off, but she dug in again. The rope dropped off her feet as she untied the last knot. The cell phone lay on the table where he'd tossed it before he'd left. She grabbed it and punched 911. *Quade, please be on duty.*

"What is your emergency?"

"My name is Sid Smart and I'm at the old chicken hatchery on Finnell Street—" She wanted to say more but a car pulled up and stopped outside.

Him.

She knew it.

The knife, she pitched the phone down and headed toward the table. Her leaded movements felt like a make believe slow-motion murder movie. She snatched the knife from the rough wooden table, ramming a splinter up her fingernail. She winced but kept moving. Positioning the knife handle between her hands, still tied, she jumped behind the door just as the knob turned and Roy Manly slipped inside.

He saw the dangling rope. "God-damn bitch!" He slung the door shut.

She leapt out, just as he turned and saw her, his eyes stretched wide.

The roar in her head blocked out all other sounds. She felt a cold fearlessness push aside her terror. She felt like she had risen above herself, and looked down, watching, as she raised her arms over her head, as her breasts glistened in the bare bulb light, as the cold night air sent a shiver across her chest.

Manly stood before her, his legs spread wide, eyes registering shock. She spread her legs, one foot in front of the other, for leverage, and swung the blade downward, hard and fast. The knife found little resistance. It penetrated deep into his chest, right below his breast bone. Warm blood saturated her hands, his blood.

She felt the knife slip in her hands, so she squeezed it tighter and pushed until she felt it sink deeper. Then she twisted it and let go. As soon as her hands released the blade she wondered if she'd made a mistake, letting it go. Maybe she should have pulled it out and stabbed again.

Frame frozen, she watched him, standing in front of her, staring at nothing.

Infinity stretched out before her.

A trickle of blood oozed from the side of his mouth. His eyelids fluttered and his eyes rolled back in his head until only the whites stared back at her. After an eon, he fell to the floor. The last thing he said was "fucking bitch."

"Damn right," she whispered back.

👁   👁   👁

Quade tore through the door. Roy laid in his own blood, spread-eagle, the knife still in his chest. Blood pulsed through his shirt and puddled on the floor.

"The best I've ever seen him look." Sid said.

Quade hadn't seen her yet and jumped when she spoke. He turned toward her voice. "My God, Sid!"

He took off his coat and threw it over her before they walked out into the rain, his arm around her shoulder, more for his own comfort than hers, she felt. An old man sat in the back seat of the patrol car. One of the officers saw her looking and said, "It's Big Daddy. We found him sitting in Manly's car when we drove up."

Dizzied by sirens, whirling lights on top of patrol cars, and voices shoving questions in her face, Sid ducked her head and pulled the coat tighter. Quade pushed them aside, and eased her into the back seat of his patrol car.

Numbly she watched Ben run toward her.

"Sid, are you okay? What happened?"

She cleared her throat and shook her head.

Quade thumbed toward the shed and Ben saw Manly's body,

sprawled in red, just before an officer spread a sheet over it.

"You're going home with me." A smile softened Ben's orders. "You might be okay, but I'm not."

She pulled back.

Quade turned away, walked toward his officers.

"Just business, I promise." Ben took her by the elbow.

She let him lead her across the street and inside his house. She knew she couldn't go home and spend the night alone.

They sat on the sofa all night, covered with blankets, sipping hazelnut coffee, as Sid recounted Roy's confessions. It all made sense now, the prostitution ring, Roy's involvement. All the others who participated were now dead. Big Daddy had used his business as a front, working the women on both ends of the business. Making beds and turning tricks.

Twenty Five

If someone today asked Sid what she thought of Roy Manly, she'd have an answer, but until a few months ago she'd never even heard his name. Neither did she know what he'd been doing in the early seventies while she made babies and baked casseroles for potluck dinners at the church. Now, she stood beside his casket. His daughters—Jewell and Emma—stood on either side of her. Rahim and Andrine stood behind them. This time Sid hoped Andrine was mistaken about the 'no death' thing.

A big pile of heavy black gumbo dirt awaited its return to the six-foot deep hole shoveled from the earth.

The bright sun hurt her eyes. Rain to rival Noah's flood had ceased after three days, and now she felt like a bat in daylight. The ground squished beneath her feet. Steam rose from the earth as the sun vaporized the standing water.

Squinting, she put her hand over her eyes and stared at the bottle of Jose Cuervo dangling from Emma's hand. Sunlight danced across the clear glass and made prism rainbows flit off of gravestones.

The daughters had pooled their dollars and bought a modest but decent casket, more for themselves, than for him, Sid knew. Now, Roy Manly lay in that casket.

The funeral attendants solemnly stepped forward and lowered the box down into the prepared hole. The automated action of the equipment buzzed inside Sid's head. She waved her hand beside her ear as if shooing away a mosquito.

The rest of the world seemed to hold its breath.

There had been no wake. There had been no viewing. No minister held a Bible or said a prayer or sang a hymn. Sad, Sid thought, then decided the only song appropriate was Martina McBride's *This One's for the Girls.*

Jewell snatched a clump of the thick wet dirt with one hand, and brushed a tear off her face with the other. Then she stepped forward. Her shoulders shook. The humidity frizzed her naturally curly hair. Her hazel eyes stared straight ahead.

Slowly, almost zombie-like, Jewell's arm rose out over the casket. She held the pose, palm down, for at least thirty seconds. Sid counted. No one moved or said a word. Finally, her fingers opened as if in slow motion, and the clod of dirt plopped heavily on the wooden box. It sounded hollow as it hit.

As she stepped back inside the threesome, Jewell glanced at Sid. Her lips, turned up at the corners, did not match her empty eyes.

The three of them stood there, shoulders back, spines straight.

As if given a secret signal, Emma cleared her throat and pushed her hand through her hair. The freckles on her face looked stark against pale cheeks. A shiver shook her body and she stepped to the excavated hole.

Sid saw a red aura encircle Emma as though someone had covered her with a red blanket. She unscrewed the cap on the bottle of tequila, raised the bottle to her mouth and guzzled down a big swig of the clear liquid. Then she turned the bottle upside down over the casket and emptied most of the spirits on top. It splattered as it hit the polished wood, and then became one with the mud around the bottom. She stopped, checked the remaining contents of the bottle, and returned to her place in line.

The grave diggers stepped forward and filled the grave, packing down the last bit of dirt with their massive tools. No one said a word. The scrape and thud of shovels grated against the silence. When they finished, the men stood and wiped their brows with large handkerchiefs. Given the nod, they left.

Sid motioned to Quade and Ben, waiting in the car, and the two men came and stood behind them. A fluffy white dog walked up from out of nowhere and lay at Jewell's feet like a guardian. A squirrel, halfway up a tree, ceased its stride, flicked its tail and hung motionless. A mockingbird alighted on a nearby tombstone and stopped its singing.

Sid held her breath. It seemed that the earth waited too. Her eyes burned from too many tears shed in the last few days: tears not for Roy, but for Jewell and Emma, for Nancy and Ethel Elaine, for herself, and for women everywhere who suffered abuse from men. Never again would she be silent.

Emma slipped out of her shoes and with Jose Cuervo in hand, crawled and slid her way up to the top of the grave. The mud clumped on her feet and squished between her toes. It splashed on her bare legs and the hem of her skirt, but she paid it no mind. Her arms rose out to her sides and her head fell back, skyward. A rhythm must have played deep in her soul because a movement started at her feet. They squished in the mud, faster and faster. Sid saw the clench of her jaw and the tension in her shoulders. For an instant, Sid shut her eyes, and tried to shut out the pain. She felt like an intruder, watching Emma. But not watching made her feel complicit with the demons, so she forced her chin off her chest and dragged her eyelids open. When she did, she saw Emma's jaw relax as she swayed to music that only Emma could hear.

The energy in the air around them shifted. Exhausted, but safe for the first time in her life, Emma tipped the bottle up to her lips and swigged the tequila to the last drop, then pulled her arm back and flung the bottle off into the distance. The little white dog chased after it. Standing next to the empty bottle, the dog clawed a hole in the soft wet earth, then grabbed the neck of the bottle, dumped it into the hole and covered it up.

☞   ☞   ☞

They'd seen Jewell, Emma and Rahim off, all eager to get on

with the rest of their lives.

"I'll never forget you, Sid," Jewell cried, as they embraced.

"Never," Emma said. "For the first time in my life I don't have to look behind me. I know I'm not there yet. I still have a lot of healing to do, but at least there are no more secrets between Rahim and me. We've got a chance now." She pushed back from Sid. "And I'm so glad you weren't *purple polyester pants*," she said, laughing. "If you had been, I'd have walked away that day. I swear."

Maya Angelou's words echoed inside Sid's head. She turned and faced the young women, and looked each of them in the eye. "You, Jewell, and you, Emma—both of you make me proud I spell my name WOMAN."

Emma turned to Jewell and hugged her. "Thanks, little sister, if it hadn't been for you we would've never even started on this journey. You're the bravest woman I know, except for Sid, of course." They held each other and laughed. Tears rolled down their faces.

"I agree with you Emma. Jewell is the hero in all this." Sid stared Jewell in the eye. "You get some counseling, okay?"

The young women waved as they drove away.

👁   👁   👁

Sid sat in front of George, who leaned back in his chair with his shoes off and his feet propped on his desk.

"Quade called me this morning," Sid said. "They've arrested Tom Huff for grand larceny and transportation of stolen goods across federal borders. The police confiscated all their files and found enough information to charge Huff and his goons for tampering with Warren's car. Seems they got wind Warren suspected them. The guard at the gate admitted he'd been forced to write out the postcard with the eye warning. I guess that's why he got so nervous that day when I asked to see Warren's car."

"Interesting." George grinned at her and clasped his hands behind his head. "You still getting any more threats?"

Sid shook her head. "The only thing I'm not sure we'll get closure on is the arsenic in Warren's fireplace. Rather suspect that was done before I ever took over, and I'm not sure we can prove Huff did it."

"No more Bible burning?"

"Not even that. I need to make a call, though. May I use your phone?"

"Mine's yours."

Sid scooted her chair closer to the desk, lifted the receiver and dialed Sam's church office. Her words caught in her throat, she cleared it, then spoke into the phone. "Dorcas, this is Sid. I wanted to thank you for sending the tape. I know that was difficult—cost you a lot. I'll bet. Yeah, I'd like that. Let's get together some time and talk. Okay. See you." She closed off the conversation and hung up the phone.

"That was big of you, Sid." George wiped his eyes with a handkerchief.

"Whew. Guess that's that," Sid said. "Getting mighty tired cleaning up my own mess. One of these days, maybe…"

"Seems to me you've found not only your niche," George said, "but also your voice. You're a darn good investigator, Sid. You just need to check in with your boss a little more." He nudged her in the ribs and chuckled, but she knew he meant business, for he'd bawled her out good when he'd heard what had happened in the chicken hatchery.

"I'd sure hate to see you quit now, Sha. Besides, I'm short handed these days. You wouldn't leave an old Cajun high and dry, would you?"

"There's a lot I still don't know about this business, George, but I must say, it's definitely not boring."

"Next August, the South Texas Private Investigation Association has their conference on the River Walk in San Antonio. What say you and me go? I'll introduce you around, and you can pick up some techniques."

"Sounds good."

Sid could benefit from learning what the hell she was do-ing.

"I have a referral for you, if you want it." He threw out the choice morsel as if tempting a dog with a fresh ham bone.

Sid looked at him through her eyelashes. "What is it?"

Picking up a pink slip of paper, he flipped it back and forth between his fingers, looked at Sid, eyebrows raised, lips stretched thin.

"Give it to me." She snatched the paper out of his hands.

"So, do I take it that you're interested, Sha?" A grin played across his face. He pulled at his tie and straightened it over his belly. "Say, you still planning on changing the name, or at least that hideous sign? I know it's bugged you."

Silent while she read the note, she looked up from the paper. "You know what I've learned? I learned my dufus older brother was smarter than I've given him credit. Warren was onto some-thing when he named the business. I don't care what I've been taught about the gulf between the spiritual and the physical. There is a connecting link—and that link runs through me. No, I think I'm going to keep the name and the eye just as they are." She stuck the note in her handbag, walked around his desk and planted a kiss on his cheek. "Annie's put together a list of War-ren's open cases. Hopefully now I'll have time to work through those. No telling what that'll bring up."

George walked Sid to the door, his hand at the small of her back.

THE END

Author
Sylvia Dickey Smith

Sylvia Dickey Smith was born and raised in Orange, Texas - the land of Cajuns, cowboys, pirates and Paleo-Indians. She entered this world backwards - feet first and left-handed - and has been described as doing things backwards ever since! At seventeen, with a year of high school to go, Sylvia married a "preacher-boy" and soon thereafter became known as the preacher's wife. Years later, she and her family lived on the island of Trinidad, W.I. for a few years, where she developed a love for other cultures, races, religions - she virtually found her voice.

At age forty she took her first college course, and in less than six years graduated with honors from the University of Texas at El Paso, earning a B.A. in Sociology and a M. Ed in Educational Psychology. Sylvia founded her own business conducting management effectiveness training, individual and marriage counseling, and assertiveness training for women. She also facilitated therapy groups for sexual offenders on parole, and for adult survivers of sexual abuse. For several years she served as an adjunct professor, worked in the field of rehabilitation, and directed operations for a long term care facility. Currently living in Round Rock, Texas, when Sylvia isn't writing she's busy scheduling and conducting writing workshops and promoting her books around the country.
Visit Sylvia's website! www.sylviadickeysmith.com

Printed in the United States
121513LV00003B/61-84/A

9 781603 180061